# IN THE INTEREST OF N.K.

## A Novel

S. A. O'Laughlin

# DEDICATION

To my family for your patience, support and encouragement.

## CAST OF CHARACTERS

| | |
|---|---|
| Bridget McGarrity | lawyer, guardian ad litem |
| Diane | Bridget's secretary |
| Aunt Irene | Bridget's aunt |
| Aiden | Bridget's son |
| Walter | Bridget's partner |
| Tim McGarrity | Bridget's brother |
| | |
| Naomi Kline | Bridget's client |
| Cheri Kline | Naomi's deceased mother |
| Elaine Kline | Naomi's grandmother |
| Steve Ross | Naomi's father |
| Jay Kline | Naomi's uncle |
| | |
| Officer Bennett | police officer, Wisaka Nation |
| John Wapello | attorney general, Wisaka Nation |
| Joe Monroe | political activist, Wisaka Nation |
| Scott Monroe | Joe's brother, Wisaka Nation |
| | |
| Nick Harmon | social worker |
| Rob Small | juvenile court officer |
| | |
| Chief French | chief of police, Broken River |
| Judge Strickland | judge, Lincoln County |
| Mark Evans | Lincoln County Attorney |
| Barry Van Ekes | lawyer for Cheri Kline |
| Alan Barshefsky | lawyer at Whitfield & Barshefsky |
| | |
| Chet Russell | headhunter for Sun Family Foundation |
| Abby Baker | Bridget's client |
| Cal Roberts | owner of Buyland |
| Nurse Connie | head nurse at mental health unit |
| Pat Edwards | waiter and Bridget's former client |
| Dave | file clerk at Lincoln County Courthouse |
| Travis/Skinny Boy | worked with Dave |

# Chapter 1

Death wasn't her job. As a general practice lawyer in a small town in the Midwest, Bridget McGarrity dealt with the living and their many problems. Fender benders, adoption, addiction problems that turned into other problems, and occasionally a broken contract or broken heart. But not death. And certainly not a corpse.

After traveling an hour and a half through a sea of corn and soybeans, a towering digital sign with blazing red dice announced Bridget had reached the reservation. The sign was the highest for one hundred miles, dwarfing fast food signs and grain silos. A beacon of entertainment in rural monotony, the casino was no less spectacular, an enormous structure shaped to resemble a Native American feathered headdress. She drove past the casino and followed the road to the community center where she hoped she would find her client. Instead, an ambulance stood in her path, emergency lights flashing across two squad cars.

Most people would pass by and continue on their way. But Bridget drove straight towards the lights, and quieted the gnawing feeling that the call regarding a client's arrest and the squad cars might be connected.

As she stepped out of the car, her heel sunk deep into the earth. Being out of the office usually meant grabbing a coffee or going to the Lincoln County Courthouse in Broken River where she practiced law. Yet here she was—bushwhacking through an Indian reservation in pumps. She kicked the shoes off. Her bare feet pressed against the soil as she held her shoes like hand weights, the edges of her linen pantsuit lightly brushing the ground. An officer stood twenty feet ahead, his back toward her. He spat a brown mass onto the gravel, unloading an ounce of tobacco juice. Another uniformed official paced and squinted at the ground, consumed by his task.

She stepped closer and held up a shoe to block the sun, stopping just behind the officer, the smell of chewing tobacco strangely comforting. Her eyes followed the direction of his gaze to a wooded area with a sizeable soupy puddle and a toppled tree.

And there she lay.

A tangled mess of dark hair covered her face. Her arms clutched to her chest, and her knees bent upward—a consoling fetal position; maybe she'd tried to warm herself. Between a thin shirt and jeans, the pale flesh of her back and belly was exposed.

Bridget held her breath, forcing a church-like stillness, and stepped closer. Glass-like eyes stared lifelessly into emptiness. The mouth was agape, frozen and rigid. Her face was expressionless. An awful end of a tortured soul who would never conquer the world she had desperately tried to navigate.

The officer raised his palm. The blue and red patch on his sleeve, the colors of the Wisaka Nation, glowed under the ambulance lights.

"Stop there," he said.

She obeyed, but her gaze was fixated on the body. She looked past the officer, searching in vain for a slight rise in the chest. Nothing. Rigor mortis had already set in. She gulped back tears and looked away. It was so quiet here. The wind shifted, and a welcomed breeze cooled her. The air was fresh and the noise from the highway and activity from the casino a mere din. Death shouldn't be a part of this landscape.

She raised her hand while gripping the shoe like a reticent student asking a question.

"I know her."

# Chapter 2

Saturday was supposed to be routine, and the day had started out quietly enough. That was until an official from the Wisaka Nation called and said they were holding her client for stealing her grandmother's car. She had no idea how Naomi Kline, who was only 14, ended up at the reservation.

But what should she do? After several calls, she didn't get good answers. After fifteen years of practicing law, she knew to head straight to the jail to help a client in police custody, especially over the weekend. Anyone arrested on a Friday or Saturday might have to wait until Monday before seeing a judge. Why would the reservation be any different? So, she hopped in her car and headed southwest, away from Broken River. Her afternoon bike ride with her son, Aiden, and her partner, Walter, could wait.

Naomi was an alright kid. She was a budding star on the track team, sarcastic and often outright rude in a typical teenage way, a defense mechanism typical of someone her age and in her situation. Her parents had been largely absent from her life and her grandmother was raising her. Naomi's mother was mentally ill, which caused plenty of chaos in the child's life.

"The casino is the other way," the officer's tone grew deeper, louder.

"That's my client's mother. Her name is...was Cheri Kline." She looked away, upward, spotting half a dozen vultures coasting the gale winds, circling, and waiting. "The birds didn't—"

The officer folded his arms, and his six-foot-plus frame glared down at her.

"And you are?"

"I'm Naomi Kline's lawyer and...over there is, that...is her mother." She stumbled over her words as she said them. "I met her before, at a court hearing."

Cheri was at court before she had been committed for mental illness when she sought help from the state to raise her daughter. The Department of Human Services stepped in and declared Naomi a "child in need of assistance" or "CINA"— pronounced "China" for those in the business.

The officer frowned. "You're a defense attorney? Let me escort you to your car."

She nodded. Of course nobody wants a defense attorney at a potential crime scene. She then looked at the body again. Her hair was disheveled, her left cheek pressed to the ground, and her right hand loosely clasped to her chest, peacefully, like she was sleeping. A plastic bottle of Hawkeye vodka lay covered in dust about three feet from her. She hadn't even noticed the bottle before.

The officer raised his arm to guide her away from the scene. "Ma'am, your client is at the community center. I'll escort you to your car."

"Right," she said in a daze. Together, they walked toward the car. She tucked her pumps under her arm, stumbled for her car keys as her hands shook. She dropped the keys.

"Sorry, I need a moment."

She pressed her eyes closed and took another deep breath. It felt like yesterday when she had faced a similar tragedy. When Bridget was thirteen, her parents had died in a car crash, and an unlucky rookie cop delivered the tragic news. She and her little brother had landed in foster care for years before the authorities finally handed them over to her mother's sister, Aunt Irene—a lawyer-turned-hippie in California who was dragged back to the Midwest to care for her niece and nephew.

She tried in vain to suppress images of her parents in the photo of the mangled sedan in which they perished. The gruesome picture was like a recurring rash, striking in times of distress or high emotion, and invaded her consciousness more than she cared to admit. Despite that, Bridget at least understood what had happened to her parents, the cause of it, and the finality. Naomi would need the same finality and an explanation.

Bridget looked over her shoulder again, at Cheri.

Mentally reviewing the two-inch-thick manila-colored court file, *In the Interest of N.K.*, she recited the facts in her head. Cheri Kline suffered from mental illness and could not care for her child. The grandmother, Elaine Kline, had usually cared for Naomi because Cheri was often absent, her whereabouts unknown, drifting from institution to institution. This time, though, Cheri had returned to take her child away from Elaine and enlisted the help of social services to do it. Naomi had also developed an attitude, refused to stay with her grandmother, and wanted to be with her mother.

The social report hadn't detailed substance abuse or alcohol. The file described Cheri's psychotic episode after stopping her medication and landing in the mental health unit. Too bad she hadn't stayed in the hospital.

"Officer, they're taking the body away?" She shuddered at the word "body." She took a deep breath and tried to pull herself together. "What about pictures? Fingerprints, soil samples, and evidence-gathering. You know, the CSI stuff. It's a crime scene." She gestured at him with her shoe, like a schoolteacher with a pointer, her hands grasping her shoes even tighter to keep them from shaking.

"You think so? Glad I found an expert," he said.

Bridget inched forward, unable to stop herself. "The bottle...did Cheri drink herself to death? On a warm August night? She's what, 35? Cheri wasn't a drug addict or an alcoholic. She had no history of alcohol or drug abuse. She battled mental illness for sure... Something's off. Please look deeper into this case."

A swarm of gnats hovered on Bridget's neck where sweat had dripped under her collar. She raised her hand and shaded her eyes from the sun. Her stomach clenched and she leaned against her car, a green Grand Am, a car that would not give up.

The officer folded his arms. "You're not looking so hot. You should be on your way."

"I'm fine," she lied, feeling acid build in her throat. "My client is at the community center. Honestly, I'm not sure where that is."

He radioed on a walkie-talkie, directing two EMTs preparing her for transport, an ambulance ready to serve as a hearse. He jangled keys in his hands.

"I guess a police escort will get you along your way."

# Chapter 3

Bridget sat shotgun with the officer at the wheel of a black SUV serving as a squad car. She gazed at the fields and homes of the Indian reservation, home to the Wisaka Nation. A plume of dirt trailed behind them on the unpaved road, which needed a fresh layer of gravel. She secured a seatbelt across her chest and took deep breaths. The police officer's eyes never wavered from the road.

Officer Bennett didn't say a word and handed her a bottle of water, which she quickly emptied.  The water and the air conditioning slowly revived her.

"Not the Saturday you thought you would have," he said.

*No, it wasn't.*

"I did not get your name."

"Bridget McGarrity. I'm a lawyer for Naomi Kline, and the child's *guardian ad litem*."

The court appointed Bridget to represent the child. Another lawyer was appointed to Cheri. If Naomi's father ever resurfaced, the state would offer him a lawyer as well. Then a gaggle of other professionals would help the child in need, including a county attorney representing the state and a pack of social workers.

She continued, "The court appoints a guardian ad litem to determine what is in the best interests of the child. I am the eyes and ears of the court, and I'll submit a report of my impressions. It's common to appoint a child in need—"

"I know what a 'guardian ad litem' is," he said.

"Right." She felt her face flush. Had she insulted him? Perhaps it wasn't such a great idea to be here, away from her usual surroundings. "And you are?" she asked.

"Officer Bennett. Is the child's dad Native American?"

"I'm not sure. Why do you ask?"

"First time here?" Officer Bennett shifted a wad of chewing tobacco in his mouth.

*Was it that obvious?* She had hoped her first time on an Indian reservation would be as a tourist or gambler, not a lawyer who knew little to nothing about tribal law.

The reservation was two hours from Broken River in Lincoln County, where she practiced law. Broken River boasted a couple of tech companies, a small college, and enough trouble that kept Bridget busy. The Wisaka Nation was its distant, quiet neighbor.

"The putative father is Stephen Ross. And I've never met the man," she said.

"Putative father," thought Bridget. Too often, fathers were "putative." Meaning absent. Paternity was sometimes a theory or a sad tale, only to be outdone by the mother.

Bridget cracked open the window for fresh air, then closed it hastily after getting a face full of dust. She brushed the dust off her tan linen pantsuit and wrapped her ash-blonde curls into a bun, removing an elastic from her wrist, ready for the purpose. She searched through her leather handbag for a tissue, futilely.

Instead, she found an orange-flavored candy, emergency sweets for her six-year-old son, and popped it in her mouth, savoring the sugar and artificial flavor.

The CINA case should have been relatively straightforward. Mom, who hadn't been much of a mother, decided she needed help from the state. Grandma wasn't too thrilled with Cheri doing anything, while Naomi complained about her grandmother. Social services would provide counseling to help the family decide about Naomi's care and keep an eye on the child. Not too difficult a case because at least Naomi could be with her grandmother if her mom couldn't keep it together.

That was yesterday.

As they drove back toward the community center they took a route that avoided the casino, a road marked "Reservation Traffic Only." A hand-painted sign showed the way to the Tribal Offices, Health Center, and Community Center. Patches of field corn spotted the landscape; the reservation was engaged in what everyone else did in the Midwest.

"You grow corn here," said Bridget.

"Indigenous peoples have been growing corn for millennia. So, yes, we grow corn and soybeans—" said Officer Bennett.

"—and pray for the success of ethanol. Corn is important for the entire state's economy. Whether it's for feed or ethanol. Good for Indians, as well. I mean Natives, or Indigenous peoples. Um, what should I call you?"

Bridget smiled. He didn't.

"You can call me Officer Bennett," he answered.

"Right."

Bridget sunk into the seat, determined to keep her mouth shut. After a mile or so, the Buyland discount store came into view. A giant cement island amidst the reservation, the only one of its kind for miles. Located near the highway, it opened its doors to the rural surrounding communities.

Protesters stood in front of the store, forming a line. Some held signs hand-painted with messages saying "Native People Don't Buyland", "Shame on Buyland" and @Buyland#colonizer #NativeJustice#sovereignty. Two tribal police cars were parked at the front entrance.

She struggled to understand the scene, hoping they had nothing to do with her case.

"What are they protesting?"

"The Buyland store. It's been in the news. Some want to shut down Buyland, and some want it open," he said.

Bridget's eyes met his sideways glance. "I did read the story. A Buyland manager hurt a young employee?"

"Sexual harassment, but Buyland offered a different story. They say the employee was lying, and a thief. Then fired her."

The controversy over the Buyland store had been in the news about a month earlier. The store allegedly improperly handled an employee, a teenager, who claimed a supervisor harassed her and then fired her when she complained. Last she read about it, Buyland claimed it fired the employee for theft.

The squad car slowed to a stop by the railroad tracks and parked at the community center. The building sported a stately depiction of a Native American warrior head with the inscription in deep red: "Wisaka Tribe of the Mississippi." A directory on the wall listed a one-stop shop for government services: Health & Human Services, Housing Authority, Tribal Offices, Diabetes Center, Alcohol & Drug Abuse, and a courtroom.

"I'd like to speak with the attorney here for the county. The county attorney...I mean," Bridget stammered. "About the charges against Naomi for auto theft."

"The attorney general?" Officer Bennett spoke slowly. "You can ask at the community center."

At least it wasn't a no, thought Bridget. The reservation was holding Naomi because either Lincoln County filed charges, or the reservation did, and she was unsure of which. If the reservation was anything like a county attorney in Lincoln County, they rarely dropped charges.

Her young client in custody faced mourning the loss of her mother at a juvenile detention center, and she didn't intend for that to happen. Now was the time to be tough, she thought, as she pressed a hand to her forehead in a failed effort to rub away the worry. She calmly exited the SUV and brushed a wrinkle out of her suit.

"Thank you. I feel much better. And my car, can I—"

"We will get you back to your car. No reason for you to extend your stay here. Unless you want to stop at the casino?"

She trailed behind Officer Bennett as they walked through the tiled hallway to a metal door.

"Excuse me, but are you Bridget McGarrity?" said a woman, presumably a clerk. She pushed up the large, framed red eyeglasses on her nose that complimented her straight, shiny black hair.

"Yes."

"Naomi is in the conference room. Better go see her now before that man takes her away."

# Chapter 4

Bridget walked briskly down the hallway toward the conference room where a man stood outside, jostling keys in his hand.

"What are you doing here?" he asked. The clerk stepped back and listened to their exchange.

"Rob. Always a pleasure," said Bridget.

Rob Small, who was more large and square than small, was the "JCO" or juvenile court officer. He licked his dry lips that were crusted with a yellow glob that looked like mustard. His presence wasn't a good sign because he was likely here to transport Naomi to juvenile detention in Lincoln County.

"You can see the kid in court on Monday," said Rob. He popped a piece of gum in his mouth to cover the wafting onion smell from lunch.

She hesitated, considering whether to confront him.

"Excuse me, Rob, I intend to see Naomi now."

Through the thick glass of the conference room, Bridget peered at her young client. Naomi sat in a chair by the windows, her lanky legs tucked under the chair and her jeans torn at the knee. Her black hair, streaked with blue highlights, was a tangled mess. And Rob had already worked his dark magic: Naomi was handcuffed.

The clerk stepped up quietly and stood between Rob and Bridget. "I gave Naomi something to eat, and I'll let her stay with you," the clerk said to Bridget.

"Thank you," she said, taking a moment to concentrate on how she should contend with Naomi. So young and so alone. Comfort was an excellent place to start.

"Rob, could you remove Naomi's handcuffs. Please."

"No can do, counselor. Handcuffs are standard protocol for the juvenile delinquent," said Rob.

The clerk folded her arms. "Sir, you can't do that here."

"Do what?"

"Put a child in handcuffs," said the clerk.

"Naomi has zero history of aggressive behavior. It's unnecessary," Bridget added.

"Stealing a car and running away is aggressive. The kid's a flight risk."

The clerk abruptly turned and stomped down the hallway, her hair swishing from side to side as she hurried away.

A JCO's job was to keep children in check, deliver news more often bad than good, and compel acceptance of his authority and position. If Bridget didn't give him the appropriate praise, his delicate ego might be dented. That might make her client's and her life bumpier. To put Rob at ease, she pressed her lips together to mimic a smile.

"Kids can get rough. I get that, and we're both having a hell of a long day. A drive from Lincoln County during a weekend is tedious, and who wants more complications? Today is different. You do know her mother's body was found today? I just identified it."

Rob raised his eyebrows. So, he didn't know.

"More reason for restraints."

"The charges against her won't likely stick. Just a tip for you."

"Says the defense attorney. I'll wait to hear from the county attorney," Rob grunted, his bulbous nose reddened. His smugness was irritating, but she bit her tongue.

"Take the probation contract now." Rob thrust a piece of paper at her, which she scanned briefly. It was a standard probation contract, detailing rules Naomi needed to follow to stay out of juvenile detention, including staying with her grandmother and, of course, pleading guilty. Given that Naomi had fled from her grandmother, Rob's request to return her to her grandmother's care was not appealing. This all had to wait.

Rob pointed to the signature lines at the bottom of the page, one for Naomi and one for Bridget.

"Sign here. Then I spring the cuffs."

If she signed, Rob would recommend releasing Naomi back to her grandmother instead of detention to the judge. If she didn't sign, then it would be off to the juvenile detention center. She might be there a long time.

"Naomi and I will review this before either she or I can sign. And it's not valid until we get in front of a judge."

Rob snatched the paper from Bridget's hands and crumpled the sheet. So much for a peaceful hearing. Rob's ego was already bruised.

Bridget grabbed the crumpled paper back from him. "Remove the restraints while I speak with her. If you don't, I'll be sure to alert the court and social services of your civility. This crushed paper will be marked 'Exhibit A.'"

Soft steps tapped behind her. It was Officer Bennett. The clerk must have asked him to watch over the exchange between her and Rob.

"Everything OK here?" asked Officer Bennett.

"Fine," said Rob.

Officer Bennett looked at the window and then at Rob. "Sir, you need to remove the restraints now. That is not what we do here."

"She's being transported back to Lincoln County, and handcuffs are protocol."

The two eyed each other.

"Welcome to Wisaka Nation. May your stay be short."

Rob Small shrank as Officer Bennett stood unwavering, staring him down.

"Fine," huffed Rob, smoothing a greasy strand of hair off his face. "But leave the sad news about Naomi's mom to the social workers. Not you," he pointed at Bridget.

Rob bounced the keys from hand to hand as he swung open the door. Officer Bennett remained outside, and Bridget followed.

# Chapter 5

Naomi didn't budge when Bridget entered. She stared at the tiled floor, one foot trying to remove the peeling sole of her gym shoe. Her wrists and ankles were bound to a single chain secured with a broad leather belt encircling her narrow waist.

"Certain you'll be safe, counselor?"

"I'll be fine, Rob. Thanks for your concern over my wellbeing."

Naomi stood, and despite her youth, she had an inch over Bridget. She extended her cuffed arms. After Rob unshackled her, Naomi rubbed her wrists and examined a rip in the elbow of her shirt. She flung her tangled ringlets from her face and lifted her chin in defiance. Rob lingered in the room.

"I will speak now with my client alone."

"Right," Rob grunted as he left the room, the cuff keys clinking in his hand.

Delivering bad news was often part of the job, but this situation was a first. Rob was right—social workers were trained grief counselors. News of her mother's death should wait for a social worker when they got back to Lincoln County. She was unsure how Naomi would react.

"Let's concentrate on getting you out of here and home."

From years of criminal defense, she learned to focus first on getting a client out of jail. Details of what landed them there could wait. Rarely was a person who was recently arrested prepared to tell the truth because the need to explain their predicament was too great, and people could say the craziest things to be released.

"My mom, where is she? Please."

Naomi had her own concerns. She wanted answers and wasn't prepared to wait for anything.

"I—" Bridget hesitated.

"Mom was crazy mad. I told her to get fixed in the hospital, get the right meds. She was so off. Wouldn't stop talking and said she was going to save me from Grandma. But she called the cops. As if! No help there. So, we skipped out."

"Elaine Kline, your grandmother, alerted the police?"

"Yes. Elaine called the cops." Naomi scowled and continued to talk rapidly. "I wanted to stay with my mom because otherwise she would be back on the streets. So, I decided it had to be me. I grabbed the keys and we left. I told her we should go back to the hospital, but Mom said no. I had to talk to her, but I couldn't find her after we stopped here. Please, where is she...."

Bridget sighed. Counselors be damned.

"Sit down. I have terrible news." Bridget gently placed her hand on Naomi's shoulder and guided her to a seat. Naomi immediately started sobbing and shaking her head. She knew.

"Your mom was found on the reservation today. She passed away during the night."

"No. You're lying. Dead? That's not true!"

Bridget held her hand lightly over Naomi's. "I am so, so sorry. It is true. I saw her and I identified her." Bridget choked on her words. She couldn't say the word "body." "The officer drove me out to see her, to the place where they found her."

"No, no!"

She squeezed her knees to her chest and screamed into her legs, rocking back and forth. What to say when there was nothing to be said? Bridget lightly placed her hand on the child's back. As if someone flicked a switch, Naomi jolted to standing and pounded a fist on the wall.

"It's not right! My mom said people were out to get her."

"Naomi, this is an awful day. The worst day. We'll take care of you right now and get you home."

Bridget pressed her hand to her chest, trying to suppress her own distress. Naomi needed a place away from judges, the cops, and a JCO to grieve. When her parents died, at least she didn't have to deal with a criminal charge and handcuffs. That came later.

"I am trying to get charges dropped so I can take you home. If that doesn't work, the JCO will drive you back to Lincoln County for a detention hearing—"

"Him? He's gross. He creeps me out."

"Will you stay with your grandmother? I know you ran away from her, but the only other option is the youth shelter. Or if the charges stick, then juvenile detention. A foster home will be hard to find on short notice. Tell me your—"

"Send me to juvie. I hate Elaine."

"Social services will give you counseling and your grandmother to help you cope. I will visit the house and give a report to the court—"

"I hate you, too. Go away."

Bridget sighed. Why should this be easy?

"You go ahead and hate me."

Naomi started crying. "Mom tried to kill herself before. I grabbed the keys. I drove. I hate her, too. Why should I care? I never saw her anyway."

Rob hovered outside, either oblivious or insensitive to their conversation, but Officer Bennett prevented him from entering the room. She was beginning to like Officer Bennett.

She stepped outside the room.

"You should've left this to the social workers." Rob jangled his keys, but his tone had softened as if he was trying to appear nice around Officer Bennett.

Ignoring him, she said, "Officer, may I speak with the attorney general?"

Rob shook his head. "Listen, I've spent enough time here. Let me transport the kid back to Lincoln County like I'm supposed to. I'll take care of her; we'll see you in court on Monday."

The thought of her in the car with him for over two hours was too much. Rob had exhibited the empathy of a lizard.

"You can wait."

And she cocked her head. She would mess with Rob in her own time and in her own way.

# Chapter 6

The courtroom was small but efficiently designed with four wooden pews for a jury, one long conference table, and a judge's bench crowned with a wooden emblem of the Wisaka Nation. As Bridget hovered by the conference table, a man sporting a tie, leather boots, and jeans entered. A long braid rested on the middle of his back.

"I'm John Wapello, the attorney general of the Wisaka Nation. Have a seat."

She shook his hand. "Thank you for seeing me on a Saturday, Mr. Wapello."

"Call me John. And not a problem. The Buyland protesters are keeping me busy. What can I do for you?"

Bridget pulled the file out of her tote bag and laid it on the table.

"Two points. My client is Naomi Kline, the subject of a CINA case. You have her in your custody."

"Officer Bennett brought me up to speed."

"She's accused of stealing a car. Has a complaint been filed?

If so, I'd like a copy of the charges."

John leaned back and folded his hands on his stomach. She didn't understand his hesitancy. In Lincoln County, her request would have been standard protocol.

"You are a hoot. Two points? Here's my first point. Are you admitted to practice law on the reservation? You do realize you are in another jurisdiction."

Bridget mentally slapped her forehead. She needed a different approach.

"My client called. She's fourteen, so I came. I'm her attorney and also her guardian ad litem, acting in Naomi's best interest. And not much chance of appearing in court on a Saturday. I would never let a fourteen-year-old navigate this mess alone. Given what has happened, I'm glad I came."

John smiled, leaning toward Bridget. "Cool! That sounds better. Did you enjoy the drive out here?"

"I can coordinate with local counsel, if needed."

"You mean the public defender."

"Yes."

"Not everyone would make the trip out. Bridget McGarrity, right? Is that Irish? The Irish really do turn beet red, don't they?" She smiled politely, feeling her face burn as if on cue. He continued. "The Wisaka Nation has its own constitution, laws, police force, courts, and school. We also have our own bar association."

She was being scolded like a child, and maybe she deserved it.

"Let me officially welcome you. Here is a list of attorneys from our bar association who have co-counseled with outside attorneys."

He slid a piece of paper with names and numbers across the table.

"The charges against Naomi—" said Bridget.

"The charges are from Lincoln County. Not us. A Juvenile Court Officer is en route to collect her and bring her back to Lincoln County."

Rob.

"He's hovering by the door outside," she said.

John folded his hands on the table like he was beginning a lecture. "Auto theft is a felony and wouldn't be handled by the reservation."

"A Class D felony. Naomi could face up to five years if tried as an adult," answered Bridget.

"That's right. The federal government has jurisdiction for serious crimes, even if the crime did occur on our land. No matter, though. Whatever Naomi did or did not do occurred in Lincoln County and does not involve us. You probably have heard of the case called *McGirt v. Oklahoma*? The supreme court affirmed that."

Bridget nodded, "...I did hear of that case. Tulsa is located in a reservation."

"I think Tulsa and most of Oklahoma chose to forget that."

"The tribe can't prosecute its own crimes?"

"You see the dilemma, and I deal with it every day. You only need to step outside and look at the protesters. The Buyland store argues it doesn't have to abide by our courts. We're arguing whether we can even handle the case."

Bridget closed her file. "I have one more request. You're the attorney general, and Naomi's mother died on this reservation. I would love to tell her that everything is being done to discover the cause of her mother's death. Can I tell her that?"

"Officer Bennett told me of the tragedy. The mother—"

"Cheri Kline," said Bridget.

"Cheri Kline died of complications of drugs and alcohol," said John.

"A woman died here, a young woman. Yes, she battled

mental illness, but she wasn't a drug addict. Her death deserves an investigation."

"My hands are tied, remember? I cannot prosecute car theft. And murder, I cannot prosecute murder. Those crimes are felonies, and we are back to the cold realities of jurisdiction— Wisaka Nation doesn't have it, not for a serious crime. Your federal government does."

Bridget stood up abruptly, unable to hold her frustration. "Then call the FBI and have them investigate."

"I did." John continued. "Officer Bennett informed me of the circumstances. We have ordered an autopsy with the neighboring county. Our officers are taking pictures now and collecting evidence. We will share findings with the FBI. But frankly, everyone tends to ignore us in these matters. But I'll do what I can."

"Thank you. That is at least something."

"I'll be honest with you. I don't think the FBI will pay attention, and our neighbor county doesn't like to do our autopsies. They think we should have our own medical examiner and morgue. A death concerning a woman who battled mental illness with no signs of a struggle with drugs and alcohol will not be at the top of their list."

"Thank you for trying." I'll call them myself, she thought.

"And Bridget, if Naomi is a Native American, we need to be informed. A CINA case involving an Indigenous child doesn't belong in state court."

"I am aware of that, but there was nothing in her file that says she is a Native American. I'll make inquiries."

The door swung open, and Officer Bennett emerged through the door. Naomi was by his side. Rob trailed behind, the keys to the shackles rattling, a grim reminder of what awaited the child.

The room fell silent as all eyes fell on her. Bridget broke

the ice.

"Sit next to me," she said.

Naomi looked down. Her silence was deafening. John Wapello spoke slowly and looked directly at her.

"Naomi, my sincerest sympathies to you and your family. Ms. McGarrity, may I speak with Naomi about her mother, nothing about the charges, of course."

"Briefly and in my presence," answered Bridget.

John nodded. "I didn't know your mother, Cheri Kline. Was she a member of the Wisaka Nation?"

"I don't know."

"It's OK. We can do this another time."

Naomi looked at the ceiling, her eyes pooling in tears, and she wiped them away.

"She was here about protests and reservation rights. She said that, at least. Elaine is from Oklahoma and lived with Indians."

"Thank you. That helps tremendously. OK, then," said John. "Ms. McGarrity, any CINA case with a child with Native American heritage should have been flagged. The Indian Nation must be notified of the child's Indian heritage because the tribe's interest may be superior to anyone else. The Federal Indian Child Welfare Act requires it."

"I've heard them talk about Indians. I didn't steal no car."

Bridget lightly covered Naomi's hand with hers. "I understand. I'll look into it. Social services may know more."

Naomi leaned back in her chair and turned her head away. Rob straightened like he was preparing for Naomi to fight. Officer Bennett's eyes were on Rob.

Bridget's cell phone vibrated, flapping on the table like a caught fish. She grabbed the phone and looked briefly at her new notifications. There were two communications: one from Elaine Kline and the other from the Juvenile County Attorney in Broken River.

"Time for us to go, Miss Kline," said Rob.

"Excuse me. One minute." Bridget scampered to the window to listen to her messages. After an awkward couple of minutes, she returned to the table.

"Rob, time to change your afternoon plans." He let out a noise—a combination of a laugh and a grunt as she leaned back in her chair. "Check your phone. There's a message or two you might have missed."

His face paled as he raised the cellphone high, searching for a better connection and looking like a proud cheerleader with a baton.

Bridget cleared her throat. "If I may?"

"Please do. The suspense is killing me," said John.

"If Mr. Robert Small is able to check his phone, at least two phone messages should be there. One from Naomi's grandmother clarifying she never wanted charges filed. She simply didn't know the location of her car and was concerned, so she contacted the police. The second should be from the Lincoln Juvenile County Attorney confirming no charges for auto theft will be brought."

"What? I don't think so. She's going to Lincoln County with me. I need an order or something."

Bridget folded her hands calmly on the table. "Officer Bennett, you can release Naomi into my custody. A social worker is waiting for her in Broken River."

"Good enough for me. I'll make sure the Lincoln County attorney sends the confirmation. You'll get your order, Mr. Small," said John.

"Fine. Take the kid home." Rob wouldn't look at Naomi and Bridget.

"Is that alright with you?" she asked Naomi. She nodded. "Then it's a deal."

With a heavy foot, Rob stomped out of the room. Naomi rubbed her wrists as her dark eyes looked off into space as if her mind had transported her elsewhere, to a safer, happier place.

John held open the courtroom door. "Nice to see a new face. Let me know if you're interested in becoming a member of the bar. Lincoln County could use an attorney who understands what we do here."

Bridget studied him for a minute. John was a prosecutor giving a helpful hint to a defense attorney. Why was he being so nice?

"The drive isn't so bad if you don't mind corn and soybeans," he said.

A small crowd had formed in the hallway, and John shook his head. "This day doesn't end," said John.

"I'll escort you to your car," said Officer Bennett.

# Chapter 7

The crowd ignored them, and Bridget sighed in relief. She had had enough for one day. They were a mishmash of people, some casually dressed looking like protestors and others in suits ready to do business. The clerk Bridget had dealt with earlier was shaking her finger at one of the suits. Another woman with a press badge and microphone stood in front of a camera asking questions. Officer Bennett directed Bridget and Naomi past them.

"What's the crowd about?" Bridget asked.

"It's about Buyland again. The U.S. Marshal has decided to solve our problems for us. They will keep the store open and stop protesters from closing it," answered Officer Bennett.

Outside the community center, grim-faced protesters waved signs and two squad cars hovered nearby. A dozen officials wore black t-shirts with "US Marshal" in yellow on the back. John Wapello made a beeline toward them, and a few protesters hissed as he walked by.

"The Buyland should shut down. That's what my mom

said," Naomi said, her voice faint. Both of them paused, examining the crowd and trying to understand what was happening. Officer Bennett tucked fresh tobacco in his cheek, hung a thumb on his belt, and stood by Bridget's car far from the crowd.

"Some agree the store should close. Yet Buyland provides jobs, which doesn't happen every day, even if they do not want to follow our ways here, our laws, and be in our courts." His voice lowered. "It's best that you go. And I'm very sorry to hear about your mother."

"Then find out who hurt her," said Naomi.

"You can tell me why and how you ended up here. That would help."

Naomi looked at the ground and then at the sky. Anywhere other than at Officer Bennett.

"Why don't you start, Officer? How did you find Naomi?" suggested Bridget.

Bennett frowned. "Fine then. This young lady was parked outside the community center, sound asleep in the driver's seat."

Naomi's face flushed.

"I drove here with my mom. She said she had to meet a guy and we drove to a house, but I waited in the car. She never came back. I walked up to the house and asked, but they said she had left. I drove around and found this building." Naomi looked at the ground drawing a line in the pebbles on the pavement. "I guess I fell asleep."

Officer Bennett nodded. "Do you know what house?"

"It was dark. A guy named Monroe? I think she said that. She talked about a lot of people." A fresh wind blew the hair from Naomi's pale face. She stood still, unmoving, an exhausted calmness. Bridget closed her eyes for a moment as the breeze revived her.

"You can figure that out, I'm sure, Officer? I think we

should head back."

"Yes. Thank you, Miss Kline," said Officer Bennett as he walked back to the crowd and stood near the U.S. Marshals.

Naomi kicked a stone, sending it across the parking lot. The effort seemed to exhaust her as her slim, lanky frame sagged.

"Ms. McGarrity..." said Naomi.

"Call me Bridget." She opened the car door.

"Don't lawyers drive fancy cars like Cadillacs?"

Bridget squinted at the faded green veneer of her Pontiac Grand Am. A new rust patch was developing near the bumper. "This car gets me to where I need to go. The last of the series before they discontinued the line. She's a resilient old car."

Naomi slipped into the front seat and sank into the plush upholstery.

"In Broken River, you'll meet a social worker, Nick Harmon."

"And I'm not going to Elaine's right now?"

"I don't think so, but you might reconsider."

"Don't I get to say what happens? You're my lawyer, so you have to do what I tell you to do!"

"I am your guardian ad litem and your lawyer. The 'lawyer' part means, yes, I do what you ask. The 'guardian' part means I find what's in your best interest, even if you disagree with me, and I report to the court. I remain your guardian during the duration of the case."

"What if you decide something I don't like?"

"Sometimes the child has two different people performing that job, if there is a conflict between what is best for you and what you want."

"What happened to my mom?" Naomi whispered as she looked outside the window.

"I don't know," Bridget said.

"You can figure it out, right? You can make things happen.

That's what my mom said."

When Bridget's parents died, she and her brother had no one; social services and a disinterested neighbor were it. Even her court-appointed lawyer, her personal advocate, ignored her. She swore she'd never be that type.

Naomi rested her forehead on her knees. To lose a mother is awful, the worst. It's like losing a home, a permanent state of homesickness, and a feeling you could never shake, thought Bridget. How could she help her?

"Lawyers aren't the police."

"But you're a guardian ad... whatever. Finding out what happened to my mom is in my best interest," said Naomi.

"You do have a point."

"Promise you'll try?"

"Yes, I promise."

"Glad to hear you say that, Bridget."

She used Bridget's first name so casually, it disarmed her. Her younger clients usually resorted to "ma'am", "the lawyer", or even "sir."

They both fell silent as they drove past the Buyland store. Protesters stepped aside as U.S. Marshals opened the store trailed by Buyland employees. The federal government will help open a store. But won't investigate the death of a poor woman, she thought.

"You contact me when you like."

But Naomi didn't hear. She had already fallen asleep.

# Chapter 8

Monday morning started with the usual ban. Phone calls and paperwork would consume the bulk of her day. Bridget grimaced at her desk stacked with files: a brief to submit, a client who urgently needed a visit in jail, another who needed a divorce like ten years ago, and a statute of limitations running out fast.

She rubbed her neck as she assessed the two piles of files on her desk—the "hot pile" and the "not-hot pile." Usually, the not-hot pile was the large, distended beer belly of a mountain, sloping toward the slimmer hot pile. Today those piles were dangerously reversing into two bloated stacks. The file *In the Interest of N.K.* hovered between the two awaiting its sorting.

She grimaced as images of Cheri's body raged through her head. She picked up the *In the Interest of N.K.* file and walked into her office lobby, sat on the red chrome chair in the reception, and gave it a spin. The office building was a former Maid Rite restaurant converted to a commercial space with three offices and a small conference room where the kitchen used to be. The drive-through window was now the office window of

Diane, her secretary. The reception desk was the former Maid Rite white laminate counter along with two red-topped chrome bar chairs. She took another spin, walked to Diane's office, and placed the file *In the Interest of N.K.* on her desk.

"You wouldn't believe my weekend."

After bringing her up to speed, Diane tsk-tsked.

"Never a dull moment here. Not sure you can take another complicated case. The schedule is packed," Diane said as she reached to answer the phone.

Diane was the primary face of the McGarrity Law Office. She came at 7:45 and left at 5:00; she was never sick and never late. Faithfully, she answered phones, wrote briefs, kept the books, and covered for Bridget when needed. Diane was also a slob. Enormous piles of paper topped her desk and floor like whipped frosting on a cake, leaving only a jagged path from the door frame to her chair. The shades to the single office window had never been opened. Bridget inherited Diane and the dysfunctional filing system from a former law partner. The crazy filing system also made Diane indispensable. Only she could find anything in the nooks and crannies of the office. Yet nothing was ever lost.

"Did you check your voicemail?" said Diane.

"Voicemail is so last year. Anything spicy, or can I delete?"

Diane frowned. "I think it's a voicemail from Cheri Kline, the kid's mother. From last week."

"Oh."

Ambling back to her office, she glowered at the bright red light on her phone. The voice mail light was always lit, and she had grown accustomed to it, relying instead on Diane to field calls for her.

She hesitated. Cheri Kline wasn't her client; Naomi was. In CINA cases, she didn't talk to a parent unless Cheri's attorney authorized it—usually. And that "usually" depended on who the attorney was. In this case, Bridget didn't need to look through the file for authorization because Cheri's attorney was Barry Van Ekes. In the last five years, Bridget never received a letter from him, and he never returned phone calls and even missed court hearings. His lethargy and neglect made his clients desperate, which was likely why Cheri had called Bridget.

She pressed "play" as a woman cleared her throat, her breathy voice shaking.

"What I'm calling for is I need clarification on Naomi. I want you to put my mother on the stand and make her swear under oath...."

Cheri talked fast, jarringly, and rambled on from everything about the government to religion and the environment.

"... Miss Bridget, if you could help me, I'll give you every penny I have. I know you're God. You're a guardian, like an angel for my Naomi. They're trying to put me away, and I need the law. I need the law, ma'am. I'm sorry to bug you with this. I'll be at 5E. That's if I don't make it. That's where they'll put me. I'll expose what they're doing first. I need friends. Thank you, ma'am, very much."

Bridget replayed the message. If she didn't make it? She knew Bridget was God? That was a first, she thought. She played the message again. And again.

Parents rarely sought out their child's attorney as diligently as Cheri had, and she'd never received a call like that.

The framed law degree appeared to laugh at her. At first, she had hungrily devoured the classes and lectures during law school. Hours in the library, reading about the groundbreaking cases where the weak and innocent always prevailed. Practicing law was a different story. After five years in a Chicago firm and an eighty-hour workweek, the glamor of justice and winning every case became distant goals—lost but not forgotten. She represented large corporations and as an associate she had only met a client twice. The experience left her unprepared for the job of a solo lawyer when she moved back to Broken River. What she really needed was the calm of a Zen monk, the ruthlessness of a ninja assassin, the fangs of Cujo, and the patience of Mother Teresa to do this job. A sugar daddy would have been lovely.

The next steps for Naomi's case were predictable. Social services had taken Naomi to the youth shelter after she had dropped her off. She would receive counseling and would likely return to her grandmother's home. If that failed, there would be a search for other relatives or a foster home, or the father could resurface. The case would be closed. Story complete. Or was it?

A folder from the hot pile slid to the corner of her desk. So many cases needed her attention. She shoved it aside.

She grabbed the telephone directory of the Eighth District Bar Association and placed it on Diane's desk.

"New project, Diane. Our client, Naomi Kline. The reservation is investigating her mother's death, or at least trying to. I want to make sure this case isn't ignored. I need your help in contacting the county and the federal authorities—"

"Federal authorities? The FBI?" said Diane.

"Yes, thank you. And federal because of a little thing called jurisdiction. It's a problem. The Wisaka Nation doesn't have jurisdiction to prosecute a serious crime."

"Goodness, then who else would care?" Diane balanced a pen behind her ear.

"Exactly the problem. Apparently, no one. I've been told that the Feds don't care and won't thoroughly investigate. That doesn't sit right, and that child will not have peace."

"Or you."

Bridget paced back and forth in front of Diane's desk. The action felt good.

"Gather your weapons lawyer-style. It's time to lock and load." She raised a fist in the air.

"I'll load paper in the printer." Diane yawned.

Within minutes Diane had phone numbers and addresses to every federal agency in the district. Bridget and Diane sent a flurry of letters—certified, regular, facsimile copy and email attachment. The certified mail made them look serious. Fax, because they still used faxes. Email, who knew? They called government bureaucrats who took messages.

Two hours later, only one agency called back. "We will get back to you," they said, "We'll take a second look at the investigation," they said, but made no promises. In other words, the feds might or might not pay attention to a drug crime or a particularly gruesome murder, but a dead, troubled, possibly drunk woman? "No" was the clear and consistent answer.

Bridget called the county, even if doing so meant an awkward conversation. Usually she was defending her clients from prosecution, not soliciting help. The Lincoln County Sheriff was unavailable, and the call was forwarded to an intake clerk who incredulously asked whether Bridget wanted a crime investigated so the Sheriff could throw her client in jail.

In a sing-song voice, the clerk explained. "Wisaka Reservation is not even in our county. They've got their own deal. Dearie, unless the crime was here, there's no reason for the Sheriff to rally West. You might ask the city."

Bridget cringed as she heard "dearie," but said nothing. It was probably the clerk's dream to explain jurisdiction to a defense attorney.

"Great suggestion. I'll do that."

Bridget frowned at the phone headpiece. The clerk was right—the city. Why not take a tumble down another step on the bureaucratic government ladder, from federal to state, county...oh, why not the city? She walked to Diane's office again.

"Let me know when I should hire part-time to sort that pile."

"I've never lost anything. Your files are impeccable, as usual." Diane handed Bridget the phone messages.

"I will not touch your desk—today. I need one more number—Chief French."

"Will do," said Diane.

Bridget cracked a knuckle. Hank French rattled her. Chief French had been the police chief for Broken River for at least a decade and knew Bridget well. Way too well. The younger Officer French had dealt with her on more than one occasion when she was a runaway teenager. While she languished in foster care, Bridget was a frequent flyer at the Broken River PD for all the wrong reasons. He had become well-acquainted with her situation.

Chief French took the call himself.

"Bridget McGarrity, counselor. Always a joy. Even though you joined the dark side."

"Criminal defense is not the dark side, Chief. Not this time. I'm calling about a CINA. I'm hoping your office will investigate a case."

Bridget explained Cheri's death and the lack of an investigation.

French chuckled. "Still making social workers run in circles? You had a CINA case until the child stole a car. Charming kid. You know I'm bound by the law and jurisdiction."

"Again, the theft charges were dropped. And Cheri Kline's death may have a link to Broken River. She drove straight to the reservation from here."

"OK, counselor. Here's what I'm going to do for you." Chief French gave an extra emphasis on "you." She'd feared she had just sold her soul for a favor. "I'll send an officer to ask a couple of questions and see if anything smells. Give me a holler on the horn in about a week if you don't hear from us sooner."

"Thanks, Hank. I appreciate it." Bridget smacked the phone

in its cradle with a thud. Waiting a week was unbearable. As a lawyer, she was used to the tools that made people jump—she could issue a subpoena, ask for a deposition. Here she was like anyone else. Reverting to a mere complaining citizen without legal tools was frustrating.

Diane walked into her office with a stack of papers representing a month of billing. She placed the file on the corner of her desk along with twenty other files.

"I'll have to create my own jurisdiction. How about Planet Bridget, where judges, jurisdiction, and orders aren't needed? Where the world does as I tell them because Bridget McGarrity knows best. I should draft my own rules."

"Make sure you get a retainer. And your bag lunch is here," said Diane.

"My who?"

Diane annunciated the words slowly. "That man—the salesman type, who left messages about a business proposition. You didn't tell me more. He said it was urgent. You said it wasn't."

"I forgot about that, and I don't think I have the time."

"I've never seen anyone buy you lunch and certainly not deliver it, too."

"Maybe something will surface with Naomi."

"You really think anything can be done? It's another poor kid who ran out of luck. At least she has a grandmother."

Bridget sighed. Diane was right. There was little more she could do. She had done what could be done and had talked to anyone who would listen to her, which is more than a lot of lawyers would do. She took Naomi's file and chucked it in the not-hot pile.

"I'll talk to Naomi myself, but I've done what I can. So, let's see who's buying me lunch today."

# Chapter 9

A man wearing a dark suit stood in the lobby. He had a medium build and a square-shaped head with sharp cheekbones and looked like a cover page for corporate success, except for the paper sack with takeout from the only sushi restaurant in town.

He called last week and asked her out for lunch to inform her of "the great job opportunities out there." The call intrigued her enough to agree to lunch but not in a public place. Depending on the opportunity or whether he would be recognized, she didn't want any gossip that she was looking for a new job. So, she agreed to a fifteen-minute sack lunch at her office.

"Bridget McGarrity?" The man held out his hand, the size of a baseball glove. His gold watch looked like it could do double-time as a barbell. "I'm Chet Russell."

"Nice to meet you, Mr. Russell."

"And you, Bridget. Call me Chet, and thanks for your time. I would've taken you to a decent restaurant."

"This works better for me because my day tends to be rather

unpredictable."

"May I call you Bridget?

"You just did."

"Excellent. You are quick."

As he unpacked lunch in the conference room, Chet talked.

"I know you're busy, so I'll get straight to the point. I'm a consultant for a nonprofit startup called Sun Family Foundation. The foundation wants to partner with larger law firms across the state to address the needs of underprivileged children. It's fantastic—a new enterprise and people are motivated."

She sighed. "To be honest, if you're looking for pro bono work, my hands are full. But leave the literature, and I'll consider it."

"Oh, no, I get my fifteen minutes. Hear me out. I'm only in town for a few nights. Wasabi?"

The square jawbone widened into a Ken doll grin, his pearly white teeth popping. Chet took out the sushi boxes and chopsticks. Her stomach growled, and as she sniffed the miso soup, her shoulders loosened.

He continued. "You're young, but experienced. Committed to helping families. And a fighter."

"Thank you."

"You're aware of the pro bono ethics rules? Every lawyer must provide pro bono services or donate to an organization that does."

"Yes, of course, and I do my fair share already."

"I'm sure, and you're qualified to do it. But it's getting harder to do pro bono work for corporate attorneys. Everything is so specialized, even representing the poor. A few firms prefer to donate rather than take on a pro bono case. That is where Sun Family Foundation, a nonprofit serving families in need, comes in. Headed by a lawyer who is an expert in representing the needs of the disadvantaged."

"Listen, Chet, this meal is delicious, and lunch hits the spot, but where is this going? My pro bono cases end up being a client who skips out on their bill."

"Let me be clear. I'm recruiting, and Sun Family Foundation is looking for a director."

Bridget dropped her chopsticks. "Director? OK. I didn't expect that."

"You're perfect. Bridget McGarrity, an orphaned teenager, who was thrust into foster care. A survivor and a winner."

"My background should be sealed."

The sun lowered in the sky, and the light shone through the latticed shades, casting a fractured light across Chet in a stripe pattern like he was behind bars. His pale eyes squinted to narrow slits in the September sun.

"I used to work in politics and learned to dig up pasts. Social workers love to talk about success stories, especially ones that become lawyers. You're the poster child of the foster care system."

The Ken doll pearly whites popped out of his head as he chuckled. She tried to envision herself in a new job. A chance to help families before social workers and the courts got involved, and even prevent the tragedies before they ever happened. Bridget wouldn't have to worry about overhead or finding the next client.

Her head began to ache. Perhaps it was the smell of his cologne, his tailored suit, or too much wasabi. Her thoughts went to her clients and the thought of leaving them behind. Clients like Naomi, languishing in the youth shelter, not that she had been able to do much for her.

"I have an ongoing law practice, and I can't just walk away. But I'm happy to look it over."

Ken doll-cum-Chet folded veined hands on his crossed legs, revealing shiny leather dress boots.

"I've left out the sweetest part. I've found a buyer for your law practice. How does two hundred thousand sound to you?"

That was triple what she made last year—one of her better years. She cleared a bit of seaweed stuck in her tooth.

"Two hundred thousand? Why not half a million?"

"Oh, my, and you are a negotiator! I like that about you. That amount might take some doing, counselor. I'll talk with my people to see if we can butter the bread a bit. We are looking for a commitment now."

An urge to bolt flashed through her—to run, or kick him out. "Uh, sorry, Ken—I mean Chet. Mr. Russell. I'm a bit flummoxed. Why the rush?"

"We're ready to go. We have the startup funds, and waiting will only increase expenses."

"It took years to build my practice."

"The contract is for three years, and we'll have you off your cases by the end of the week. The wonderful thing is you don't have to move. You can stay right here in Broken River. Now, I won't lie, there will be some travel. I'll be sending you to Cedar Town soon to meet a donor who will be a future board member."

He crossed his legs and casually placed his hand on the conference table, his big watch catching the light. Was it a Rolex?

"Bridget, this is a unique opportunity. Now, don't make me look elsewhere when I have the right person in front of me. Families here need you."

It was a great opportunity, and she needed time. She looked at her twenty-dollar watch. She had already sat with him for over an hour.

"I have an appointment that I must make if I want to relieve the babysitter on time. She gets grumpy when I'm late. And my wallet lighter."

Chet opened a leather folder. "This is the contract, ma'am." He flicked the crisp paper with his finger. "This I shall leave here for your review."

He spread the pages across the conference table like he was a dealer laying cards on the table. She leafed through the contract.

"Who prepared the contract?"

Chet abruptly stood and closed his briefcase. "I see your hesitation. This is a rare and wonderful opportunity for the small town. You would have an office and staff. That fine lady by the door would be able to come with you. You wouldn't have to chase clients who don't pay bills or make trips to distant counties or reservations—"

"How d'you know about the reservation?"

"I'm good at what I do. This may all be overwhelming, I know, but you think it over tonight. I'll be in touch tomorrow."

Her heart throbbed in her chest. Was it the MSG in the food or nerves? "It's a lot to take in."

She walked him out of the office to his car, a bright and shiny white SUV with a Maryland license plate. Probably a rental.

"Remember, we'll talk tomorrow!"

Back inside, her thoughts were muddled. Diane never budged from the computer screen as she managed the front desk.

"Should I start writing my severance package? Or fire me, and I'll collect unemployment."

"No one is going anywhere."

"OK. Don't forget your appointment with Abby Baker. Not that you would forget."

"No, I never do."

"Just the same."

She ambled back to her office and absorbed her surroundings with fresh eyes—the walls, wood flooring, even the red chrome stools she couldn't part with. Despite the difficulties of running a small-town law office, she rarely thought of quitting, let alone selling. She had never heard of anyone actually selling an ongoing solo law practice. Jilted spouses, abandoned kids, and petty criminals didn't start bidding wars. What was interesting about her clients? Did it matter? The entire experience with Chet was confusing. Yet he was probably right—the job was a once-in-a-lifetime opportunity, especially for this town. And for that price, she would have college tuition for Aiden in one day.

Her hand brushed across Naomi's file in the not-hot pile. Why had Chet mentioned the reservation? She stuffed it into her briefcase alongside Abby Baker's and left the office. Her thoughts bounced back and forth in her head like a tennis ball. Her cases were people, not a commodity to be traded.

# Chapter 10

The apartment housing was a recent development off the main roadway. What the development lacked in landscaping, it replaced with decorative stones. Abby Baker's apartment was one of a large complex of modestly-sized apartments. A half-mile away, the utility plant towers hummed ominously and spewed a constant cloud of steam over the complex.

As she pulled the Grand Am into the parking lot, the wasabi in her stomach growled in protest. The meeting with Abby should be quick, leaving enough time to pick up Aiden. Abby had refused to come to her office, so Bridget decided to go to Abby. She could've skipped the visit altogether and just crossed her fingers Abby would show for court. Lawyers weren't obligated to chase clients who refused to communicate, but, alas, in the world of court-appointed cases, chasing clients was often part of the job. If the client was a no-show, the judge might grill her on her efforts for the client. And for a good reason, the lawyer was the sole conduit to the accused—a lawyer who could discuss the rough ride of justice candidly.

After parking the car, she walked through the litter-free parking lot and past an empty commercial garbage bin. She ran a hand through her curls, detangling a knot, and noticed they were unsteady. It had been an eventful couple of days. If someone had told her she would spend a Sunday identifying a body, then entertaining an offer for her law practice the next day, she'd have called them crazy.

A powerful stench of cigarettes seeped from under Abby's door as she knocked. No one answered. The hallway carpeting dampened the sound, and dramatic music from a TV show was audible. She knocked again.

A large woman opened the door. "I thought it'd be you."

Abby hobbled back to a loveseat, a spitting distance from the television, which blared loudly. While sitting back down, Abby groaned loudly. Her hips spanned the width of the loveseat and her small head balanced like a grapefruit on her wide shoulders, her body too big for her head. Abby stared at the television, ignoring Bridget, who analyzed Abby's lack of cooperation. Given the way she was moving and that she was unable to engage in conversation, it was likely Abby was in pain, disabled, and possibly even impaired.

Despite the apparent disabilities, the apartment was clean and had one bedroom, a bathroom, a kitchen, and a main living area. In the corner of the living area was a spare mattress with blankets. Bridget sat on the only chair available, a faux leather armchair next to the loveseat. She opened Abby's file folder and clicked a pen.

A man holding a toddler stepped out of the bedroom. He was shirtless and sported a chest blackened with tattoos. The numbers 515, the area code for the capital, were tattooed across his shoulder. Bridget tried not to stare as a cigarette hung from his mouth, the smoke wafting above the child's face.

"Don't mind him." Abby's eyes fixated on the talk show.

"Sorry, Abby, I must have missed in the file that a man and a baby are living with you. Or that you have a baby. I thought that room belonged to your son."

"No, dammit, I can't live with my son because we fight too damn much. He's living at the foster lady's house, and she's real nice to me. That there baby ain't mine." Abby giggled. "That's my friend's. He's needing a bed for a few days."

Abby's hands flapped a moment, and she reached for an already opened bag of cheese curls.

Bridget closed the manila file; she was wasting her time. If Abby didn't want her son back, this visit was in vain.

"The social workers said you don't want to go to the hearing next week."

Abby threw the remote on the loveseat like a petulant toddler.

"I ain't got no ride."

"Social services will provide transportation. You should sign the release form, so that way, they can understand what your disability is."

"I ain't signing nothing." Abby's eyes remained glued to the TV, and the muscles in her jaw rippled like a boxer's abs.

"You have a good case, and we can fight it together. Your son can come home."

Social services claimed Abby had tried to commit suicide while her teenage son was present in the apartment and had removed him from her home last month. At first blush, the situation sounded awful, but closer examination revealed that the suicide attempt was a few scratches on her arm with a fork. Her son freaked, understandably, and called the police, who took Abby to the hospital. Social services alleged she had neglected the teenager by failing to get a sitter when she was hospitalized because he had stayed with friends for two days. Now Abby faced child endangerment charges and a CINA case.

Social services intended to observe the family for a while and expected they would drop the case once Abby received help. The case wasn't so different from Naomi's. Once Cheri was treated, Naomi would've returned to her mother or grandmother, but unfortunately, that didn't happen. No reason this case should be easy either.

"At least before you make any major decisions. I need you to understand the charges and your situation before you—"

The baby wailed, and the man carried the child to the bedroom. Bridget's eyes followed him.

"We need to talk. Not in front of your... um... guest."

"Don't mind him. He's a friend and gives me rides."

"He'll drive you to court?"

"Don't you trick me! He ain't here that day," Abby stomped her feet and jutted her chin. Red blotches spotted her pasty white face. "He's taking my son's bed and watching the baby. I love babies!"

Abby laughed as the baby cried louder and louder.

"Why don't we talk somewhere private? Otherwise, our conversation won't be confidential."

The baby continued to howl. The air thickened as her breathing slowed and every parental cell in Bridget's body burned. Pick up the boy and comfort him, she screamed silently in her head.

"Who the hell cares? I don't understand and don't wanna go to court. It don't matter to me. I'll hire that other attorney."

"Do you want a new attorney? I'll make that happen."

Abby smiled at her. "No, sweetie, I like you. I like that other attorney, too, from Cedar Town. He wears bow ties. A lawyer should wear a bow tie. I'm going to make money with him. Not you, baby."

Bridget didn't probe any deeper. The airwaves were saturated with lawyer advertisements, promising big money, and confusing the public.

The tattooed man left the bedroom, leaning back in the corner, cigarette dangling from his mouth. He swayed, eyes burning red. The smell of alcohol emanated from him, even from across the room. The child's cry spoke to Bridget. Someone pick up that baby.

Abby said, "Oh, honey, get him? Would you? I can't get up. My back hurts. Bring him to me."

"No," he growled. "He'll quiet down. Kid's gotta learn."

The cigarette smoke and alcohol and her client's indifference made her nauseous. As she stuffed the file folder into her handbag, the tattoo man did the unthinkable—he flung his burning cigarette straight at the baby.

She clenched her jaw as she looked at anything but Tattoo Man. She feared a confrontation, but the skinny baby tugged at her heartstrings. The Tattoo Man stared with icy eyes. She tied her hair into a tight bun. Could this week get any stranger? Yesterday, she identified a body on the reservation, and today, she was watching a crime in progress.

She rubbed her temples, trying to summon wisdom and energy. Nothing came. At least, nothing useful. Instead, she heard screams from her younger brother, Tim, so many years ago. Bridget could hear the monotone voice of her foster mom in her head. "Your brother doesn't behave, and now he is choosing the chair. Do you need to choose the chair?" Every night for weeks, Tim "chose the chair," his piercing cry lasted for hours until he would fall asleep on the floor in a crumpled mess. Bridget had forgotten her foster mom's name. She, however, never forgot the crinkle of plastic cigarette packing stuffed with a yellow lighter on the side. The foster mom would smoke cigarette after cigarette while sipping from a clinking highball glass, her face blank, as her little brother cried. Banished to her bedroom, the foster mom would never let her help him, comfort him, or talk to him—be a big sister.

When she complained, the caseworker answered. "It's a safe home. Foster parents are hard to find." The next day, Bridget packed what belongings she and Tim had, and she skipped school. She waited the entire day in a park across from her brother's school. At 2:40 p.m. when school let out, she picked him up and walked to Aunt Irene and Uncle Billy's. That same evening, they enjoyed sloppy joes and a movie. An impulsive, passionate decision was when she was at her best, especially when it came to social services.

Here she was again—a child in imminent danger. No court order was needed to tell her immediate action was necessary. If she called social services, days could pass before the department investigated or sought a court order. Trying to look nonchalant, she shifted her weight to one leg as the secondhand smoke filled her lungs.

"Abby, you're right. Do what you want. Kids can be real brats, and then they don't appreciate you! I know because I got a whiner myself at home. Can I bum a cigarette? It's been a long day," Bridget asked coyly.

Abby and Tattoo Man laughed, and he tossed the cigarettes and lighter to Bridget. She took one out, placed it under her nose, sniffing the fragrant, minted tobacco. It had been a long time. She lit the cigarette, inhaled, and coughed.

"Not my usual brand. But I'm lucky 'cause I don't deal with it no more. My ex manages that now, but dammit if I still don't gotta send them child support checks every month. Now they garnish my paycheck. Your friends in government can help?" Bridget gestured towards his shoulder where the man's 515 tattoo was.

Tattoo Man chuckled and inhaled, a wheeze that sounded like years of chain smoking. "You get it, man. I ain't shit paying child support. Dammit, this boy is mine, and I do what I want."

"Took the kid back, huh? Show 'em how it's done." Bridget walked over to the kitchen and ashed in the sink.

The baby boy continued to howl, and Tattoo Man walked toward the child.

"Fuck ya." Tattoo Man slurred his words as he swayed. "Shut it, you little shit."

"Stop yelling! Bring the baby here, and I'll hold him." Tattoo Man did nothing, and Abby did nothing, fixed on her couch, and the baby howled.

Bridget took a deep breath and said, "I have a real knack for babies. May I hold him? I'll walk the little crier around the complex, and he'll be snoozing for the next two hours. Guaranteed."

She felt for the car keys and jammed the cigarette in the corner of her mouth. As she walked toward the bedroom, she made goo-goo sounds. The red-faced baby sat on the floor and sucked on a finger. Tattoo Man turned away, retrieving the packet of cigarettes near the loveseat. Bridget understood the silence as approval and played peek-a-boo. She picked up the child.

With a child in one arm and keys in her pocket, she headed to the door.

"Handsome little shit," said Bridget. The two cackled like grinding gravel. "I'll be back in five."

"You don't have to walk him," replied Abby, her attention never leaving the TV.

"That's OK. I don't mind."

She jiggled the baby and turned the child forward, so he could look in front of him instead of the stranger holding him. The child quieted as they exited the apartment. She tossed the cigarette on the sidewalk and glanced behind her. No one followed.

Her tone softened as she spoke to the child. "Good baby,

time to go. What's the worst that could happen?"

Kidnapping charges for one. Her advice was never to put yourself in a situation where you must explain yourself to the police. So much for expert advice. She power-walked towards the car, placing the child in the back seat.

"There you go, buddy. My tote bag—that can be your own booster seat." She secured the seatbelt around him. "That'll work for a quick ride. The gooey Cheerios are from my son, Aiden. Enjoy."

The boy blinked at Bridget, his tired eyes never wavering. She swept away the mess from the back of the car. "You're too young for Cheerios."

"Bitch! Goddammit! Get back here!" yelled Tattoo Man.

Bridget slid into the front seat of her car, locked it. "Thanks for the cigarette!" She waved as she slowly drove the car, baby on board, leaving the scene. The baby chewed his fingers, eyes unblinking.

"This may come back and bite me in the ass!" she said out loud, slapping the Grand Am's dashboard. "But I feel much better. How 'bout you? Would you like a song?"

She launched into a breathy version of Old MacDonald. The baby cooed and resumed chewing two fingers.

# Chapter 11

The hospital room at Northeast Memorial bustled with activity. A nurse took the baby's vitals as Bridget securely held him in her lap. A medical attendant peeked in, cooing at the baby as she eyed Bridget from head to toe. The staff was all smiles, and she guessed word had gotten out that a lawyer had escaped with a neglected baby, and she was the hospital gossip for the day.

Bridget sent a series of texts to Aunt Irene, who confirmed Aiden was at home with Walter, and she needn't rush.

Another medical aide entered, carrying diapers and clothes for the child. The nurse undressed him, humming softly as she gently held the boy, rubbing his back as she wiped his face. The woman looked familiar, and her heart skipped. She nervously picked at her medical gown.

"Elaine, right? Naomi Kline's grandma?" asked Bridget.

Elaine looked nervously from side to side. Attorneys can make a person nervous, and Elaine didn't likely want to broadcast that she required a lawyer, which could signal trouble at home, thought Bridget. Elaine looked nothing like her granddaughter; she was short, fair-skinned with blue eyes and light brown hair.

"Good to see you again, Mrs. Kline. My deepest regrets about your daughter, Cheri. A coincidence seeing you here."

"Thank you, and not really a coincidence. I heard a lawyer brought in a baby and had to come myself to see. And here you are." Elaine tapped a baby bottle several times on her wrist to test the temperature of the formula.

"My house is way too quiet, Miss Bridget. Cheri's gone, and Naomi's at the shelter. I'm going to visit her today. Lord, I've made mistakes, but I want her home. I suppose I can talk with you to make that happen?"

"I represent Naomi, so, yes."

Elaine handed the baby bottle to Bridget. "The child is calm with you. Why don't you feed him?"

"Me? Ok, but you are the expert here."

"Not really. The doctor should be in shortly."

The boy grasped the bottle greedily, his quiet sucking sounds filling the room.

"He needed that. I could use a drink myself but perhaps a different flavor."

Elaine washed her hands in the sink as Bridget laughed at her own joke.

"I am so sorry about your daughter, Cheri. I hope to attend the funeral. So, I assume I will see you there?"

Elaine's face paled, and she smoothed the wrinkles from her hospital uniform even though there were no wrinkles.

"The what?"

"The funeral or memorial service?"

"Lord, I can't afford a funeral. I'm not one for ceremonies. She'll be cremated this week."

"I think Naomi would like a ceremony."

Elaine frowned. "We'll see if she makes it back."

A doctor entered the examination room.

"And what do we have here? Let's have a look at you, little

guy," he said. The doctor slipped the stethoscope around his neck, and the boy whimpered as Bridget untangled herself from his grip.

"Is there something specific I should look for? Our conversations are private," said the doctor. Bridget thought about the medical files on her desk that contained everything from a client's drug use to conversations about hemorrhoids and hangnails.

"Our conversations are private? That's a good one, doctor. Given what's happened to this child, every social worker, county prosecutor, and defense attorney will devour your notes."

He said nothing as he went to scrub his hands. He probably had no idea how much his chicken scratch notes would be scrutinized.

"Sorry, I didn't mean to be rude. Please make a thorough examination of the child," she said.

"You're the child's relative?"

"I'm a lawyer."

"The child's lawyer?"

"No."

"The parents' lawyer?"

"It's complicated." She smoothed her hair back into a bun. Hopefully, she looked better than she smelled.

The doctor raised his eyebrows. "You're just 'a lawyer'?"

"I really can't offer much more at this point. Sorry."

Elaine cleared her throat. "She saved this boy and brought him to the hospital."

He looked at her down the length of his raised nose. "That's a switch."

Another nurse entered. "Social services are here for the boy."

Bridget slipped out of the examining room, nodding discreetly to Elaine. How this would end for her and Abby, Bridget didn't know. Lawyers should defend their clients. Not implicate them in crimes or be a witness against them. She strolled down the hallway when her vibrating cell phone broke her reverie.

"Hi, Aunt Irene."

"Glad I caught you. I picked up Aiden and brought him home. Walter's home."

"Thanks." Walter was usually home.

"About the cookout on Saturday. Will Walter mow the lawn before Friday? I bought rolls and Tim is bringing steaks..."

Bridget wasn't listening. "Aunt Irene. I need fresh ears."

"Ears. Of course. Do you want to pick up corn?"

Bridget fanned herself with a legal pad and sat down. "No, I've got a situation."

Aunt Irene had practiced law in Broken River but dropped her business to move to California to live the alternative life on a commune. She and her brother had brought her back, but Aunt Irene had retired for several years.

"A crisis? Of course! Oh, Mighty Isis!" said Aunt Irene.

"Dedicated foe of evil!" answered Bridget.

"Defender of the weak."

"Champion of truth and justice."

By the end of the recited dialogue, based on the short-run 70s TV show, her chest loosened. Aunt Irene was hooked on the old TV show, *The Secrets of Isis*, and got Bridget hooked, too, and the goddess Isis became their inside joke. When life became desperate, they called for the powers of Mighty Isis, like the heroine in the show.

Bridget recounted her afternoon to her.

"You did what, Princess Warrior? Better polish that metal breastplate," said Aunt Irene.

"Funny."

"Bridget, baby, you're still causing mayhem for anyone you think unfit. Whether it's a foster parent, real parents, or, God forbid, a JCO."

"Gentle on the psychoanalysis. The kid was in danger, and I acted. Quickly." She emphasized the "quickly," long and loud.

"Retract your claws, honey. Not every disadvantaged kid is your little brother needing to be saved."

The more they discussed, the more she worried. Lawyers should defend clients, not rat them out. Abby could face criminal prosecution for aiding abuse and allowing Tattoo Man to live in her apartment, which might break the government rules for subsidized housing. The court would appoint Abby a new attorney, and in defending her, the attorney might go after Bridget.

The best-case scenario was nothing would happen. The worst-case scenario was the State could file criminal charges against Bridget for kidnapping, with a nice topping of disciplinary sanctions from the bar association. A call to 911 instead of fleeing with the child might have been prudent, but slow. Too slow.

"Other repercussions could come your way. The possibilities are endless," said Aunt Irene as Bridget paced.

"You make it sound sexy."

"Better hustle your butt down to the courthouse. Pronto. Get yourself off the case."

"I'll go in the morning."

After walking back to the examining room, she peeked in one more time. Elaine held the boy as the doctor inserted an I.V. The baby needed medical attention. Her instincts weren't so off.

Her cell phone vibrated, and she swore to herself as she saw Walter's name flash on her phone because it was her turn to cook, and she forgot.

"Late summer heat means confusion. I'll pick food up on the way home."

"Hi, Mommy. I found potato chips."

"Aiden? Where's Daddy?"

"In the garage."

"Can you find him for me?"

Aiden screamed on the phone, "Daddy!!!"

"I meant, go get him."

"I don't think he heard me."

"Are you fine?"

"Can you get pizza, the crunchy kind?"

"Taco pizza?"

Taco pizza—a pizza covered with ground beef, refried beans, extra cheese, and topped with crunchy tortilla chips. She begrudgingly agreed as she imagined the oncoming heartburn the pizza would give her.

"Go downstairs and sit with Daddy while he works. And stay away from the potato chips. I'll be home soon." She ended the call and glowered at the silent phone. "And thank you, Walter, for having my back and your humbling childcare skills. I love you, too, darling. And thank you for understanding my—"

She was going to scream but bit her lip as a patient glowered. Better to scream in a closed car.

# Chapter 12

"Mommy! You didn't forget dinner, and I told Daddy. And you're late," said Aiden.

"Really?"

"Aunt Irene said so."

Bridget kicked off her shoes at the front door and kissed his forehead. She would not admit to being late to Aiden. Once she apologized for being late, and he returned the favor with the daily greeting: "Late again, Mommy?"

"Did Aunt Irene tell you I have taco pizza? Where's Daddy?"

"I dunno."

She took the pizza to the kitchen, served Aiden a slice, and walked to the garage.

"Her Highness shows," Walter's deep bass voice resonated from the garage. "I need a second."

She headed to the sofa, put her feet on the ottoman, and scowled at the pathetic state of her stockings. Aiden jumped over his Lego bricks, pizza slice in hand. He sat in his favorite chair across from her, legs crossed and his free hand under his chin, like a psychiatrist analyzing a patient. He leaned slightly forward and whispered.

"Were you in jail again?" Aiden asked.

"No jail today, and you need a plate."

He jumped over the ottoman with another slice, but this time on a plate.

She assessed the spectacle on her legs—pantyhose with runs. She tugged at them, and the tear deepened.

"Nylon is natural. Petroleum products are natural, and gas is natural from mother earth. To earth, you must return."

"I'm never gonna wear those either," said Aiden.

"Smart kid. Why don't you give Mommy a moment?"

Aiden didn't move. Bridget cracked open her eye, finding her son standing above her. She groaned as she heaved her tired body up and hugged her son. "Two more hugs," she whispered, and then she pried herself from his slender arms.

She dragged herself up the three steps to the bedroom, closing the door quickly before her son tagged behind her. She slipped on her cutoffs and a favorite sweatshirt. As she pushed up her sleeves, Bridget considered going for a run, doing tai chi, or yoga. She had already skipped out making dinner. Beer at home felt better.

Walter emerged from the garage, rubbing paint off his hands. "I thought taco pizza gave you heartburn."

"So does starvation." Bridget opened a beer and took a generous gulp as he turned on the TV.

"Hard day saving the disenfranchised?"

"A bit more chaotic than usual," she said and grabbed a slice.

"Parents don't embrace their inner June Cleaver anymore." Walter ruffled Aiden's hair.

"June Cleaver? A baby boomer reference?"

Walter rubbed her shoulders as the stress of the day slipped away. "Ah, the touchy Gen Xers. And I'm not a baby boomer."

"You're close enough."

"I like to keep my distance."

"Buddy, let's give the TV a rest," she said.

A news broadcast captured her attention, and Bridget didn't move.

"The Midwest can look forward to more muggy, hot weather. That's not the only thing heating up. At the Wisaka Reservation, tension is rising between different factions of the Wisaka Nation and the Buyland discount store...."

"Weren't you there over the weekend?" asked Walter.

"... U.S. Marshals were deployed to help open Buyland after protesters blocked the entrance. Protesters allege the store improperly managed an employee—a supervisor allegedly sexually harassed a teenager...Buyland claims it fired the employee for theft and wants to fight the case review in federal court, not in the tribal courts. Authorities deny any connection to the body of a woman found dead on the reservation due to exposure..."

Bridget turned the TV off.

"You were on the reservation because of a new gambling habit? Not because of a dead woman. Right?"

A lock of his ash grey hair toppled toward his face, covering a smudge of light green paint. She brushed pizza crumbs off her face and kissed Walter on the cheek. Walter worried too much about Bridget; she didn't want to fuel the fire.

"How is the painting coming along?" asked Bridget. "You know, Aiden shouldn't be in the house alone while you work."

"You're changing the subject."

"I am. At least leave the garage door open. He didn't know where you were."

"He's OK. Isn't that right, buddy? Six years old and the big man on campus."

Aiden slid open the porch doors and Walter followed him into the backyard. She was looking forward to a quiet evening engaged in a benign, boring activity, like staring at a white wall, rocking back and forth in a straitjacket while mumbling incoherently. But the news report nagged at her, and she gave into temptation and pulled out her laptop and looked up Buyland. Wherever she went, Naomi's case pricked at her consciousness.

The discount store had opened two years ago, and the community touted the opening as the darling model of cooperation between corporate and Indigenous' interests. Within two years, the honeymoon was over. Buyland fired a junior employee after complaining about sexual harassment but claimed the employee underperformed and committed petty theft.

A group on the reservation, headed by Joe Monroe, sought to close the store. Monroe advocated fresh leadership for the Wisaka Nation, a re-negotiation of Buyland's lease, and organized protests to get his point across. U.S. Marshals got involved, forcing the store to open under court order.

"The protesters I saw yesterday," she said to herself.

Both the tribal government and Joe Monroe's group were unhappy about how the store was managed, but the tribal government wanted the store to stay open. Buyland tried to avoid a Native American courtroom and argued the lawsuit should be in the federal courts. She rubbed her neck. Not again— jurisdiction. Who rules whom, what, or where? She'd heard the word "jurisdiction" too many times in the last couple of days.

The house was quiet, and she snapped the computer closed. She peered outside as Walter and Aiden were kicking a soccer ball.

"To bed," said Bridget.

"Ten minutes more?"

"I clock out at eight o'clock. You don't want to be around when your parents turn into gelatinous blobs of Jell-O."

"Green Jell-O? Yum."

Aiden skipped up short three steps to the upstairs, then turned around and skipped down for a last hug of the day. Soon he will leap over all the stairs entirely, thought Bridget.

After putting Aiden to bed, she walked out to the backyard. The sun had set, and faint stars dotted the sky.

"A glass of red?" asked Walter with a smirk.

"My favorite color. Hellmart's best for $2.99?"

"I thought you weren't shopping there."

"I wasn't. Not until $2.99 wine and the mortgage."

"And the price of oil paints." Walter ran his hand through his gray hair and fastened it into a ponytail. "I could've made dinner. Call if you're late."

"I called Aunt Irene."

"You can call me."

She looked away. Walter wasn't exactly attentive to details like dinner. She slumped in her garden chair, visualizing a moment of peace before bed. A steady breeze gave respite from mosquitoes.

"Wish the rabbits would eat the mosquitoes instead of the lilies," said Walter. "Let's go inside. The mosquitoes love me."

Bridget didn't answer. Her thoughts wandered to the two crazy cases, Abby and Naomi. Her work made Walter nervous, so she rarely shared details about work. Still, Cheri's death had already hit the news, although she doubted her name would be in print. Walter should know, just in case. She slapped a mosquito on her neck and followed Walter inside.

"You should know about a couple of cases I'm working on in case it hits the news."

She told him the basics, leaving out names and people. Walter stood up abruptly, fetched the bottle of wine, and started pacing.

"Wish you'd find safer work."

"I was offered two hundred grand for my law practice," she

said in a flat tone.

Walter choked on his wine, dribbling on his white shirt. Bridget detailed her exchange with Chet Russell.

"That's great news!" Walter said.

"You're a bit too happy. Not sure it's for me. The offer is hard to believe."

"I would believe in two hundred grand in the bank." He took Bridget's feet from the aging wool ottoman and started massaging.

"They want me off my cases immediately."

"Even better. I mean, I shouldn't say that. I get worried." Walter finished his glass of wine.

She'd worked so hard in law school and moved back to Broken River and started her law practice. Wearing pantsuits and sensible shoes was a compromise and an accomplishment. Broken River had expected her to fail, and she had every excuse, given her background. She drew intense satisfaction in messing with the same people that messed with her.

The sky darkened with storm clouds, and Walter closed the window to the kitchen. He placed the cold pizza in the refrigerator, shutting the door too hard. A panoply of refrigerator magnets cascaded to the floor.

"The Native American case, you're too close. I mean, a woman died."

Walter was never an easy read when it came to whether he was ticked. Years of painting and renovating houses gave him calm and patience. She reassembled the magnets and photos.

"I like the office job in a corporation. Sounds safer," he said.

"Don't worry about me."

Walter had his quirks, and one of them was worrying about things, especially Bridget. Ignoring his quirks worked for her for the six years they had been together. Aiden's arrival in the world was an unexpected joy after a weekend of impulsive fun. She had just met him, and she resigned to be a single parent. Walter wrote her a letter, asking for permission to be a part of her life and their future child. How could she deny her child a father when she herself missed her own? Bridget agreed and never looked back.

"Tell me about your day. How about complementary colors? I don't get why they call it complementary."

Walter scratched his chin. "I'm making significant progress on the new piece. It's innovative and different. Expressionism didn't do well at the art fair last year."

"Didn't do well" was an understatement. Concerned mothers covered their children's eyes as they rushed past Walter's art booth.

"I'm really close this time."

Walter's voice trailed off as he headed toward the garage to continue the world's next great masterpiece. She rubbed her temples and stretched out on the couch, the sounds of cicadas creaking rhythmically outside.

Maybe Walter was right, and a change wouldn't be so terrible. She said to herself, "Sun Family Foundation. Hi, I'm the director." The title sounded so official and service-oriented. She tried it out again, "Hi, I'm the director. Let me take your order." Would she have to be nice all the time?

***

Thud. Bridget lay on the shag carpet of the living room and jerked her head back, smacking it on the coffee table. She had fallen asleep on the couch and rolled right onto the carpet. The clock ticked quietly—it was four a.m. As faint dreams of screaming babies and a running teenager slipped from her consciousness, she stretched the sleep from her limbs and rose slowly as blood rushed to her head.

*I'll have no rest until I finish this case*, she thought. A new career can wait.

She headed to the kitchen and grabbed a glass of water and her briefcase. She flicked on the light as the brightness blinded her momentarily. Bridget needed a home for Naomi to close the case, and understanding why Cheri died might help her get a decent night's sleep. She began skimming Naomi's social file, which contained pages of family history drafted by social workers. Stephen Ross was her father, but his whereabouts were unknown. If Naomi rejected her grandmother, Elaine, he might be an option. Naomi also had an uncle, Jay Kline, who lived in Washington, D.C.

Elaine Kline looked stellar on paper. Her husband, a general physician, had passed away several years ago, shortly after they moved from Oklahoma. The file was silent whether Cheri lived on a reservation in Oklahoma where they had adopted her.

The report primarily centered on Cheri's behavior and difficulties caring for Naomi, whom she had had at only age eighteen. Recently, conflicts with Elaine had escalated because Cheri had decided she wanted to raise Naomi without Elaine but could not do it on her own. So, Cheri had contacted social services, which started a CINA with Cheri's cooperation and approval. Cheri had seen this as an opportunity to become a mother again.

Social workers made plenty of notations about Cheri's behavior and were critical of her parenting skills. The file offered no actual diagnosis or other general medical histories. Except Elaine provided a statement that Cheri had been diagnosed with schizophrenia, which was usually controlled. Until now. Absent was a single reference to drug abuse or alcoholism.

Sleeping was useless at this point, and she shoved the file aside. The next court date was months away, which was too long.

Stirring things up was a better option. She'd get everyone in front of a judge and see what they would say.

Bridget took out her computer and typed out a page and a half, requesting an emergency hearing. She put the caption "Request for Emergency Hearing" in bold capital letters. In the motion, she summarized the tragic events of the last week and stated placing Naomi with a different family member was urgent. Labeling the request as an "emergency" also helped. Getting in front of a judge was like requesting an audience with the pope after the state budget cutbacks. She slapped the computer closed after she filed the paperwork electronically. The clerk would have the motion at nine a.m.

Bridget folded her arms. The Land of Bridget requires more than pencil lifting and filing papers, she thought to herself. Her own research, not social services or self-serving statements from family, might give Naomi and Bridget answers.

"Kiddo, I'll learn what I can about that night and her condition," she declared to herself. That was the minimum she could do, especially if she took this new job. She made a promise to Naomi to do her best. She had witnessed a tragedy, and no one could speak for Cheri. Yes, she was deeply connected to the case and also wanted closure.

Face scrubbed, teeth brushed, and a fresh suit, she groaned at the mirror and frizzy hair. Despite her efforts, she looked like a frazzled, pale housemaid who could use psychiatric treatment—which was fitting because that was exactly where she was headed.

# Chapter 13

By the time she reached the hospital, after getting Aiden to school, it was after eight o'clock. Because Bridge knew her way around, she walked straight to the elevator past a bright-eyed volunteer eager to help. Tucked away in the east wing on the fifth floor was the mental health ward nicknamed "5E", which was where the county's worst cases were handled—the suicidal, the withdrawing alcoholic, those suffering from drug addiction or mental illness. It was where Cheri Kline had hospitalized herself voluntarily. A formidable, unmarked metal door faced her. She pressed the buzzer and smiled in full view of a peephole. After a long two minutes, a medical assistant opened the door.

"May I help you? Visiting isn't until this evening," she said.

"Today I'm not visiting anyone. I'm a lawyer. May I speak with the head nurse? Is Connie working this shift?"

The nurse nodded and let her enter as the heavy electronic door locked shut behind her, echoing in the hallway. The reception area was a cross between an emergency room and a jail. White tiles and vinyl chairs for easy cleanup were in front of a

TV, and yellow humming electric lights blinked across the no smoking sign. Not letting patients smoke was often the double whammy for the 5E drug addict. The patient had to stop not only the illegal drug that was killing them now but also nicotine which would eventually kill them someday.

Patients tended to be unruly at 5E, which Bridget experienced firsthand. She was there monthly for mental health commitment hearings, which were like a mini-trial conducted around a conference table. The patient, along with an attorney like Bridget, had the opportunity to challenge the doctor or family member who sought to commit them for mandatory care.

At the nurses' station, Connie stood with a chart in one hand with a phone pressed between her shoulder and ear. Every week she donned a different hairstyle, and today she sported two tight buns, like big auburn headphones with painted black eyebrows and blood-red lipstick completing her original look.

"Hey, honey! Don't your type haunt us on Fridays?" Connie's scratchy voice cracked.

"I was in the neighborhood. Chasing ambulances, hustling clients. Leaving my card in the emergency room. The usual."

"Love your style. What d'ya need, sweetie?"

"The file on Cheri Kline. Her daughter, Naomi, is my client. I don't have the latest updates, and I was hoping you might help. She left 5E after two days, and the hospital file might reveal why."

Connie frowned. "If I give you that file, the hospital will fire me. Then someone will sue me. Probably you."

"Not at all! Cheri signed a release. Check the file. And Connie, I'm here every month. I would never cross you. God only knows what you'd put in my coffee."

"Don't start me fantasizing," Connie said with a snort. "Still gotta say no, honey."

Bridget sat down in a chair across from Connie.

"Cheri Kline died shortly after she left here. Her daughter, my fourteen-year-old client, has many questions."

Connie pulled out a pack of cigarettes from her purse. "Damn it all. I'm taking a break. Need to feed my addiction." She opened a cabinet and placed a file on the desk. "Do not look at that open file on my desk labeled Cheri Kline. And make sure a copy of that release makes it to the file."

Connie opened the file, winked, and left the nurses' station. "Thank you!"

The police had brought Cheri in last week for a 24-hour hold after picking her up at Elaine Kline's house. The 24-hour hold was a little-known secret the county rarely discussed. Police could bring a person to the psychiatric ward for assessment, and after 24 hours, the patient walked unless either a psychiatrist recommended commitment, or they agreed to stay. Cheri agreed to treatment. Initially. The doctor's notes detailed Cheri was having delusions because of schizophrenia. She complained about the medication's side effects, and the doctor recommended a longer stay. She had received Haldol, which was followed with Xanax and Risperdal, an antipsychotic. After four nights, Cheri left.

The file reported no substance abuse, and she guessed that the hospital would have tested for substances. The file didn't give her a straightforward answer. She guessed Cheri had left the message on her voice mail while she was at 5E.

"You lost your glow, honey," said Connie, the smell of cigarettes following her.

"Cheri was pretty sick. Why'd you let her leave?"

"Let her leave? Back the truck up, honey. She left because she wanted to. I remember Cheri. We'd have preferred her to have stayed a little longer to make sure her medications were working right."

"But she left."

"If a patient ain't a danger to herself or others, she walks.

You know that. And that woman wouldn't hurt a fly. Not what I saw. Her mom must be hurting. She was really helpful, staying with her. She's a nurse's aide, you know."

"Elaine Kline?"

"Yes, she works mostly on the third floor but is up here on occasion. Shouldn't the cops be handling the case?"

"This time, no. Cops don't care because they can't care. They found her on the Wisaka Reservation, but the reservation doesn't have jurisdiction, and the feds and the state can't be bothered."

"That's what I would call crazy. What's her little girl going to do?"

"What about drug abuse? Fentanyl pills and an empty bottle of vodka were found next to her body."

Connie's painted eyebrows compressed to a mono-brow. "Honey, I doubt the fentanyl or the vodka belonged to her. Cheri wasn't a drunk or a drug addict. Not when she was here, and I doubt ever. She was just plain ole crazy. A schizophrenic trying to sort out the real from fantasy."

"How do you know she didn't abuse drugs?"

Connie pointed to a medical report. "Her blood tests were clean, too clean. So, we tested urine and hair, and it also showed nothing. She wasn't taking her prescribed medication. And frankly, I've been around. We can spot drug addicts pretty well here."

"Could she have committed suicide?" asked Bridget.

Connie shook her head. "Makes little sense. We watch for signs of suicide, and Elaine helped her, and the meds stabilized her. Cheri was a real sweetheart. I wish I had more answers for you, honey."

Bridget had hoped 5E would confirm Cheri had been suicidal or abused drugs, but she learned the opposite.

"I owe you one, Connie."

"I like flowers and sandwiches. Now, go save that little girl."

"Working on it, and now I need a judge to agree with me."

"You tell him I'm watching!" said Connie.

# Chapter 14

"Let me get this straight. You visited your client at her home and left with a baby?"

Judge Strickland's eyes narrowed as he clasped his bifocals, dangling from thumb and index fingers as if he preferred grasping the stem of a martini glass.

"Any other chicanery, Ms. McGarrity?" he continued.

The word "chicanery" echoed off the walls of the courtroom like a judge's gavel; he hammered every consonant through a clenched jaw.

"No," Bridget answered.

"What's your role here, counselor?"

"I'm Abby Baker's lawyer. You appointed me on the case, and I'm requesting that a new attorney be appointed."

"Your decision about saving a baby is perplexing. State your grounds in support of a new attorney."

Really? Bridget thought. Judge Strickland was playing her because confidentiality rules prevented her from revealing details about Abby, and the judge knew it. She cocked her head and used her nicest, nonthreatening voice.

"*Necessitas non habet legem.*"

Strickland leaned back on his bench. "*Necessitas non habet legem*? Necessity has no law."

"The principle that supports that emergency demands immediate action, and a person may break the law for the greater good."

"I know what it is. Cite a case or statute."

"I can provide the court a brief later. However, I will bill the state for my costs."

That comment reminded the judge that his actions cost the state money. He was a conservative, and the extra costs might agitate him enough to make him back off.

"Mr. Evans, what is the position of the State?"

Mark Evans's head jolted up. He was a brand new county attorney and fresh from law school. He had either dozed off or had moved on to the next file. Abby Baker's case was probably one of the fifty cases he had dealt with that morning.

"Proceed? Um, no objection to Ms. McGarrity's withdrawal from the case," answered Evans.

"Mr. Harmon, would the Department of Human Services provide a status of the child?"

Nick Harmon, the social worker assigned to Abby Baker's case, stepped up to the front of the courtroom. His long, black, curly hair cascaded over his shoulders. Today he sported a black Hawaiian shirt with a print of yellow palm trees and baggy, green Bermuda shorts. He looked like he just stepped out of a Jimmy Buffett concert.

"Gladly. The department had no knowledge that a man with a child was living with Abby Baker, let alone a baby. Ms. McGarrity saved the day, and the baby is in protective custody and doing—"

The judge interrupted his cheerful summary.

"Ever think of calling 911, Ms. McGarrity?"

Her answer was an unblinking glare because there was nothing she could say, at least out loud. Was it impulsive? Yes. Was it well-planned and thought out? No. But the baby was safe and in a better place. Judge Strickland grabbed a file from across the desk. Bridget dreaded the inevitable disapproving grimace from Judge Strickland. He knew her well. Too well. Bridget had faced Strickland's grimace as a sixteen-year-old runaway in handcuffs. It was a problem she dealt with a bit too often in Broken River, and everyone seemed to know her past.

"I had good intentions, Your Honor."

The judge's chicken beak lips widened into something resembling a smile.

"The path to hell is lined with good intentions, isn't it?"

She screamed—inside, leaving only a restrained smirk she hoped looked like a smile. She closed her folder. Bridget needed no proof that Judge Strickland had made it his personal mission to scold her at every opportunity.

"Your representation of the aforesaid individual, Abby Baker, is ended. Your motion to withdraw is granted, and it is also moot because Ms. Baker has new counsel."

She felt an enormous weight lift as she grabbed the file to her chest, like hugging a teddy bear. Abby Baker already had a new attorney. In less than twenty-four hours.

"Abby got a new lawyer, a private attorney. Righteous, huh? From that big firm in Cedar Town, Whitfield & Barshefsky," Nick Harmon said.

Whitfield & Barshefsky was one of the bigger firms.

"That firm doesn't take a client who makes less than six figures."

"It's an interesting choice, I grant you that," said Judge Strickland.

Bridget could not imagine Abby finding a lawyer from

Whitfield. Abby wouldn't even answer the phone, read her mail, or go to the courthouse.

"One more matter, counselor. Early this morning, you submitted an emergency motion in the Interest of Naomi Kline," said Judge Strickland.

Bridget swallowed. "Yes."

"Your motion is granted. Mr. Harmon, can you please make sure that all the parties are aware? The hearing is Thursday."

Bridget smiled in relief. Despite the verbal lashing, she was two for two with Strickland this morning. She was off Abby Baker's case, and Naomi would have her hearing this week.

"And counselor, I will preside," said Strickland.

Her smile faded.

***

On her way out, Bridget stopped at the clerk's office to review Naomi's court file for any recent activity. A disheveled county employee erupted from the boiler room, otherwise known as the file room. He shoved a request form across the greasy counter toward Bridget, which she obediently completed. The court file was two inches thick, even though the case was only two weeks old.

"Thanks, Dave. You may need to clear a shelf for this one," said Bridget.

Dave grunted while smoothing down the sides of his mustache.

"I have people for that," answered Dave.

"I see you've hired help."

Behind the filing counter stood a young, skinny man with a concert t-shirt under a crisp oxford shirt. A black tattoo on his neck with the number '515' peeked over his shirt collar. His hair was bleached at the ends, his hands veined like a tangled vine.

"Interesting tattoo. Pretty open-minded of the county to open jobs to ex-convicts."

Dave sneezed. "What? Of course not."

"Sure about that? The tattoo with a three-digit number on his neck. That's an area code—his territory. Usually, we deal with local codes. Boy, are there problems when a 563 is jailed in the 515."

Dave leaned forward, whispering. "This kid won't last till next week. He's already misfiled three documents today."

"At least he can lift the heavy files for you."

Her hand brushed over the stiff green cardboard and leafed to the latest filing from Cheri's attorney, Barry Van Ekes, entitled "Report to the Court." Bridget skimmed the pages, and her stomach dropped.

What a piece of work! The report was a two-page, single-spaced diatribe against Bridget. Barry might as well have titled it, 'Let's All Come Together and Hate Bridget.' He also accused her of purposeful interference with Barry's representation of Cheri Kline. What Barry skipped was that he never returned client or even attorney calls. She leafed through the document until the signature page caught her eye.

Barry had an additional address to his signature block—to Cedar Town. She recognized the address. The office space was near the Alliant building overlooking the island in the middle of Cedar Springs River. That was prime office space and pricey.

"Dave, did Barry Van Ekes open another office?"

Dave squinted over the file. "He hasn't notified the Clerk's office, but that address belongs to Whitfield & Barshefsky firm. I bet Mr. Van Ekes is local counsel."

Van Ekes local counsel for Whitfield? He had more ethics reprimands than any other attorney in Broken River. Why would a firm like Whitfield & Barshefsky partner up with him?

"Since when does Whitfield & Barshefsky need local counsel? Cedar Town is only an hour-and-a-half away."

Dave shrugged his shoulders. "Can't say. Mr. Van Ekes was here all morning looking through files."

Dusting off the file with a grunt, Dave placed the file carefully into a mesh metal basket. The newest employee gave her a sideways glance. His armpits were saturated with sweat even though the file room was air-conditioned.

Bridget handed him another form request. "Also, I'd like to review the Abby Baker file. Whitfield & Barshefsky filed an appearance."

"Looks like they're taking a liking to Broken River."

The paperwork for the appearance was standard, and the letter stock was expensive with a watermark. Van Ekes wasn't listed, but the new attorney was Alan Barshefsky himself, a partner in the law firm.

"Dave, what do you know about Whitfield & Barshefsky?"

"They are a hundred miles away in Cedar Town."

She tapped her foot. "Really? What do you know?"

"I like to know as little as I can." Dave snorted loudly. "Big firm, lots of lawyers, and corporate matters."

"That I know. How many cases do they have in Broken River?"

"Couldn't say. They only deal with Broken River in big money cases."

"Like my case?"

Dave giggled. "Didn't mean to laugh, but that's funny. You're not a corporate gal. No offense."

"None taken."

The lamest attorney in town was working for Whitfield & Barshefsky. The big boys had just filed an appearance in Abby Baker's case, a CINA case, and also had an interest with Barry

Van Ekes in Naomi's case even though neither case was a money maker. The only thing the two had in common was her. Was she missing something? Sweat beaded on her brow.

# Chapter 15

"I'm here to see Naomi Kline."

Naomi's court hearing was on Thursday and preparing her for it was the best way to prevent problems with Judge Strickland. After refusing to go to her grandmother's, the youth shelter was the only option. The youth shelter was remote—about a half-hour drive outside Broken River. The shelter stood next to the juvenile detention center, and both buildings were made of gray concrete slabs occupying about an acre of land.

Bridget entered the front lobby, rang security, and spoke through a small speaker embedded in the wall. An attendant cracked open the door, panting with a slight wheeze.

"Are you family? You need a court order," she said.

Bridget suppressed a smirk because the woman was lying; a court order to visit was unnecessary. More likely, she didn't want to deal with family so close to the end of her shift.

"I'm her lawyer."

"I already heard that one today."

"For Naomi Kline?"

"Yeah, that's right, for Naomi. The guy looked official enough, but I told him to show the court order, and he was not happy. He said he'd be back, and now you show."

"What did he look like?"

"White, male. Clean cut suit and dressed nice. Looks like your lawyer type. I didn't let him come in." Her round cheeks reddened.

"Odd. A lawyer doesn't need an order."

"He didn't know that, but you do, Miss. Got identification?"

She'd underestimated the woman. Guarding entry to the shelter was an art form. Bridget showed identification, and the attendant's apple cheeks lifted.

"Alright then."

As the door opened, the smell of bologna drifted past the gray steel doors. Bridget scrunched up her nose; she knew the scent. It was the smell of her youth and the months she stayed at the shelter.

The lobby served as a conference room, and Bridget lowered herself onto the worn chair with the fewest rips in the vinyl. Naomi walked in. Her face was sullen and pale, her gaze fixed on the floor. Her baggy plaid shirt hung off her like a loose curtain, and her fatigue and grief were palpable. This case wasn't getting any easier.

"Hi, Naomi, sit down. I'm here about a court hearing. The judge, social workers, and family will be there. I thought a meeting would be better than calling."

Naomi looked outside through the window as her silence filled the room. Bridget thought about giving her a hug, making a joke, anything. Law school hadn't prepared her for this meeting.

"My dad?"

"Not sure. Your father's whereabouts are unknown, but the social workers will try to contact him. The court will decide where you'll live. The judge's name is Judge Strickland, and he will want to know your thoughts. The social worker also will give theirs, and maybe Elaine, too. You've had a couple of days to think about returning to Elaine's."

"My dad will find me."

Naomi jammed her shoe into a chip on the linoleum tile.

"The judge might dismiss the case. You're not a 'child in need of assistance' if your grandmother will take care of you. And, yes, to your dad if he shows and checks out. Do you have questions about tomorrow's hearing?"

Naomi's gym shoe upended the corner of the aging tile, and she slammed her foot, crumbling it to pieces. The rubber on her white sneakers was peeling off. Could she ask the court to allow her to take the kid shoe shopping?

"That linoleum is hideous. Shall I help you rip it out?"

There were many firsts this week, too many. Naomi's chocolate brown eyes didn't blink as an uncomfortable silence drifted between them. She shifted her weight in her chair, then played with a loose piece of rubber sole on her high tops. Usually girls her age were anxious and talked a lot, and she'd been more animated at the reservation. She feared being in a youth shelter was an upsetting experience. Naomi's calm was unsettling.

"What do you want? What can I do to help?"

"I want Chinese," said Naomi.

"Huh?" Bridget stammered, trying to imagine what this could mean. "Chinese?"

"Chinese. Orange chicken and broccoli."

Naomi was hungry and disgruntled and had the same dislike for bologna as Bridget. That was a good sign.

"Let me talk to the attendant."

Bridget walked to the window and looked outside, watching the frayed basketball net flap in the window. The youth shelter was on a concrete island in an endless sea of corn, stretching to the horizon. Few ran from the shelter, knowing civilization wasn't close. That hadn't stopped Bridget, not when she had Aunt Irene waiting a half-mile away in a car. Naomi acted differently than she expected. Bridget had always wanted to flee, get out, and complain. Naomi was content to order in.

She turned around in disbelief. In Naomi's hand was Bridget's wallet, and her tote bag was wide open. Naomi grinned mischievously.

"Orange chicken."

Naomi waved Bridget's wallet at her. The kid had just pickpocketed her. Should she laugh or cry? Instead, she burst out laughing as she snatched the wallet back, along with the tote bag. She thumbed through it, and nothing was missing.

"I guess that's my signal to leave?"

"And get orange chicken?"

"Is this how you normally order food? Steal a wallet?"

" 'Normally.' " Naomi grimaced as she bent her fingers into quotation marks. "It's Elaine's wallet, and she doesn't share, so I help her share. I figured you share, too," said Naomi.

The kid's face beamed pink; Naomi was enjoying herself. Bridget was entertainment to an otherwise dull day. Unfortunately, she was developing the wrong skills at the youth shelter.

"You're a brat. And I'm nuts, but I'm also hungry," said Bridget.

And I'm going to miss dinner at home. Again. She knocked on the steel doors, alerting the attendant.

"We're going out to get something to eat. I'll have Naomi back in an hour."

The woman snapped her gum.

"Whatever. You're the lawyer."

# Chapter 16

At the Asian Garden restaurant, Naomi and Bridget were an unlikely pair. Naomi with her torn jeans, long dark hair, and lanky body, dwarfing her pale lawyer in a light gray suit. They both ordered orange chicken.

"Great idea. This is a better place to talk," said Bridget.

Naomi ate every piece of chicken, leaving the vegetables untouched.

"On Thursday, a hearing will determine what happens with you. Before we sit in front of the judge, I'd like to hear from you."

"The shelter is like jail, and no one can get in. Right? I'll stay there." She shoved rice from one edge of the plate to the other side.

"The shelter is temporary. I'm pretty sure the judge—"

"Mom didn't stop her medication because I gave her meds. Somebody hurt her on purpose."

Big tears dropped, and Naomi's chin quivered. Bridget didn't know what to say. Taking a child out to lunch wasn't enough to override the tragedy.

"I'm so sorry about what happened. We don't have to talk about anything. I'm glad you're getting a decent meal. I can tell you cared about your mother."

"I did, but I'm not sure she cared about me. She was always gone. When she showed up this time, she said she had a plan, and we were going to leave. We'd get our own place away from Elaine. She said you're my lawyer and would get us a place." Naomi shoved the vegetables over to the side of her plate. "What happened to her? I don't understand. The police never even talked to me."

So much for social workers doing the heavy lifting. The child knew little about her mother and how she was found. Bridget recounted to her young client everything she learned from her visit to 5E, and the drugs and alcohol found with her.

"My mom drank nothing but grape pop!"

"The nurse at the psychiatric ward didn't think it made much sense either. The social workers also never said anything about addiction."

Naomi stared at Bridget. "The nurse thought it was strange, too?"

"Your mom's bloodwork showed she wasn't on any drugs. They even did additional tests for urine and hair, and it also showed nothing. Unfortunately, she wasn't taking her medication either."

"She took her medication. I saw her."

"This is tough to hear about your mother. I checked her medical records, and it showed she was off her meds. It's pretty common, though, because the medication for her condition often has undesirable side effects."

"Who said that? Northeast Memorial? That's Elaine's hospital." Naomi smoothed her hair and tied it into a knot on top of her head. "When are we going to court for my mom?"

Maybe never. Tell a fourteen-year-old that the world

doesn't care? That no one would investigate her mother's death?

"Not sure. And an investigation is unlikely. I'm sorry. Let's focus on you. You like the shelter because it's safe, but it's only temporary. Why don't you like your grandmother?"

"Elaine calls me a foster kid. When her son, my so-called uncle comes, I have to leave because he doesn't like my mom or me."

"That's awful."

Bridget had heard much worse; still, she didn't deserve that.

Naomi slumped in her chair. "I'd like to go back now."

As they stepped outside, the thick, moist August heat clung to her skin like a leech. Her car keys were moist after sitting in a cold restaurant for an hour. On the ride back to the shelter, Naomi was quiet, too quiet.

"Do you have another lawyer?"

Naomi rolled her eyes. "Yeah, I have a ton of lawyers."

"A man saying he was your lawyer tried to see you today at the shelter. A man."

"Really? No idea."

"One more question, why don't you call Elaine Grandma?"

Naomi played with stations on the radio. "My mom said to call her Elaine. My mom called her Elaine, too. Never Mom."

"Anything else you can think of that you want the judge to know, or even not know?"

She shook her head, opened the window, and wind tousled her long hair. "Road trip?" she smiled.

"Another time."

The youth shelter hadn't changed much, a concrete block with wired windows; shades obstructed any view inside making it more like a prison than a shelter. Bridget pulled into the parking lot, slowly navigating the car past a large pothole. She wrote her cell number on her business card and handed it to Naomi.

"My office and cell number for emergencies. Nick is also a good person to talk to."

"The hippie guy with the long hair? He's going to help find out what happened to my mom?"

"He's not the police, but he can help—"

"Not interested."

Bridget hesitated for a moment, as did Naomi. "Next time, how about getting you new shoes? Aren't you in track?"

"I don't want shoes. You're gonna help me, right?" Naomi asked.

Bridget didn't have the answers that Naomi needed but that was something a child couldn't understand, and why should she? It wasn't right. And what about the new job and Chet Russell getting her off all her cases within the week?

"Thursday is your court date, and we'll see."

"The hippie guy told me the case might be over if I stay at Elaine's because then I'm safe. Well, I'm not going to Elaine's."

Naomi turned her back to her and waved at security.

"You're welcome for the chicken," Bridget said in the empty lobby. Naomi would be hard to help, and she knew that. Having a happy client wasn't always the goal. It wasn't not like anyone had a parade at the end of one of her cases. Winning a court hearing wasn't like winning the Super Bowl.

\*\*\*

As she walked to the car, she removed her gray suit jacket and tossed it in the back seat. She slid into the faux leather front seat and kicked off her pumps. Her cell phone rang.

"Hi, there! I took the liberty of dropping off additional paperwork at your office. The next step is withdrawal from your cases and then a nice check."

"Chet Russell?"

"The one and only. I don't mean to pressure you, but we need that yes and signature on the line. Today would be great."

"I can't stop practicing law in one day."

"Sure you can. You're special, and the community will reward you for it. You deserve this," said Chet.

"That's more compliments than I've had in the last decade," she said.

"It's the truth."

"How many lawyers have you approached to take over my cases? I'd like a say in all of this."

"Of course! That's your compassion speaking, and it was insensitive of me."

"I could start with Sun Family Foundation but finish the cases on my own time."

"I love that passion, and you're a leader, but that is a no-go. This foundation needs you in at 100 percent. You're going to love your new work, new office, and cash in the bank. No more driving around to youth shelters in a beat-up Grand Am."

Her grip tightened around the steering wheel. "Youth shelter? How did you know?" She squinted as she looked around the shelter for Chet's car. She saw only corn, soybeans, and the shelter had only one recreational element, a basketball court with a pumpkin-sized pothole and a fraying basketball net that flapped in the wind.

"That case is on the docket tomorrow, an emergency hearing in a CINA case. Fancy lawyering for poverty law. You can ask a new attorney be appointed tomorrow," said Chet.

"Thanks for the compliment, but what is the rush?"

"Waiting makes donors nervous," he said. "A foundation of needy families awaits you. We'll be in touch. Tomorrow."

He abruptly ended the call, and her head was spinning. She

wasn't sure she could say no to the job offer. She started up the Grand Am, which growled and sputtered to a slow start.

The phone call had left her rattled. The thought of her dropping her cases by the end of the week felt very wrong, if not impossible, especially this case. As she pulled out of the parking lot, the steering on the Grand Am tugged to the right, which was one of the car's many quirks. Too often, it felt as if the car was trying to drive her instead of the other way around. Sort of like Chet, pulling her in a direction she did not want to go.

She wiped the dust off the dashboard. "I do the driving here. And we'll see what happens in court tomorrow."

# Chapter 17

Bridget arrived early at the courthouse, ensuring she'd have time to meet and talk to people before Naomi's hearing. CINA cases were unlike any other court hearing and often involved several caseworkers and families, sometimes leaving only standing room in the courtroom. Given all the potential dynamics among so many people, Bridget familiarized herself with everyone appearing as much as possible before court, primarily if she was representing a child. The fewer surprises for Judge Strickland, the better.

Nick Harmon sat outside the courtroom on a wood bench, dressed in psychedelic tie-dye. He sat next to Naomi and offered her a piece of bubble gum as he popped one in his mouth.

Naomi wouldn't have any of it. Her face was downcast and grim. She fidgeted with her hair repeatedly, eventually crowning her head in a jumbo bagel-sized hair bun. Her back was to Elaine, who was dressed in hospital work clothes and patted down her smock with a jittery hand.

Bridget broke the ice. "Good afternoon, Elaine. Glad you could get out of work." Elaine secured her handbag over her shoulder and nodded. "Steve Ross? Naomi's father? Is he here today?"

"I haven't seen Steve in years," answered Elaine.

"Elaine is lying." Naomi whispered in Bridget's ear.

Nick bounced slightly from side to side, making it impossible to focus on his hippie tie-dye shirt. His red high tops tapped to an imaginary beat as if he were listening to a tune that only he could hear.

"Not sure if the State Attorney could find Dad," he said.

The clock ticked perilously close to two. Judge Strickland ran a "rocket docket" and wanted everyone in their seats at the beginning of the hearing.

"Anyone else, Nick?"

At the end of the hallway, Barry Van Ekes studied his cell phone.

"That's all me knows, m'lady," said Nick, mimicking some accent.

Bridget headed toward the empty courtroom. Like baby chicks in a row, Naomi, her grandmother, Barry, and Nick followed. The judge's bench sat authoritatively on a raised platform. As if signaled by an unseen conductor, a door opened abruptly to a swish of black fabric as he entered.

"All rise! The Honorable Judge Strickland, presiding. This court is now in session," said the court reporter as everyone dragged themselves to their feet.

"Please be seated," Judge Strickland continued. "Let the record reflect that this is the matter of Juvenile Court Number 16394, In the Interest of Naomi Kline...." The judge continued the colloquy of Who's Who and summarized the status of the case, all who were present, including the tragic passing of Cheri Kline. Her absence cast a funeral-like somberness over the courtroom.

Barry stood. "Your Honor, I request permission to withdraw

from this case."

"Sit down, Mr. Van Ekes."

Judge Strickland's face smoothed, and the hardened judge turned into a caring grandpa as he continued.

"Naomi, I would first like to express my condolences to you. And to you, Mrs. Kline. I will do everything in my power that the law allows to keep you safe. You have one of the best attorneys in the county sitting next to you. She understands, and she cares, as do I. You also have caring social services with many resources. If anything troubles you, I will hear about it. And they will hear it from me."

Bridget sighed. Strickland wasn't the easiest judge, but this was a side she hadn't seen. It was lovely.

"Now, Mr. Van Ekes. What is it? I've read your motion."

Barry Van Ekes stood, straightening his crooked tie. A lawyer should never wear anything crooked, thought Bridget.

"Your Honor, to be clear, this case ended before it began. Thanks to counselor Mrs. Bridget McGarrity, I never had contact with my client, as stated in my report to the details of that engagement. Mrs. Bridget McGarrity interfered with my attorney-client relationship by having direct contact with Cheri Kline. She..."

Bridget stood. "Mr. Van Ekes, please call me Ms. McGarrity. Mrs. McGarrity was my mother, and she died when I was a teenager. Your Honor, the allegations are unwarranted and mean-spirited. Cheri Kline has tragically passed, and these comments are hurtful and inappropriate."

"My client called your office," said Van Ekes.

"My secretary put her through to voice mail. I did not speak with her directly."

"Seems pretty fishy to me, Your Honor. You were also at the Wisaka Reservation when she died. What was your involvement with Cheri Kline?"

"What are you talking about? Barry, this is outrageous. A child is in this room, who is the victim's daughter. Yes, I identified her without Mr. Van Ekes's permission. If this tirade is going to continue, I request a separate hearing."

What was Barry implying? Did he try to link her to Cheri's death? Bridget's fingernails dug into the palms of her hands. Barry, that slime ball.

The judge raised his finger again, and all fell silent. Strickland didn't need a gavel.

"Enough. Anything else, Mr. Van Ekes?"

"No."

"Your application is granted. You're dismissed from this case."

"Thank you, Your Honor."

Barry sat down, crossed his legs, and sat back. Judge Strickland stared him down.

"Mr. Van Ekes, that is an order. Leave the courtroom."

"Oh, right."

Barry screeched the office chair across the tiled floor and left the courtroom as Bridget bit her lip to keep from smiling. A hearing without Barry Van Ekes was a good day.

"Now, the State's attorney. I've spent a precious 15 minutes searching the file for what type of notice of this hearing the State gave to the father."

"My apologies, Your Honor," said the county attorney, Mark Evans.

"Apologies are nice, Mr. Evans. Now, do as I ask. Explain what notice was given and the State's due diligence."

Evans leafed quickly through the file and then scanned another file. He had been less than a year on the job, fresh from law school. The silence in the room pounded as everyone watched him shuffle through papers. Bridget placed her green ballpoint pen on her pale pink legal pad. She was glad not to be on the other end of Strickland's ire, for once.

"An attempt at delivery at the last known address. The sheriff's affidavit shows a failed delivery."

"That's it?"

"Yes."

"Publication? Did anyone search the internet? Ask anyone who knew him?"

The judge placed his chin in his hand with his elbow perched on the bench. Mark looked down at his file folder as if hoping something would miraculously sprout from it.

"He didn't update his address with the state or with Child Support Recovery Unit. I believe he's on probation. From another state. Yes. Sorry, I can't say. My apologies to the court."

"'My apologies to the court?' Should I explain the basics on notice to the county attorney's office? Shall I read to you the statute that these proceedings cannot continue without notice to the parents? Cannot. Do parents include the father?"

"Yes."

"Yes, what? Should I read aloud the statute?"

Mark's face turned even paler as he clutched the pen.

"Actually, Your Honor, the State was considering dismissing the case."

The judge's face softened. "Naomi, has anyone asked you where your father is?"

"He called me, before my mom..." She folded her legs up on the chair, hugging her chest. "What about the reservation? My mom said she met him there when he worked at the Casino. Mom said our great grandma was an Indian princess."

As if a gale force wind blew across the courtroom, papers shuffled frantically as the judge, the state attorney, and Nate searched their files. Naomi perked up in her chair, baffled by the sudden ruckus. Elaine clutched her handbag a little closer.

"I didn't know, Judge. There's nothing in the file.

Indigenous law cases are rare in this county," said Mark.

Strickland lowered his reading glasses. Nick's foot tapped slightly slower, a more cautious beat.

"Mrs. Kline, would you like to add something?"

Elaine smoothed her skirt. "Since my husband died, I don't know. He managed everything. My husband did all that when we lived in Oklahoma."

"What does social service have on Naomi's father, Mr. Harmon, and Naomi's heritage? Does she have Native American heritage?" asked the judge.

"The file doesn't have information as to the birth parents, but I'll look into it," said Nick.

Bridget said, "At the Wisaka Reservation, the attorney general requested that he be informed of these proceedings. Given the recent tragic event, the Wisaka Nation would be in a better position—"

The courtroom door opened, and a tall man in jeans, leather boots, and a vest over a flannel short-sleeved shirt entered. He remained standing, listened, and then clapped loudly and slowly.

"All right. Yes! The lady lawyer is right," said the tall man as he walked towards Naomi, who was already standing. "Naomi, baby. God, I'm so sorry."

They hugged, and Naomi closed her eyes as she rested her head on his chest.

"Naomi's father, I presume?" asked Strickland.

"Guilty as charged. Steve Ross, sir," he said in a booming voice with one hand around Naomi's shoulder and the other in a pocket. "I wanted to say how awesome this is. Naomi, you're here."

"Let us get a few details before we proceed. What is your address, Mr. Ross?" Strickland demanded.

"I'm working on that one, sir. I've been on vacation," he smiled, tipped his cap down, and winked at Bridget and Naomi.

"As of a year ago, Mr. Ross's address was in Illinois Penitentiary, serving five years for felony assault," said Mark.

"Bar fight gone bad. I don't roll with the bikers no more."

"This is going nowhere fast," said Strickland.

"Your Honor, if I may speak," said Mark. "The State would like to dismiss the case. The father has been located. The child has regularly resided with the grandparent and was safe in her custody. Ending the case would eliminate the need to send notice to the reservation."

Here it comes, thought Bridget. Strickland was going to kick the case. If the State had no interest, it wouldn't continue.

Judge Strickland sighed.

"Are you making a motion?"

"Yes."

"Write the motion, and then file the motion. Send it to the concerned parties. After that, I will rule on it. Mr. Harmon, I assume social services will make a diligent effort to sort out whether this case needs to be referred to an Indian court, as well as Mr. Ross's intentions. I will continue this hearing for one week. That means I will see you in seven days. Whole days, including weekends. Does the prosecution understand?"

"Yes, Judge," Mark answered.

"Today is Thursday. What day would that hearing be, Mr. Evans?"

"In a week. Friday. I, uh, think."

Judge Strickland hung his head in disappointment, obviously enjoying torturing the new county attorney.

"Ms. McGarrity, please assist our venerable representative of our great state."

"The hearing is continued to Thursday," Bridget said.

"Clear?"

Mark nodded. His face was so pale that he looked like he might faint.

Strickland explained that Naomi should stay with her grandmother; Naomi elbowed Bridget, whispering in her ear.

"My client prefers the youth shelter or her father," said Bridget even though she knew Strickland wouldn't go for it. Steve Ross could not even provide a home address.

Strickland frowned as if Bridget were a corrupting influence and asked, "Naomi, is that true?"

"Yes," she answered softly.

"Mrs. Kline, can you make Naomi feel welcome during this difficult time?"

Elaine nodded her head furiously. "I've taken care of Naomi since she was little. I was so afraid something like this would happen. Cheri has always had issues and would disappear for years. Since my husband died, things have been, well, I just—"

"Very well," said Strickland. "In my experience, teenagers cannot be placed somewhere where they don't want to be. During that time, I want everyone to work very hard. Ms. McGarrity, you will visit the Kline family with social services and file a report before the hearing. Mr. Ross, it has never been a better time to find a job and a home."

"Mister, being where I been the last couple of years, I was able to sort out what's important."

"Naomi, can you stay with your grandmother for a week? For me? Give it a week. And if you have any problems, talk to your attorney or Mr. Harmon."

Naomi slumped in her chair away from Elaine.

"OK."

Strickland gave his closing remarks, and with another swish of black fabric, he exited the courtroom. A collective exhale was released by all.

\*\*\*

Outside the courtroom, Naomi sat hip-to-hip next to her father. Nick gathered information from Steve, and Elaine stood a few feet back. Her lips were pressed in a thin line.

"We have one week, so I would like to schedule a house visit."

"I'm sorry, a what?" said Elaine.

"We'll visit your house while Naomi is there, and I'll submit my report to the court."

Elaine shook her head, brushing her hair off her face. She looked frazzled. "You're still on this case? You're not supposed to be on the case."

Nick jumped in, "I get that was confusing. The case probably will be dismissed next week, but the judge is being extra careful. So, no, Ms. McGarrity is not off the case. None of us are, and in fact, we have a lot of work to do if we're to be back here next week."

Elaine huffed. "I'll wait downstairs for you, young lady, and we'll head home." She glared at Steve when she said "home" and then marched toward the stairwell. So much for the nice façade she performed for the judge.

Nick said, "It's OK, Bridget. I'll talk with her, and we'll send a counselor."

If she had doubted Naomi about Elaine before, she didn't anymore. Elaine's reaction was odd. She could understand her dislike of a home visit, but she was genuinely surprised that Bridget was staying on the case. Why would she assume that Bridget was off the case?

Bridget's phone vibrated as she glanced at the sender. It was Chet Russell again. She hadn't even thought about withdrawing from this case as he requested. At this point, it was unimaginable and almost cruel, and she doubted Strickland would even let her. Had Russell contacted Elaine, but how would he even know about Elaine? CINA cases are sealed.

She let the call go to voicemail.

\*\*\*

The setting sun blurred her vision as Bridget headed home. A trio of red-tailed hawks swarmed the open road. One broke from its brethren, obstructing her path as it skillfully reversed its course in the direction of the car, as if urging her to follow it to someplace far away. Not today. Instead, she was elated to be heading home. The last weeks were plagued by missed dinners and tardy homecomings. Today she would finally be early and do a little work from home. Bridget's cell phone vibrated again, and after the third ring, she picked up.

"I'm almost there—about two minutes."

"Mommy?"

"Aiden, what's up? Where's Daddy?"

"I don't know."

"Look in the garage, sweetheart. I'm sure—"

"The police are here."

# Chapter 18

As if in a dream, Bridget drove slowly into the cul-de-sac, past the brown ranch house, past the white split level, and finally stopping by her house with blue aluminum siding. A neighbor held a coffee cup, calmly watching the spectacle. Another spied discreetly from behind his window sheers. Parked in Bridget's driveway was a squad card with "Sheriff" emblazoned in red letters on the door. A young officer, working hard on a piece of gum, nodded as Bridget parked the car.

"Are you Bridget McGarrity?" he asked as his radio crackled. Light brown stubble brushed his chin—he had probably just learned to shave.

"You're old enough to drive a car?" said Bridget.

"For God's sakes," said Walter, who stepped outside as Aiden trotted behind him. He dashed out to his mother, but Walter held him back.

"OK. Yes. I'm her. It is I. The Bridget. Is that better?" she talked as though she were suffering from a brain injury.

"You reside at 1321 Pinnacle Drive?"

"Officer, give me the papers and go catch a criminal."

"You have been duly served. Have a great day, counselor."

The officer walked lightly, almost skipping, to his squad car. A joyous day when an officer can make trouble for a defense attorney. Glad to make your day. She turned her back to the curious neighbors and retreated into the house. Ignoring Walter and Aiden, she ripped open the package. She eyed the caption in dismay.

In the District Court in and for Lincoln County,
File No. 23 C003125
Abby Baker, Plaintiff, v.
Bridget McGarrity, Defendant,

Petition At Law, Action for Legal Malpractice.

Comes Now the Plaintiff, Abby Baker, and for her cause against Defendant, Bridget McGarrity, states as follows that Defendant provided legal services to Plaintiff and was required to render the same legal services as a reasonably competent attorney and provide reasonable care...

Bridget could read no further.

Abby Baker suing me? For malpractice? Little Abby, who harbored the baby snatcher?

"This makes absolutely no sense. I don't understand, how?"

"You don't understand? If you can't understand, we're in trouble." Walter rubbed dry oil paints into his hands.

"The lawsuit's nonsense, but don't worry. I'll take care of it."

She leafed through the papers, coming to the signature line on the last page—it was the law firm Whitfield & Barshefsky, from Cedar Town, signed by Alan Barshefsky himself. Abby Baker hadn't signed. She covered her mouth in dismay. Was this what Chet meant by managing her cases?

"I have a new paint job, another Victorian. I wanted to

surprise you. Hopefully, they'll still want me near the house after all this. The lawsuit won't hit the news, right?"

"I'll take care of it. I know it's upsetting, frightening, and people get sued, but the lawsuit is baseless."

Bridget tried to believe herself, repeating words she often recited to distraught clients. It will be OK. Yes, it will cost. Yes, it will take time to sort out. You should win. You may win. Think about settling.

"I don't know what's happening, but I'll take care of it. And nothing will resolve itself overnight. I'll get Aiden's dinner."

Walter stuffed a clenched fist into his jeans pocket, headed to the garage, and hesitated.

"You're worried about dinner? Aunt Irene is on her way. Please—go."

Walter stepped closer, put his arms around Bridget, and held her tight as her throat tightened.

The neighbor with the coffee cup stepped back inside, but the other neighbor continued to leer through his sheers. She wanted to stay home, hug her son, give him potato chips for dinner, something happy, but instead, she was cast from Eden. Who was she kidding? Walter was right. Home was not the place to fix this mess, and she needed to get to the office.

Kicking off her work shoes, slipping on her favorite jeans, and even a shower to erase the grime of the day would all have to wait. She rolled her newly served papers into a cylinder and headed to the car.

# Chapter 19

"Diane, coffee, please. Make it strong."

Bridget had never asked Diane for coffee, never asked her to do anything that wasn't strictly job-related—no mindless errands, buying birthday presents or the like. The look on her face quieted Diane because her demand for coffee was that of a desperate person, not a person in charge.

She flipped on the computer and looked up the firm Whitfield & Barshefsky. Online public records showed Barshefsky had not represented a single individual in the last five years, only corporations.

Whitfield & Barshefsky's website listed about twenty lawyers, all with professional headshots and knock-out resumés to instill wonder and confidence in the potential client. Not a single lawyer listed legal malpractice or even medical malpractice. Not even a low-level grunt associate listed pro bono work in poverty law. Why Barshefsky had made the leap from corporate law to representing the poor and mentally disabled baffled her.

"Why the hell me?" yelled Bridget out loud.

Diane walked in with the coffee, and the aroma loosened the tension in her chest.

"I hope that language wasn't for me," said Diane.

"Just having a great conversation with myself. An awful day."

"I'd rather not know." Her blasé response was a sturdy tree in a windy storm.

"Thank you. You're a saint. At least, somebody doesn't hate me."

"Love...with a paycheck."

Like a dog caught in the garbage, Bridget reluctantly handed the complaint for malpractice to Diane. She kept her eyes low as Diane read and braced herself for criticism. None came.

"Abby Baker? She called today with questions about the 'papers,'" said Diane.

"Abby Baker called about why she is suing me? That is precious. Does she even understand she has another lawyer?"

Bridget reached for the lower desk drawer and grabbed a fifth of whiskey she kept. The unopened bottle had sat in her desk for years, a gift from a former client.

"I'm going to Irish my coffee, and it's almost 5 o'clock." She poured a little into her mug.

"The brown stuff, huh? Didn't know your dedication to the Irish."

"Exploring the darker sides of my heritage."

Bridget inhaled deeply as tension released, took a sip, and grimaced.

"You should stick with water."

Bridget stomped to the office kitchen and poured the coffee down the drain.

Calm down.

So what? She was being sued. A new lawsuit should be as eventful as Monday morning to a lawyer. Yet the lawsuit hurt because it was aimed at her. How could she be sued for malpractice? A malpractice suit was a scar on her reputation.

How and when did Barshefsky come to meet Abby? Abby must be a pawn. She felt like one as well.

The lawsuit was filed with lightning speed. On Monday evening, Bridget brought Baby Doe to the hospital, and the next day Judge Strickland released her from Abby's case. Barshefsky had already filed his appearance in Abby's CINA case. That took less than a day. The malpractice suit against her had been filed yesterday, on Wednesday, only two days later. All this within the same week. Why? Barshefsky couldn't be making money off Abby's CINA case or the malpractice suit.

And when had Barshefsky met with Abby and agreed to take her case? Abby rarely left her apartment and wouldn't even go to court for the sake of her own son. She didn't seem the type of person to go lawyer shopping, and it was more likely that a lawyer had shopped for her. Abby had mentioned another lawyer at her home, and Bridget assumed she was talking about a TV commercial.

"When Abby called, what exactly did she say?"

"She didn't have a clue. That gal still thinks you're her lawyer even though I told her to speak with her new attorney."

"Barshefsky filed this thing without even talking to Abby. That's unethical."

They could have met earlier, before Baby Doe. But why? Bridget thumbed through Whitfield & Barshefsky's paperwork and Abby's signature wasn't anywhere.

"Her signature isn't on the pleading, which he should have included for this type of case."

Bridget gave Diane the task of researching Whitfield & Barshefsky to look for the type of companies it represented, industries, their current cases, and even any civic groups their attorneys belonged to or donated to.

"Try to find a connection."

Diane yawned and looked at her watch. "Sure, after I contact the insurance carrier."

Bridget spun around again on the chrome chair.

"Barry Van Ekes added the address of Whitfield & Barshefsky to his signature block."

"Van Ekes? Oh, jeez. Cedar Town can have him."

"Van Ekes knows my cases and my clients, at least some of them. He would have access. He was at the clerk's office looking up cases. I bet those cases were about me."

"Barry might have to resign from the McGarrity fan club."

Bridget returned to her desk and checked out Whitfield & Barshefsky's web page again. Van Ekes wasn't listed. Bridget called Whitfield firm asking for Barry Van Ekes. The receptionist denied all knowledge of him. She then tried calling Barry at the number she had, and it went directly into voicemail. No surprise there. Bridget sent him an email requesting him to call.

Diane plopped the day's mail on her desk, which was Diane's signal—it was five o'clock.

"I can stay longer."

Diane never offered to stay, and her offer was comforting. "That's OK. Please let me know if you have any ideas."

Besides contacting her insurance carrier, learning that Abby was clueless about her lawsuit, and spending the last hour web surfing the plaintiff's attorney, she had accomplished nothing.

The office phone rang.

"Law offices," answered Bridget.

"Glad I reached you!"

"Chet Russell," Bridget's stomach dropped, but she didn't know why. "Meant to call, but the last couple of days haven't gone as planned."

To put it mildly. She pulled out the contract Chet had left earlier this week and leafed through it as they spoke. The paper the contract was printed on was beautiful, slightly off-white. Her office would never bother with that expense. She held the paper up to the light—it had a familiar watermark. Her heart started to race. Then, she scuffled through her files, found the malpractice suit, and also held it up to the light.

It was the same paper and the same watermark. She then found the appearance form Barshefsky had filed on Abby's CINA case. Again, the same paper and watermark. Whoever prepared the contract had used the same paper for Abby's CINA case, the malpractice suit, and Chet's contract for Sun Family Foundation.

She fanned herself with the contract. "I'm sorry, Chet, you were saying?"

"Hate to press, but we need an answer today."

She took a deep breath and folded over a tiny corner of the paper, ripped the corner off, and tore it to shreds.

"Who prepared the contract you want me to sign?" she said as her heart raced.

"So much thinking. Why don't you sign? I'll pick up the contract, have you sign all the paperwork to get off those cases, and we'll celebrate, properly, at a nice restaurant. Bring your family."

"What's the rush?"

"That's business."

"A nice new job, fancy offices with expensive paper stock."

"You can help with finding office space."

"So, you don't want to tell me who prepared the contract, but you should know my cases aren't looking too attractive at the moment."

He paused. "I know about the malpractice lawsuit. That's why I'm here. We'll take care of that. That lawsuit is a sign. Time to make the change you are worthy of."

Bridget sprung out of her chair but tried to remain calm. "How did you know about the lawsuit?"

"I make it my business to know."

"Whitfield & Barshefsky is the firm behind the Sun Family Foundation. They prepared the contract, didn't they?"

There was a long pause on the phone, and Bridget wished she had met with him face to face. Finally, Chet chuckled, deep and low.

"Can't pull the wool over your eyes. This is awkward. How do I say this? Yes."

A week's vacation to process everything that had happened since Sunday would be nice. Cheri's death, Baby Doe, being sued for malpractice, and now this offer.

"I don't understand. I'm—"

"Not to worry!" he chuckled again. "Whitfield is a large firm. The right hand may not know what the left hand is doing. The good news for you is the offer is still good. Nothing has changed other than one more reason to close your law practice. Today. That malpractice lawsuit is history if you play it right. Leave your cases behind. Step away."

"Let me guess. Abby Baker will drop the lawsuit if I work for Sun Family Foundation?"

"Exactly! We'll take care of that and all your other cases—if you're with us. My understanding is that Abby Baker insisted on the lawsuit. Whitfield, and specifically Mr. Barshefsky himself, stepped in to make sure everything was handled properly."

"Abby insisted?"

"Yes."

He was lying. She leaned against the office wall, slid down to the carpet, and sat on the floor.

"How about the main foundation donors? When do I meet them?"

"I'm looking at a two hundred thousand dollar check, a big sum for a small town lawyer. Withdraw from your cases and sign the papers. Did Diane give you the package I dropped off?"

She held the phone away from her ear, examining it as if

Chet were going to pop right out. He was making it so easy for her. Who wouldn't grab this opportunity? He had solved her problems, served on a silver plate. Two hundred thousand; she could pay off her mortgage. And the malpractice suit, a balance sheet barely in the black, and a failing car would all be part of the past.

Did she have a choice? As she closed her eyes, the only image that came to her was Cheri Kline's awful demise.

"I have a home visit tomorrow in a CINA case, a brief to write, a court hearing next week, and clients to meet. I'll consider your offer once I have met everyone involved."

"Our major donor, who requires confidentiality, requires action immediately. Tax reasons. Withdraw from your cases now."

She wanted to yell at him, confront him and say something mean. But this was the Midwest.

"Another time, Chet. You have a wonderful day."

Bridget hung up.

# Chapter 20

The next day, Nick Harmon and Bridget walked up the wooden steps to Elaine Kline's house, an old Victorian. Bridget welcomed the opportunity to focus on something different and put Chet's contract and the malpractice suit aside. Even though she felt like Chet and Whitfield & Barshefsky were circling her like hawks, she would ignore them, for now.

Elaine Kline's house had seen better days. Green awnings with yellow shutters had succumbed to age and weather, leaving bare wood, and the landscaping had gone wild, a mix of weeds and creeping ivy. The residential block had a mix of housing styles—a couple of Victorians, a brick house, and a 50s-era ranch. The adjacent house looked vacant, with spotted gray stucco and wild oak sprouting through a broken window.

"I didn't know you were coming. You're still Naomi's lawyer?" Elaine cracked the door open, stepped outside, and shut the door behind her.

With Ray-Bans plopped on his head and black curls banded together in a neat ponytail, Nick Harmon waited out in front of the house. A Hawaiian shirt with pineapples brightened the otherwise drab porch.

Nick began, "Yes, Ms. McGarrity is still Naomi's lawyer. Why would you think otherwise? I called and left a message. We talked about the visit at the courthouse."

"You can't come in now. I'm sorry, but the house is an absolute mess."

Judge Strickland had been clear not to let the Kline case wait. As guardian ad litem, Bridget would submit a report before the hearing, and the report would provide her impressions. She could go places a judge could not.

"Should I tell Judge Strickland you refused a visit?" said Bridget as Naomi poked her head through the door and stepped outside. "Hey, Naomi."

Elaine sat down on one of the plastic lawn chairs scattered on the porch, tapped Naomi's shoulder, and pointed to a chair.

"OK then, please, sit down." Elaine directed them to a dusty plastic lawn chair.

Bridget smoothed her white linen pants. "Elaine, this is a home visit, and we'd like to go inside. The porch isn't gonna cut it, unless, that is, Naomi lives outside?"

"The house...I didn't have time to tidy up." Elaine wiped sweat beading from her forehead.

"I'm a lawyer, a working mom, and I'm not from Good Housekeeping." She'd hate it, too, if a social worker wanted to examine her house.

Naomi rolled her eyes and opened the door with a grand hand gesture. "Welcome to my world."

The four entered the home. Given the house's condition on the outside and Elaine's comments, Bridget had expected a mess. She was wrong, very wrong. The house had plush, thick carpeting in a mauve pastel and was comfortably air-conditioned. The matching sofa, chair, and ottoman were white and soft. Mail scattered across the center of a spotless glass coffee table. Perhaps that was the mess Elaine was referring to?

"Please sit down," said Elaine as she sat on the chair while Naomi retreated to the carpeted floor, away from Elaine.

"She's been deep cleaning," said Naomi.

"Shush, child. They're not interested. I'll bring water."

Elaine headed to the kitchen, picked up a stack of photo frames, and brought them with her, which clattered as she walked.

"So much dust!" said Elaine.

"If you consider this place dusty, don't bother with my house," said Nick.

The walls were barren, and there was an outline and small nails where frames had hung. The only thing on the freshly vacuumed carpet were their footprints.

"She doesn't like photos?" asked Bridget.

Naomi shrugged her shoulders. "She cleans a lot and takes medication."

Nick asked Naomi for details about school, and while they were chatting away, Bridget brushed her finger across the stack of mail on the glass coffee table. An official-looking envelope with "The Office of Special Trustee" was written on the front. It was torn open. She lifted the corner of the envelope and peeked inside. It was a check made out to Cheri Kline, but Bridget couldn't tell how much without taking the entire check out of the envelope.

Bridget retracted her hand and stared at the mantel, away from the mail.

That money belonged to Naomi, or at least should. If Elaine became Naomi's official guardian, she'd manage the money until she was an adult. She wondered whether Naomi knew.

Elaine returned with glasses of water and placed them on the table, coasters in hand. Elaine rearranged the mail stack, gathering the paper in an aligned pile, angled to an opposite corner of the table.

"Naomi, why don't you give me a brief tour?" asked Bridget.

The rest of the house matched the living room. Furniture was dusted and spotless, with every piece meticulously maintained. Walls around the house were painted off-white, also devoid of pictures, photos, or paintings.

"Great place," said Nick, who had opened up his cell phone and was checking his schedule. Nick apparently did not need to see anything more because the home was acceptable, and the child was safe. Task completed. "I've gotta 'nother thing. You can sail this ship, skipper."

"Naomi, give me a hug," he said, but Naomi stepped away and folded her arms. "Or not! It's all glamor in the life of social work."

Nick skipped out of the house. Given her week, Bridget would've preferred he stayed, but she could finish the visit without him. Sometimes families opened up without the prying eyes and ears of social workers. Elaine may tell a different version of what happened to Cheri.

"My house is fine. Cheri wasn't here very often, couldn't keep a job, and didn't finish high school. I've raised Naomi."

Bridget took a sip of water and put the glass back on the coaster, slightly missing it, and the base hung off the coaster. Elaine reached over and centered the glass on the coaster. Naomi sat on the floor and put her glass next to her. Elaine grabbed it and placed it back on the table, carefully centered on the coaster as Naomi rolled her eyes.

"See? Everything's gotta be clean. Elaine takes pills for it."

"Let me talk with Elaine. Then we'll talk. OK?"

"Whatever."

Naomi stormed out, retreating to her room. That went well. Bridget crossed her legs, her white linen pants blending with the sofa.

"Honestly, I don't understand why you're here. I can care for Naomi. A medical assistant doesn't earn much, but we're fine."

The comment was one Bridget had heard a lot. Everything was fine. Go away. Bridget continued with her questions.

"Any other sources of income?" asked Bridget, cocking her head. Elaine blushed and pressed nonexistent wrinkles in her smock. Elaine looked everywhere except at Bridget.

"No, I...uh...the house is mine. After my husband died, there were a lot of bills. The insurance took care of the house, and I make do. I've managed to decorate and do stuff. I enjoy indoor housekeeping but can't stand the outdoors with my many allergies and then there's the bugs outside."

Elaine stood and smoothed the cushion on her chair, then swept imaginary dust from the table.

"Tell me about Naomi's uncle, your son," asked Bridget.

"Jay? Such a busy boy. He works in politics in Washington, D. C. You know, elections, fundraisers. I wish he would visit more."

As she talked, Elaine rearranged the pile of mail and turned it horizontally, then vertically, on the table as if trying to match the corners. She then stood and repositioned a clock on the fireplace.

"Do you know whether Cheri used illegal drugs or alcohol?"

"Probably."

"You were with her at the hospital?"

Elaine finally stopped fidgeting and sat on the plush, tan loveseat. "Yes, I was with her. Her medication was stable, and I thought she should leave. So, I brought her home. It wasn't long before she had left again."

"When is her funeral? I would like to go. Nick said you hadn't anything planned."

"No, I can't afford that. She's been cremated."

"My goodness, that was fast. How about a ceremony, a memorial service?"

Elaine was remarkably calm about Cheri's death, almost as if she was relieved.

"I suppose you're right. I should do something for Naomi and me. Cheri was the cutest little toddler when she came into our lives. She was fine until she hit 16, and the psychosis started."

Beyond the staircase, there was a rustling, probably Naomi hovering in the stairwell.

"Could you get Naomi for me?"

On cue, Naomi entered the room. She had been listening to them. *I would eavesdrop too.*

"Uncle Jay was here last week," said Naomi.

"Did Cheri get along with him?" asked Bridget.

"He's some big shot in Washington, and we have to leave when he comes."

"That's enough, Naomi. The lawyer doesn't want to hear all this. You must be busy," said Elaine.

"Is Jay a problem? I would like to meet with him, or at least talk."

"Jay? Goodness, no. I can barely talk to him. He gets upset about Cheri, though. Jay never adjusted to her when we brought her home. He never forgave us for bringing her into our lives. We took care of Cheri after her mother died when we lived in Oklahoma. My husband was a doctor working with the state. She was the perfect little baby, and that's when my husband arranged everything."

"Was that a reservation in Oklahoma?"

"My husband worked with the Osage during his residency. I don't remember much because I was home with the kids. Then we moved here."

"Was Cheri Native American?"

"I was so busy, and we didn't care where she was from. Those things aren't important."

Elaine walked out to the door and opened it.

Time to go? That wasn't subtle, thought Bridget. She eyed the bundle of mail neatly stacked.

"You realize Cheri's assets belong to her daughter. That's unless there's a will that says otherwise."

"No, poor dear, she had nothing and no money."

Bridget sunk further into the sofa, deciding if she should confront her. They could chat all day, discussing the many intricacies of the Kline family. Elaine looked like she was through talking.

She paused for a moment, considering whether her words helped. "The more you tell Naomi about her past and her mother's, the better for everyone. Hiding the past will not help the future."

Elaine faked a smile and kept her hand on the doorknob.

"Naomi, walk with me to the car?"

"It's too hot. Stay inside." Elaine headed to the sofa and began plumping the pillows where they had sat.

"True! It's sweltering. How about a slushy, Naomi? My treat."

Naomi was already heading out the door.

# Chapter 21

At the gas station, they walked back with the two slushies. Naomi sat on the Pontiac's hood, watching the turkey vultures coast on a gale wind in a turquoise sky, stretching over the flat plain as far as the eye could see.

"I hope you like bubble gum flavor with plenty of high fructose corn syrup," said Bridget.

"High fructose corn syrup is bad."

"This is corn country, and them is fightin' words."

Naomi swirled the ice and poked at it with her straw. Bridget continued, "That was my attempt at humor."

"Oh, right. I get it. You're trying. Do I have to go back there?"

"About your grandmother, I have reservations, and I will raise them with the judge. You may not like her, but the question is whether you're safe, and there aren't many options."

"I chose youth shelter. The orphanage. Juvie home, whatever. What about my dad?"

"Your father doesn't have a home yet, or a job, and that may take time." She didn't want to get Naomi's hopes up because fathers often disappoint, and Steve had not been a part of her life much.

"Orphanages went out with Oliver Twist. And you're not a criminal, so a juvie home is out."

"I'm not bad enough? I can change that," said Naomi.

"Don't. Try to be patient and focus on school."

"She lied! Said I stole a car. They handcuffed me because of her!"

Naomi kicked the wheel of the car. *And you lifted the wallet out of my tote bag.* She wasn't sure how innocent Naomi was, or Elaine, for that matter. Bridget grimaced as the cold slushy rushed to her head.

"Slushies are both a joy and a pain at the same time."

"Kind of like me," answered Naomi.

Naomi reached into her pocket and handed an envelope to Bridget. It was a check for $3,230 made out to Cheri Kline from The Office of Special Trustee—the envelope from the coffee table. In the notation line was written "Full Headright."

"Why does Elaine get that? Why not me?"

"Good question, and that's not a small sum. Do you know what the check is for?"

"I don't know, but she was looking at it while talking on the phone to Jay and said I was interfering with the state or something."

"Did Elaine say 'state' or 'estate'?"

Naomi shrugged her shoulders as she drained the last sip. She took the straw and tied it into a small knot.

"Elaine is not being honest. Your mom told you you're Native American, and I'm pretty sure that check proves it."

Naomi threw her straw against the ground, tears streaming down her face.

Bridget continued. "What happened that night? Tell me—

one step at a time. Start with the trip to the reservation and the ride with your mom."

Naomi wiped tears from her face with the back of her hand.

"My mom came home because the hospital let her go. She had the keys to Elaine's car. At first, I didn't want to go. I know my mom does crazy things and has problems. My dad was supposed to come and help."

"You drove to the reservation with your mom?" asked Bridget.

"Yeah."

"What was the car ride like? How was she?"

"She talked a lot, going on and on and never stopping. That's normal for her when she has her episodes. Said Elaine wasn't mad anymore and gave her the car keys."

"She knew you left?"

"Elaine hides stuff like keys. She never liked my mom driving." Naomi smoothed her tangled brown lock that fell to her shoulder.

"What happened then?"

"We drove to a house on the reservation. Mom made me stay in the car. After a while, she came outside. She talked about an errand and ran off, and then was gone. That was it. I asked people in the house where she was, but they didn't say nothing. She left me there."

"Who was in the house?"

"Some reservation guy. My mom talked a lot about him." Bridget showed her a picture of Monroe in the news on her phone. "That could have been him."

"What about the people in the house? Were they nice or upset?"

"They were like 'no biggie,' which made me angry. My mom told me to wait, and I did."

Naomi's throat choked as she recounted how she made

"errands" with her mom to the reservation. Twice, Naomi waited in the car while Cheri went into the same house and delivered something.

"I don't know. She delivered stuff like papers and thick envelopes. We'd done that twice."

Bridget handed the check for $3,230 back to Naomi, and they got in the Pontiac.

"You keep this. This belonged to your mother, and now you. It also tells us something about both of you."

"I waited for her in the car, but she never came."

"Where was your dad? When did you talk to him?"

Naomi took a pebble from the floor mat and threw it out the window. "Forget about my dad. He should have helped, but he didn't. What's new? If I have to go back to the witch, then let's do it."

Back in the car, the radio screeched as Naomi searched for music she liked.

"This radio is so old, it's funny."

She drove slowly back to Elaine, but bringing her there made her feel uneasy.

"You have my number."

"Do something," said Naomi, her face forlorn.

"I'll tell Nick that he should look for a foster home and assist your dad in finding a job."

"I mean about my mom. You promised you'd find out what happened to my mom."

"I'll call the reservation, and we can talk to the police together if you want. Though, you should be prepared that police's hands may be tied."

"Why?"

"It's hard to explain. It's about jurisdiction. Jurisdiction is like turf. Your mom's death wasn't on their 'turf.' The reservation police can't do much."

"She died on the reservation! That is their turf."

"The federal and state seriously mess with their turf. Any serious crime, like murder, the reservation can't do anything because the federal government should step in. These words are harsh, but there's no other way to say it. Your mother's tragic death is not enough to draw the attention of the federal government."

"The reservation is the perfect place to get away with a crime."

A lump formed in Bridget's throat. The kid was right.

# Chapter 22

"Lunching with a lawyer, I feel so important," said Nick.

"Says the social worker who can make or break a family. That's what I call real power."

They met at Steady Eddy's, a favorite restaurant in downtown Broken River, which was about a block from the courthouse, the county jail, and the adjacent halfway house. Because of the mixed population, downtown establishments fell into two categories—the nice or the seedy. Steady Eddy's in Broken River was one of the nicer ones, located across the street from a porn shop. A disgruntled date wouldn't have to go far.

Bridget nodded to the busser, who brought them water. The busboy was a former client, Pat Edwards, who was a so-called "deadbeat dad" who Judge Strickland sent to jail for thirty days for failure to pay child support. Pat nodded back and disappeared into the back of the restaurant. Nick looked at her inquisitively but knew better than to ask. With lawyers, like social workers, you never knew who a former client was and who was a friend.

A waitress sporting a blonde ponytail bounced their way.

Blondes with ponytails in Broken River were as common as aphids in a cornfield. Bridget ordered a beer instead of coffee and a turkey sandwich. Nick ordered pulled pork and water.

"I hoped you could provide insight on a couple of matters. Let's start with the Kline case."

"Hate to be a spoiler. We're going to recommend dismissal next week because Elaine checks out," said Nick.

The waitress came with their drinks. The ice cubes in the water made her teeth hurt.

"Tell me about Naomi's father."

"If he pulls his act together, wonderful. However, that doesn't matter because Elaine checks out. Darling, the Kline case is over. The child is safe."

"Maybe."

"Maybe? Let it go, honey. What are you up to?" Nick's voice went flat.

"For lawyers, 'Let it go' means retirement. Hold out a little longer for me on this case."

Nick scratched his chin, assessing her like a therapist.

"Hmm. The child of social services becomes a crusader for kids in need. I'll see what I can do. You're epic. Thought about wearing a cape?"

She felt her face redden. Her childhood wasn't supposed to be common knowledge. Yet everyone knew—Nick and even Chet Russell.

"Did you know I was a foster kid?" Bridget asked Pat as he refilled his water glasses.

"Who doesn't?" said Pat, grinning as he walked away.

"Is it possible to keep anything private in this town? My past is just that—past."

"Your past fuels your caring heart—"

"Enough psycho-babble."

"You don't love us, do you?" Nick cocked his head, taunting

her.

"Only you, Nick. I only love you."

The sandwich had warmed her stomach. Bridget grabbed the bill, but Nick snatched it back.

"One more question. Would you know anything about the Sun Family Foundation or a man called Chet Russell, who's a recruiter? They've offered to buy my law practice. Sun Family receives donations from larger firms like Whitfield & Barshefsky and helps children in need. Heard of it?"

"Nada. Sound like a righteous foundation, man. But not for you, Sister Justice. Man, can you even do something like that? Stay with us, neck-deep with messed-up families. It would be a huge loss. Damn, girl, you got it coming from all sides. A dead parent, malpractice lawsuit, and quitting. Need a hug?"

"Don't you dare."

Nick shook his head, and his black tresses brushed his shoulders as he outstretched his arms. Bridget couldn't help but smile as she took the last bite of her sandwich.

"You didn't share my client list with anyone by accident, like the Whitfield law firm or Barry Van Ekes? Like Abby Baker's address?"

"Barry? Yuck. Are you kidding? I'd be breaking a dozen laws, and I'd never mess with you."

Bridget's phone rang. It was Walter.

"Marital bliss calling? You better answer that."

"I'm getting a bite to eat," said Bridget to Walter.

"Irene called and said Tim is coming into town for the barbecue on Sunday."

Bridget hadn't seen her brother, Tim, in ages, not since Uncle Billy's funeral. Hanging with him during a happier occasion would be nice.

"Wonderful, and that would be great on the lawn." Bridget rested her head on the back of the tall vinyl booth, relieved that

Walter was calming down and had stopped worrying about the malpractice suit.

As she talked on the phone, Nick crumpled his napkin, put it on the table, and looked outside. His head jerked as his eyes followed a man pacing back and forth with a cell phone outside the restaurant. He glanced sideways at him as Nick's phone vibrated. The man looked familiar—bleached tipped hair, lanky.

Nick signaled to his phone that he was going to take a call. The lanky man walked past him outside the restaurant and turned his back. Odd. She could have sworn the two were acquainted, given the eye contact a minute ago.

Bridget straightened Nick's file on Naomi, which he had left on the table unattended. He should be more careful about confidentiality, she thought. She pushed it to the side of the table and rested her chin on a fist. Nick came back inside the restaurant, wiping sweat from his neck.

She shoved the file to Nick. "Why are you leaving confidential files on a restaurant table? You're looking kind of nervous. Distracted by your friend?"

"Who?" Nick chewed on a fingernail.

Bridget laughed. "OK, whatever you say."

"I'll say." Sweat dotted his forehead. "Our department will keep an eye on the family, and if something goes awry, we can refile."

"She hasn't been forthright about her finances or Naomi's heritage."

"Who doesn't lie to social workers? Elaine may want to formally establish legal guardianship over Naomi or an adoption, especially since Elaine isn't really the grandmother. Elaine's guardianship was over Cheri Kline."

"What are we talking about?"

"Elaine was Cheri's legal guardian, not the adoptive parent."

Bridget grabbed Nick's file and opened it. She ran her finger along Cheri's biographical information. Her birth parents were not listed, nor was there a birth certificate. It listed Elaine and her husband as legal guardians, not adoptive parents.

"Why wasn't I told of this?"

Nick's foot resumed tapping. "Not sure. We don't always get complete information from the parents. For all purposes, Elaine is the grandmother."

"I need to see her birth certificate. The court is going to want that. Call Oklahoma. That's what Cheri meant about Elaine not really being Naomi's grandmother. Does Naomi even know?"

"She's known Elaine all her life, and they're as good as family. So, when I wrote my report, I put grandmother."

"Legal guardianship differs from adoption. If Elaine's a legal guardian that affects inheritance, doesn't it?"

"Wow, yes, it does, Sister Justice! Inheritance."

Maybe Elaine didn't want to cut off Cheri's inheritance rights. Who is Cheri's family? Bridget thought about the home visit at Elaine's house. She said the house was dirty, but it wasn't. The only items out of order were the mail on Elaine's coffee table and Cheri's check.

"Naomi found a check made out to her mother for three grand. Elaine has no right to that money. Do you know anything about that?" Nick shook his head, and she shot him a stern look. "Better find that birth certificate and find out Cheri's heritage and any blood relatives. The court will want to know whether tribal notification is required. You're not dismissing this case, and I'll oppose any motion to dismiss. Got it?"

Nick scratched his afternoon stubble. "I'm truly humbled. My love for you grows and deepens. You will not sell your law practice. Can I have that hug now?" He cocked his head like a curious puppy. He outstretched his arms.

She gave him a perfunctory hug.

"You radiate strength, girl. Gotta skedaddle."

Nick took his file and left money for his bill on the table. He tipped an imaginary hat as a few patrons watched him with a sideways glance.

***

While paying, Pat Edwards walked up to the table.

"Miss Lawyer?" Bridget was used to clients never knowing her name. "Miss Lawyer", or "Lady Lawyer", "You There", "Suit and Heels" were not uncommon.

"I wanted to say thanks," said Pat.

"Sorry I couldn't keep you out of jail. Strickland wouldn't bend."

"It's alright. I've been out for two days, and I got this job. Steady Eddy is a solid place. I needed a shove."

"That is impressive, Pat."

He stepped a little closer and his voice dropped. "In jail, a man visited me. He asked me whether I was happy with you as my lawyer and angry that I was in jail. He said I could sue or something. I got nothing against you, and I told him no."

Her throat tightened as if she had swallowed a rock.

"Was he a lawyer? Did he give you a name, a card?"

"No name. I'm not sure he was a lawyer. He talked about taking care of me."

Bridget shuddered. A man was contacting her clients and wanted to know whether they were happy with her services. He had no success with Pat, but he did with Abby Baker and that resulted in a malpractice suit. She wondered how many clients he had contacted.

"What did he look like?"

"Big white guy. Casual, baseball cap. Big gold watch."

"Perfect teeth? Pearly white grin?"

"Now that you mention it."

Big white guy with a cap, a gold watch. That could be anyone. Or not. Chet Russell had a Rolex, and he wasn't just anyone. He's the one who wanted her to drop her law practice and head a foundation that she knew nothing about.

Chet's interest in her was more than a job, and Pat confirmed it. Why was he after her, was the question of the day. She wondered if anything he said was true—the foundation or the payment of two-hundred thousand for her law practice.

"Thanks, Pat."

His ample forehead crinkled in concern as he said, "Watch your back, Miss Lawyer."

# Chapter 23

Bridget, Walter, and Aiden arrived at Aunt Irene's house hours ahead of the family cookout. Walter had mowed the lawn. Bridget brushed clean an old, unused grill with a metal brush and mixed vinaigrette for a salad, and Aiden wrapped silverware into cloth napkins. Plastic knives and paper napkins in the house were an environmental misdemeanor.

After reviewing Aiden's work, Aunt Irene inspected the lawn with a white gallon of clear liquid and sprayed weeds, which Aiden lugged.

"I wouldn't want to be a plant around you," said Bridget.

"It's borax and water, which lets the grass take over and nudges out the weeds. Aiden, it's important to damage the competition but don't poison the soil."

"Lucky the grass to have you as its agent," said Bridget.

After weeding, neighbors arrived, and Aiden and a neighbor kid disappeared with fistfuls of potato chips. A neighbor acted as a grill master armed with steak sauce and tongs.

"When's your brother, Tim, coming? We all want those

expensive steaks he loves."

Family barbecues were a rarity since Tim, her younger brother, moved to Chicago. A car door slammed outside, and soon thereafter, Tim entered, holding a sack of inch thick steaks. Nothing but the best corn-fed, marbled Midwest steak.

"Baby brother! Nice of you to grace us with your presence," said Bridget.

"Sorry I'm late. Great to be here! Did you start the grill?"

Bridget smiled up at him because Tim loomed a good foot above her.

"Straight to business, and the grill is where it always is. Not much has changed here. I know it's rough with no staff here to help."

"Funny, Bridge. Jesus, great to see you!"

Both laughed and the siblings embraced.

"It's been too long."

"Uncle Tim!" yelled Aiden.

Tim hugged him and ruffled his hair.

"I killed weeds. Do you want to help?"

"Yikes. Did you use Aunt Irene's famous hippie homemade weedkiller?"

Tim and Aunt Irene greeted each other with a long hug while Bridget brought the steaks to the grill.

\*\*\*

After eating corn and steak, everyone had settled into lawn chairs except Aiden and his friends, who were intent on killing weeds. Covered in a bandana mask, Aiden dragged the homemade jug along next to him.

"Aiden, let that be. It's a natural weed killer, borax, but you still need to be careful. Glad to see that young Aiden here wants to be a good steward of the land. A hundred years ago, there were over fifty feet of black topsoil and prairie grass. Taller than a man on a horse," Aunt Irene said.

"Did you ride a horse through the prairie grass?" asked Aiden.

"No, I didn't. That was a bit before my time."

"Your great-great-grandfather, what about him?" asked Aiden.

"My great-great-grandfather, huh?" smiled Aunt Irene. "Well, no, he didn't see it either because he didn't live here. No one was here then."

"No one? Someone was here. Entire nations were here," Bridget said.

As if to finish her thought, Aunt Irene continued. "Of course, the Indigenous were here. An issue this country has yet to deal with properly. Aiden, do you know what genocide is?"

For the first time in years, Bridget wanted and needed to hear Aunt Irene's lecture on Native Americans again. She frowned a bit but was glad that someone other than herself could teach Aiden about the sins of the past. Her mind wandered as Aunt Irene lectured, but she interrupted as she launched into Custer's cavalry giving blankets infected with smallpox to the Native Americans.

"How about a trip to the Southwest and a visit to the reservations? Oh, sorry, Bridget, I forgot about last weekend," said Aunt Irene.

"No, that's OK. I've been doing my own refresher course. Ever heard of 'headright payments'? The enrolled members of Osage receive headright payments in Oklahoma."

"I remember my grandpa saying how the Osage were the richest people in the country because of oil money," said Aunt Irene.

Bridget's great-grandfather was a train conductor who came home with stories of the nation. Aunt Irene continued that the oil money in Oklahoma was targeted by opportunists who descended upon the Osage and their money.

She put her hand on her belly, regretting that third ear of sweet corn. "A headright is the distribution of that oil money. Each Osage member from 1906 received a portion and passed it down to their family members. The headright is the right to receive a quarterly distribution of funds derived from the Osage Mineral Estate."

"Listen to you," said Tim. "Someone's been doing her homework."

"That's not what's going on here with those protests," said Aunt Irene.

"The protest is about a lawsuit against the grocery retailer, Buyland, who is misbehaving, and they want the store closed."

Tim sat down again with a third plate of food. "God, this corn is good. No one can match the Midwest in corn and steak. That reservation, the Wisaka? Now that's an interesting situation. Buyland is a family-owned store, relatively small. It's remarkable that they're positioned with Native Americans, but my bet is not on Buyland surviving in the long run."

"Because you don't shop there?"

"True, I don't. My eye would be on the bigger company that could step in and buy them out."

"There is always a competitor."

"That sounds vicious as weeds," said Aunt Irene.

"Yep, sounds like weeds for your borax weed killer. Get rid of the competition, so one plant can grow," said Tim.

"How is working for the greatest Ponzi scheme?" asked Bridget.

"Investment banking? I'm doing exceedingly well, thank you," answered Tim.

This was true. He was doing very well. When did Tim grow up and become so different from Bridget? The two had shared everything growing up, although foster care wasn't a topic they discussed. Her experiences gave her compassion and willingness to fight. Tim didn't want to think about it and had moved on— to bigger, better, and profitable endeavors, which was his way of being secure. Money equals power equals safety.

"Of course, and all those protests? It doesn't sound like they're behaving themselves."

"Buyland could shut down," said a neighbor.

"Talk to them? Heck, join the protests!" said Aunt Irene.

"I'll put it on my to-do list," said Tim.

"You, Bridget?" asked Aunt Irene.

"I'll drive by and honk."

Tim and Bridget laughed. Aunt Irene never changed because the 60s never stopped for her. Bridget inhaled deeply, relishing the moment she wasn't in a courtroom or facing a malpractice suit. It was good to get away from it all.

The sound of crashing glass and a car alarm overpowered their conversation.

"What the heck was that?" asked Tim.

Bridget, fearing the worst, ran to the front of the house.

# Chapter 24

A gangly kid circled on a red bike in front of the house. He wore baggy jeans, a black concert t-shirt, and a black cap. At first blush, there was nothing spectacular about him.

Except the gangly kid was swinging an aluminum baseball bat.

As he approached the house, she realized the kid was no boy. The hair on her neck tingled, her teeth clenched. The punk was headed straight towards her.

Bridget retreated towards the safety of the house, but the crash of breaking glass stopped her. The car front window was shattered. She turned slowly, not wanting to acknowledge the sound or the situation. Then another crash. Her car mirror was smashed, and after another crack, her side window shattered.

The blue-eyed punk with pale, blotchy skin eyed her with amusement. His straw-bleached hair popped out from under his black cap, and his lips stretched into a fiendish smile revealing dark, stained teeth. He had a tattoo on his neck. His grubby hands held the handle of the bat he was cradling on his right shoulder.

"I've gotta message for you!" said Skinny Boy.

Time slowed. I'm not supposed to be here, she thought. The only dangers Bridget ever contemplated were nasty paper cuts, or maybe an unknown toxin leaching from a library cushion or ancient poisonous glue lurking in book bindings. Those were the dangers she had expected to face. Not this. She rarely represented serious felons. Maybe occasionally drunks, small-time dopers, jilted wives, abandoned kids, and a few crazies.

The bat swung in her direction.

With cat-like agility, Bridget crouched low like a cat. The bat grazed the hairs on her curly blonde head as the force of the swing sent the punk tumbling to the ground. Dear Mother Earth herself had sucked her toward the earth, protecting her from evil men wielding weapons. A car horn sounded.

"Fuck." Skinny Boy dusted gravel off his baggy jeans. "Bitch lawyer!" He stood, looking at her, smiling. He knew her and knew she was a lawyer. She should run because this attack was meant for her. She remained crouched.

"It don't matter, bitch. Just delivering a message." He did a little dance as if delivering a singing telegram. "The message is the next time I won't miss. And you're not invited to the powwow. Get it? Stay home. Bake a cake. Leave the girl alone."

Skinny Boy laughed as he jogged toward the red bicycle lying on the street. He hopped on; the bike was too small for him. Like he was a playful youth off to Little League. But he wasn't young and playful. Her heart pounded throughout her entire body. Hands shaking, she clenched them for control and stood slowly. Aiden was inside. All were safe. For now, at least. The punk made it to the end of the street and turned off the road. She resisted the impulse to go after him. Her poor, pathetic car—the Grand Am with shattered glass scattered across the street and lawn.

Bridget hung her head and sat down on the hard concrete front stairs to the house, its solidness stabilizing her. Fatigue draped over her body like a shroud as she felt a hand on her shoulder. She jumped. It was Tim. Behind him followed Walter and Aunt Irene, trailed by Aiden.

"Chicago is a lovefest compared to this town." Tim looked solemnly at her car. "You're at it again, aren't you? Messing with people and causing trouble. What're you trying to fix?"

"This isn't foster care, and I thought our past was off-topic, which suits me fine," Bridget's voice cracked.

After a long pause, he said, "You're right. I'm out of line. God, do you make me nervous."

Walter walked to the car and brushed his foot over the broken glass. He leaned over, looking under the vehicle. Tim followed him and also examined the car. He reached under the rear axle and pulled at something, holding it in his hands—a little square tracker, the thickness and size of a quarter. Aunt Irene covered her mouth, stunned.

"You're being tracked," said Walter.

"It's not like I'm in hiding," she said flatly.

"Who would be tracking you?" asked Tim. "Is this related to a client?"

Bridget nodded. She couldn't get the attacker's face out of her head. Had she seen him before? Her hand clenched until her knuckles were white as she tried to recall the attacker's words. Did he really say "powwow"? If so, the attack was about the Klines. If so, whatever she was dealing with was graver than she understood. Her client's problem now became her problem, and more likely than not, Naomi was in danger.

By the time the police arrived, her trembling hands had steadied and her breathing had slowed. A neighbor who had seen the punk riding a red bicycle called the police. She was glad a neighbor had witnessed it because at least she had corroboration.

She thanked him, explaining that the attack had been targeted at her, and her neighbor needn't worry about his safety.

Bridget provided a statement to the police and explained what she could. She told the officer about the "powwow" message and how it may relate to a client. The officer's raised eyebrow revealed he was skeptical until she described Cheri's death. He confirmed a squad car would circle the area for the next 48 hours, and they would check on Naomi Kline and her grandmother.

After more questioning, Walter took Bridget's hand and led her back into Aunt Irene's house. They sat in the den, where Uncle Billy used to read. He died last year, and Bridget missed him terribly, especially now. He had been so steady amidst the chaos of her life, providing guidance, a kind word, and a home.

"How about a toast to Uncle Billy?" said Walter.

"Uncle Billy's whiskey? Count me in," said Tim. Uncle Billy's bottle of Bushmills was still in the cabinet, neglected and alone. Tim poured two fingers into chipped ceramic mugs and handed Bridget the one with Audubon Club on it.

"To Uncle Billy."

She sipped it slowly, overwhelmed by its strength, and put it aside. Uncle Billy had protected her, cared for her, gave her a home, even though they weren't blood-related.

"Hey, deep thoughts," said Tim.

She didn't know what to say. Her thoughts were stuck, much like this heat, as if she was sitting in a sauna with no exit. Aunt Irene came in with a tray of glasses and a pitcher, breaking the uncomfortable silence.

"Iced tea is also brown like whiskey, yet more refreshing." She poured a glass and handed it to Bridget, who gulped it down. "You have always believed the world was after you, and this time you're right," she said.

Her mind tried to piece together the last week—the malpractice lawsuit, selling her law practice, and the warning from Pat that a man matching Chet Russell's description was after her. Even Nick acting shady at the restaurant when he eyed that man outside the restaurant made her suspicious. Ceaseless images—screaming infant, a cigarette-flinging man, Cheri's body—images driving through her head like a train.

"Everything's OK, right?" asked Walter.

"I'm being targeted, and it's related to one of my cases, but I'm not sure why."

Aunt Irene paused. "What about those protests? Not that I know, but big money can get nasty. You've stepped on someone's toes, sweetheart."

Bridget shook her head, thinking of little Naomi facing big players, but none of it made sense.

"One of the biggest law firms in the state may be after me, but I'm not sure it has anything to do with this attack."

Tim raised his hand for a high five toward Bridget. "B. Forget what I said earlier. You have great instincts, and you can smell danger. You learned from the past, and I buried it. You got this."

Bridget looked down, not used to the compliment. Aiden peeked into the den.

"Go home with Aiden. I'll take care of the car," said Tim.

"How?"

"I'll drive you," said Aunt Irene.

***

They drove home with Bridget in front of the dented Suburban, and Walter and Aiden in the back.

"Do we need to move out of town?" Walter said, his voice shaking. "I don't mind moving and having a new start. I could find a job in a paint store, something regular like retail with benefits. You could take that new job?"

Walter wiped his forehead and pulled Aiden closer to him. He was taking this hard, which was to be expected. Consoling words escaped her and staring aimlessly out the car window was the only thing her body, feeling like lead, would let her do. But what could she say? Lawyers don't share details about work—a client's problem was confidential, and confidentiality meant silence. Clients' secrets belonged to them, not her, and she preferred it that way. Now that her home, her family, and Bridget herself were threatened, she should have put fears to rest, but words didn't come. She wasn't sure she even knew how to talk about it. So she said nothing. You could slice the silence with a knife.

She pressed the palm of her hands to her weary eyes and wished for an immediate solution. Instead, Pat's warning at Steady Eddy's rang true. *Watch your back, Miss Lawyer.*

She knew only one thing. That punk—or whomever he worked for—had crossed a line. She would not sit idly by while she, her client, and her family were threatened. But what to do and why this was happening? She hated to admit it, but she needed help.

# Chapter 25

"I'm here to see Chief French." An officer stood behind an inch-thick bulletproof glass at the Broken River police department. He eyed Bridget cautiously as she explained herself.

"Take a seat," he grumbled.

She sat on a sturdy black stacking chair and studied the intricate patter of greasy handprints on the glass windows while she waited. After a half hour, the police chief finally showed. Chief French stood well over six feet, barely clearing the door. His sculpted handlebar mustache obscured an otherwise clear view up his prominent hanging nose.

"This way."

She felt eyes upon her as she walked through a row of desks. Police stations made her uncomfortable, but now she needed them. It didn't make it any easier that Chief French was the person she was asking for help. French was a rookie cop when Bridget was a budding juvenile delinquent. Now he was police chief. She straightened her spine, trying to shake the feeling that she had misbehaved.

His office had the same linoleum tile as the rest of the building and smelled like burned coffee and corned beef sandwiches. A mustard package lay in the corner of the metal desk. He closed the door behind him and showed her a padded metal chair.

"Sorry to hear about your car, counselor."

"The attack was a warning. Someone wants me off one of my cases. It's about the client I talked to you about earlier last week. She's only fourteen, and her mother passed away on the Wisaka Reservation. I have to be blunt—I need help. I've been threatened. A woman, her mother, is dead. I'm concerned about the safety of my client and my family."

Chief's brown cowlick perched on his head like a question mark.

"The attacker knew your client's name?" he asked.

"No, but he intimated as much."

She described the incident at Aunt Irene's, detailing what she could remember. She also shared her concerns about discrepancies in Cheri's medical records, the malpractice suit, and Whitfield & Barshefsky's appearance on Abby's CINA case.

"Please investigate Cheri Kline's death. There's got to be a connection."

"And what are you going on? That he said 'powwow'? Sure it wasn't 'pow' like a gun," Chief French spoke in a low tone that was both consoling and frustrating at the same time.

"No, it was a reference to the Kline case. Although I know this sounds far-fetched."

"A bit."

"It's the only case I have involving a Native American. Actually, it's the only one I've ever had. It cannot be a coincidence."

"The police are doing their job. We've poked around a bit and found nothing. Cheri Kline was a troubled woman with a history of mental illness. The hospital folk knew her well, and her ma. Elaine Kline, right? The hospital folk speak highly of the lady. And let us not forget about that little thing called jur-is-dic-tion." He pronounced the word "jurisdiction" slowly and somehow added another syllable to "tion."

"You have jurisdiction. My broken windshield in Broken River."

"Not sure about that, but let us take this further. If the attacker did say 'powwow,' that's the reservation folk. And they'd be better positioned to handle that."

She shook her head. "The attacker was white, and I don't think anyone from the reservation would be giving warnings like 'powwow.' That does not sound like a threat from a Native American." Bridget continued, "And then there's the bogus malpractice suit. It's like someone is purposefully trying to get me to stop practicing law."

"People get sued, counselor, and not always for the right reasons. You know that. You can grapple with that one better than I can."

"And Cheri's medical record?" asked Bridget.

"Interesting. But Cheri wouldn't be the first to hide drug abuse and alcohol."

"So, you will not investigate."

"No, I didn't say that." Chief paged through a file. At least he had a file, she thought. "The daddy, Steve Ross, has done a spell in prison. We'll talk to him."

She pressed her lips together. Chief was right; maybe he only wanted his daughter back and thought threatening her lawyer was the easiest way. "He wasn't aggressive; he was friendly and cooperative during the status hearing."

"We'll keep our ears open, and we'll question Mr. Ross. But Bridget, leave this case alone. We're running a squad by your house for the next couple of days. We're also keeping an eye on the Klines. You stick to the courtroom. I'll handle the streets."

Bridget thanked him and quickly left his office, biting her lower lip to keep it from quivering. Outside the police station, she leaned against the cold brick. Just breathe. Chief French hadn't completely ignored her, and a squad car nearby was comforting. But he was clear that was all that he was going to do. She was on her own and it didn't feel good.

*Am I crazy to think more is going on here?* She leaned against the wall, the coolness of the brick calming her as a reality of the situation struck.

If she wanted a serious investigation, she would have to conduct it herself.

# Chapter 26

Diane called and gave her progress on Whitfield & Barshefsky. After cross-checking their known clients with Bridget's clients, Diane came up with nothing. A brief background check on the lawyers revealed nothing, as expected. The lawyers at Whitfield & Barshefsky were squeaky clean, other than the occasional speeding ticket and open container infraction during college years.

"About the Sun Family Foundation and Mr. Russell. It lists him as the only officer, and no name is listed in the articles of incorporation, other than Mr. Russell's signature. I also can't find an address for the corp. Same for Chet Russell."

Russell said he lived out-of-state, and his cell number was a Maryland number. He had incorporated in state, which was an interesting choice, especially if he represented a firm from around the country.

"No information on the incorporation. Why am I not surprised? Any other goodies?"

"The Sun Family Foundation was formed two days after

Cheri died."

Just in time for him to look me up, she thought. "Mr. Russell may not be a good person."

"You think? He called again and asked me to confirm that I filed the withdrawals for all your cases. Should I look for another job?" Diane's tone was bland, almost nonchalant.

"No, you're good. I'm surprised Chet called. I basically told him that I wasn't interested, in a Midwestern way."

"What did you say?"

"I told him to have a good day."

"Well, that should do it," said Diane.

"You'd think."

"Should I keep looking?"

"Let's take another approach. You know what, I've got another idea. You call and tell him I'm in. Make an appointment in two weeks. I'll smoke him and his backers out."

Feeling a little lighter, she walked to the courthouse, which was ten minutes from the police station, and passed through security. Nick Harmon sat with a group of people, another troubled family. She nodded politely and went to the clerk's office to check her courthouse mailbox. Dave, the file clerk, was busy sorting files while working up a sweat.

"Working alone today?" Bridget asked.

"New guy worked two weeks and quit," he said.

"You must be a slave driver."

"Me? I'm a cupcake. I even ignored the bleached hair and the tattoo. At least he wore a collared shirt."

Her jaw dropped. She closed her eyes, trying to picture the clerk in her head. Then it hit her. Skinny, muscled, tattooed—her attacker also had a neck tattoo and bleached hair. Different clothes, but the same, lean build.

"Huh. That's right. Tattoo on his neck. Right?" Bridget drummed her fingers on the counter. He had worked there for two weeks, which meant he was hired right after Bridget was appointed to *In the Interest of N.K.*

"Yep. I wished they let me do the hiring around here."

The file clerk had access to all her clients' details, like Pat Edwards and Abby Baker, including her home address. There may have even been a report about Bridget bringing the child to the hospital.

"What was the guy's name?"

"Travis-something."

"How did he get the job?"

Dave shrugged his shoulders. "He came recommended, but I forget by who. He worked at a law firm in Cedar Town."

"Whitfield & Barshefsky?"

"Now that you mention it."

Travis. His face was razor clear in her head. Skinny Boy. She'd also seen Travis with Nick when they had lunch. Travis was the person who eyed Nick outside the restaurant.

"Thanks, Dave." With fists clenched, she spun on her heel and searched the hallways looking for Nick. She found him on the lower floor and grabbed his elbow, dragging him to an empty corner.

"What about it, Nick?" said Bridget.

"Huh?"

"Tell me about your friend at Steady Eddy's." Her fists were tucked under her folded arms to prevent herself from strangling him.

"Oh, dude, Lady Justice. Negative vibes. What are we talking about?" Nick's long curls wilted slightly around his face.

"Your friend. The one you pretended not to know at Steady Eddy's? The one who broke my windshield?"

Nick's hand searched for a chair behind him, and not finding one, he swayed slightly. Nick knew a lot about Bridget and her cases. Of course, anyone could find general information, but not specifics like a home address for a CINA case. If he didn't know, he was faking it well.

"You got it wrong. Travis isn't my friend. He's..." Nick shook his head and whispered. "He is or was my boyfriend. I pretended not to know him at the restaurant because I don't want people to know."

"You're gay. And? So what?"

"Shush. I care. I deal with kids, and this is a small town. I'm afraid it could cause problems for me. And the other stuff, man," he paused, scratched his stubble. "What did you say? Who broke your windshield?"

She recounted the story to Nick.

"When did you meet him?" asked Bridget.

Nick explained he had met him two weeks ago when Travis started as a new file clerk at the courthouse. After five days of bliss, everything went sour when Travis threatened to tell his supervisor he was gay, so Nick avoided him. The last time Nick saw him was at the restaurant.

"We met when I picked up the file for Naomi. Stuff was missing from that file. Remember the county attorney? Mark had no information on Naomi's father. Oh, man, creepy. He kept on asking me about my cases. You're not going to tell anyone, are you?"

"Of course I am. The police need to know you're being harassed."

"No, nothing about my private life. You don't get it. You're going to get me fired."

"They can't do that. And I know a brilliant lawyer who can help," she smiled.

"I don't want a lawsuit. I want my job. It's all I have."

She sighed. Why was helping families so tricky? "Can you at least tell the police that you knew him socially? It would help if you could also identify him."

"Sure. I'll just leave out my private life." He tapped his foot rapidly.

"You're not going to tell them, are you."

He stopped tapping his foot. "Sorry, Sister Justice, I'm not."

She could tell the Chief herself, but that may not even help. Chief wasn't exactly supportive, and dragging Nick's sexuality into the entire mess seemed cruel.

"Fine, I'll let it go for now."

"Would you stop looking at me like you're going to slug me?"

"Sorry, things have been tense."

"Am I released now?" Nick stepped backward as he gave a deep bow, tipped an imaginary hat as if he were her servant, and blew her a kiss.

\*\*\*

"I'm here!" she said, tossing her tote bag on the lobby chair of her office.

"I'm ecstatic," Diane said without looking at her. "Messages are on your desk. I've drafted your discovery response in the Simon dissolution. You're welcome. Here's the paperwork on Sun Family Foundation and Chet Russell, who wants to give you two million dollars."

"Two hundred thousand dollars."

"Also, good. Can I write my severance package now?"

She shoved the paperwork aside and took a pad of sticky notes. On each one, she wrote a name: Chet Russell, Sun Family Foundation, Cheri, Elaine, and Naomi. She stuck the papers on her desk in random formation. Chewing on her pen, she rubbed her neck and examined the sticky notes, occasionally rearranging them. Something's missing, she thought. She wrote down more names: Abby Baker, Connie from 5E, Steve Ross, Nick Harmon, Buyland, Whitfield & Barshefsky, and Skinny Tattoo Boy.

She scribbled what she knew about each name and drew arrows like a detective. After five minutes, she shoved the papers aside.

"New friends?" Diane asked, looking at the desk covered with sticky notes and the mountain of paperwork shoved in the corner.

"Everything new and weird in my life."

"I better order more sticky notes."

"Good idea. And don't expect me in the office tomorrow."

"Enjoying some 'me time'?"

"A road trip. But I'm not sure I will enjoy it."

# Chapter 27

The office of Whitfield & Barshefsky was in downtown Cedar Town, a big city compared to Broken River. The office was within walking distance of the courthouse, located on an island in the sometimes peaceful, sometimes deadly, Cedar Springs River. Although the entire city, including the courthouse and downtown, had once been completely submerged under a raging spring swell, little evidence remained of the disaster to the non-native Cedar Townie.

The offices of Whitfield & Barshefsky were a showcase of redevelopment, exemplifying Midwestern grit and stability. Impervious to the irony of using water to decorate, behind the receptionist bubbled an elaborate water fountain that sounded through the atrium.

"I'm here to see Alan Barshefsky," said Bridget.

A manicured and coiffed blonde sporting meticulously blended highlights sat behind a dark marbled credenza.

"One moment, please." The receptionist's bronzed face widened into a gentle smile.

"Mr. Barshefsky is not showing any appointments today."

Her breathy voice scratched ever so lightly, and her blonde head gently tipped downward, presumably examining a directory or calendar. The calming water fountain trickled behind her as the scent of a flower bouquet wafted through the air.

"I think he'll want to talk to me."

Her forehead developed an empathetic wrinkle. The receptionist nodded. Not a hair on the sculpted head moved.

"I'll talk to his secretary. Your name?"

"I'm here about his client, Elaine Kline."

"You are—"

"A lawyer concerning a potential claim against Ms. Kline."

Alan Barshefsky represented Abby Baker in the malpractice suit against Bridget. The law firm backed Sun Family Foundation and had prepared the contract Chet had given Bridget. And the malpractice suit would disappear once she dropped all her cases and joined the foundation. Why were they being so nice? The whole thing was too good to be true.

She had the gnawing feeling that Barshefsky had something to do with the Kline case, and she had thought long and hard about how to get Barshefsky to talk to her. Up to now, he had flatly refused.

Her hunch was that the malpractice suit had nothing to do with Abby Baker and had everything to do with Naomi.

If she guessed right about Elaine, it could explain a lot. It meant she could draw a connection between Abby and the Klines, both represented by Barshefsky. That also meant Barshefsky probably found Abby and not the opposite. And if she was right, though, she had to face another terrible truth. That this law firm, and all its resources, were after her.

The receptionist spoke inaudibly on the phone.

"You may go up to the third floor."

It was as if she had been pushed off a cliff. Whitfield &

Barshefsky were representing Elaine Kline, and the receptionist confirmed it. The firm also represented Abby Baker. They also backed Sun Family Foundation. She placed her hand on the reception desk to steady herself as she contemplated that tidbit of information. That was enough for today. Did she really want to confront Barshefsky?

Her heart pounded as she headed toward the stairwell. Climbing stairs would give her added time to figure out her next step. She reached the third floor, breathless but calmer. Another cheery face greeted her.

"Please sit down. Mr. Barshefsky will be right with you. May I get you something, coffee, water?"

"No, thanks."

I don't want to be poisoned, she thought. Bridget sat down in a brown leather chair, so soft that sitting in it felt like a gentle hug. The chair probably cost more than the entire furniture set in her living room. A man ambled towards the reception area across the parquet wooden floor.

"Mrs. Kline, I am surprised to see you here. Your son should have explained—" Barshefsky stiffened as if he had been gutted. "Wait, you're not Elaine Kline. Who are you?"

"Precious."

She sank back into the leather chair, its arms catching her descent—like the prince embracing a fainting damsel in distress. She caressed the soft leather with her hand. Alan Barshefsky's reaction just confirmed Elaine was a client.

"Mr. Alan Barshefsky, I presume? I'm Bridget McGarrity, my client is Naomi Kline, Elaine Kline's granddaughter."

Barshefsky tipped his head, observing her through his bifocals. He grinned.

"Bridget McGarrity, of course. You shouldn't have come here. There was a reason I ignored your calls."

She evaluated her foe, a middle-aged man with suspenders,

bow tie, and a belly that entered the room before the rest of him.

"Abby Baker picked a winner. Or did you pick Abby?"

"Who?"

"This gets better and better. You don't know Abby's name, yet you represent her."

"Ahh, yes. The malpractice suit must be upsetting. You should be more careful," he said.

She rested her head on her fist with her elbow propped on her new favorite chair.

"God, I love leather, the texture, the smell. Do you scent the hallways here?"

The moment was surreal, as if she were another person, the image of a big law firm's comfortable corporate life and stable community connections. She could live this life. Sun Family Foundation—would they have offices like this?

"I know Abby, but sometimes I forget a name here or there. I have so many cases." Barshefsky cleared his throat and heaved his sagging pants over his rear end.

"Oh, really?" Bridget pressed her lips as she thought of the hundred-plus names on her client list. "How many is that? One corporation? Two? And Abby and Elaine."

"I don't like to discuss such things, Miss McGarrity. And it is 'Miss' not 'Mrs.'? Walter and you never married."

He knew everything about her, had studied her like a lab rat. The hallway walls pulsed around her, along with the immaculate floor and the oil paintings. An enormous antique mahogany desk shined.

"Looks like you could hide a body in that thing. Is it a desk or a coffin?"

Barshefsky glanced nervously towards the receptionist, who was diligently studying a chipped nail.

She walked to the window that looked out over the spectacular view of the Cedar Spring River. Her Cedar Town road trip could accomplish little more, other than being stuffed into a desk and her body served as food for the river.

"Elaine Kline brought us together, didn't she?" she asked.

A hand encircled her arm, his touch oddly soft, and then squeezed hard.

"Distressing? So determined, yet so clueless." Barshefsky whispered softly in her ear, an intense heat emitting from his large body. She stepped back and jerked her arm from his grip, dumbfounded by his aggression.

"Your parents died, didn't they? Were they drug addicts like your aunt? And yet you returned to Broken River."

"What are you talking about?"

"Your aunt, the California hippie. What do you think she did there?"

This creature knew too much about her, more than she knew about him. She didn't like that. She stepped closer to him.

"Huh. Nasty piece of business, you are. But you're not the first prick I've dealt with. You prepared the employment contract for the Sun Family Foundation, didn't you?"

Barshefsky tilted his head like he was examining a fly and was about to pull its wings off. "You're in over your head. You know that, don't you?"

"You are a bad person. And I dislike bad people. I see that as your problem, not mine. Here's my warning." She pointed a finger at him. "Back off. Stay away from me, my client, and my family."

"Gladly. Get off the Kline case. Let another someone else step in, and then your life will become much simpler. If no, well, it will be bad for you."

Bridget turned her back to him and marched to the door, away from him and the stately offices of Whitfield & Barshefsky.

\*\*\*

"Asshole!" She pounded on her steering wheel. After she was out of Cedar Town, she parked the car and breathed deeply, trying to calm herself. She grabbed her phone and dialed Aunt Irene but didn't reach her. She leaned the car seat back and examined the top interior of her car. Perhaps it was too bold to confront Barshefsky, but she'd definitely learned something. Barshefsky didn't know his own client, Abby Baker, and Elaine Kline seemed to be a favorite. And he wanted Bridget off the Kline case.

A million scenarios ran through her head—moving, selling her office. She didn't want to end up like Cheri. Walter would move for her and Aiden. If Bridget stayed in Broken River, she would live with this cloud over her. Her thoughts turned to Naomi, staying at Elaine's, Barshefsky's client. What if something terrible happened to Naomi because she dropped this case? Court was next week, and another lawyer would not have a clue.

The hazy road blurred in the heat, and she rolled down the window, took a swig of water, and raised her seat upright. It was at the reservation where it all had started. The field trip wasn't over.

# Chapter 28

The Wisaka Reservation had changed little since last week, except for the absence of the U.S. Marshals. Some protesters remained, sitting in garden chairs holding yellow protest signs with red paint, "#Shame on Buyland" and "Respect our Sovereignty!" By the casino, several cars and buses dotted the parking lot. Not much would deter faithful gamblers.

Bridget pushed aside memories of Cheri's body and focused on the task at hand–finding Joe Monroe. His name had been on the news as the organizer who shut down Buyland, hoping to shake up the tribal leadership. Forcing them to be tougher on outside businesses. It wasn't clear who won that fight. Buyland was open, but the store parking lot was empty.

Officer Bennett stood outside the community center, and the knot in her stomach loosened. She had called him on the way to the reservation. An unannounced visit might cause problems. Telling Officer Bennett why she was there was cathartic. She babbled about everything, including that Cheri was not a drug addict and about the attack on her car.

According to Naomi, Cheri drove to the reservation that evening with an envelope she hoped to deliver. Officer Bennett said she had been at Joe Monroe's home. Hopefully, he had more answers as to why Cheri was there.

"I'd like to meet Mr. Monroe. I think Naomi was at his house or near there when her mother passed."

"You're not here for the casino?" Officer Bennett chided.

"Next time."

"I figured as much. I suppose you're not a troublemaker."

"No more than last week."

"Mind if I tag along?"

She sighed in relief. "That would be great."

She followed his car down a gravel road in Aunt Irene's Suburban. They drove past Buyland and the casino, heading deeper into the reservation. The area was dotted with mid-sized houses, each with dark blue address signs with white reflective lettering posted in front.

She smiled and introduced herself and said that she wanted to speak with Joe Monroe. Officer Bennett stood behind her.

A man's head peeked around the door only slightly above the doorknob as if he were squatting.

"Why Joe? Hey, Bennett, you brought the feds with you?"

"No. A lawyer," said Bennett.

"My client is Naomi Kline. I was appointed when her mother, Cheri Kline, couldn't take care of her. She died a little over a week ago."

His dark eyes scaled over every inch of her. The door slowly opened again.

"Sad. I heard about that. Hey, Bennett, what does that got to do with Joe?" he talked loudly, accusingly to Bennett.

"I'm here to find answers for Naomi, who needs to understand what happened to her mother, Cheri Kline."

"Joe's not here. I am Scott Monroe, his good-looking

brother. Do you want to wait? He won't be long."

"Thank you. I will." She headed towards her car.

"You can stay outside, Bennett."

Officer Bennett squinted in the sun, masking any irritation.

"Miss Lawyer, could you pick up the shovel in the front yard and put it in the garage?" he asked. The corner of his dark eyes turned upward, accompanied by a coy smile.

"OK," she answered.

Scott pointed to some garbage on the road and a trash bin.

He smiled, and she chuckled to herself. Odd, but she relaxed and picked up the trash. "Any other chores?"

"You can put away the shovel over there."

"Stop messing with her and let her in. She represents kids," said Bennett.

Scott's guiltless face cracked into a smile, his oval eyes twinkling as if this were an entertaining game. His head popped back behind the door. Then the door creaked wide open.

"Come on in," said the voice from inside.

Inside was a modest-sized living room with tan shag carpeting and a peeling Naugahyde couch placed in the far corner. Above it were two wooden display cases, one with four rifles and a smaller one with two military medals. An American flag draped above the display.

"Sit down on the couch. It's OK. I never sit there."

A voice sounded behind her. Bridget turned around; she hadn't seen him when entering.

"Take a load off your feet. I can't."

Scott sat in a wheelchair; his legs were missing below the knees. He was a veteran. Now she knew why the man's head only reached above the doorknob.

"I didn't know."

He chuckled. He was toying with her, making her perform good deeds for the disabled before ever stepping a foot in the door.

"I left a part of me in Iraq."

"Thank you for your service."

He opened a bag of soft mints and put them on the table with a glass of water. "Help yourself."

She drank the water and ate a mint. On the wall were two portraits of men in traditional dress. They both all looked like warriors. This man before her was also a warrior and a soldier.

"While we wait for your brother, could I ask you a few questions? Did you know Cheri?" she asked slowly, trying her best not to sound like a jerk.

"Questions. I guess lawyers ask questions like cops? There's a reason Bennett is outside."

"It's for Naomi. She wants to understand what happened to her mother."

"Sorry to hear about her, and I do remember her," said Scott. "Her boyfriend still around? What was his name?"

"Steve Ross? You know him?"

"I worked with him at the casino. Cheri was there, too, but that was a while back."

Scott wheeled himself to the center of the living room, right over the thick carpeting. His muscled arms had no problem with the thick pile rug.

"So," said Bridget, looking at the ceiling, wondering whether she would get this man to answer her questions. Charm him, she would not. His brother probably wouldn't show. "Your little brother, Joe, wants to change leadership? Be the new council leader. That's kinda cool, isn't it? He's pretty popular fighting that Buyland."

Scott chewed on another mint. "You have no idea what you're talking about, do you?"

She threw up her hands. "Doing my best here. Strange things have been happening since I took this case. Naomi feels her mother was hurt on purpose. Maybe even murdered. I've also been threatened and warned to stay away from this case."

"Yet here you are. I take it you don't think Cheri was a crazy, drunk Indian who happened to die on a reservation."

Scott's face was blank, his face frozen. She couldn't figure out whether he was being sarcastic.

"No, she wasn't. A little crazy, but not a drunk. I'd like to understand why she was here that evening."

"Death is personal, isn't it? She was here during the protests. Many people came to protest. Good people who do not appreciate how white people disturb our sovereign lands."

"You knew she was Indian?"

"Cheri's not an enrolled member, not here. She cannot live here or work in our government. I think she was Indian, at least she said she was. Many Indigenous nations come to support each other. Cheri helped."

Bridget scratched her head, trying to think of what else she should ask. "Cheri supported the protesters?"

"We worked pretty hard on getting that store here. My brother, Joe, likes to cause a stir. For a long time he has believed that the tribal council need some stirring. I enjoy working at the store. It's the first decent job I've had since Iraq."

"Does Joe work there, too?"

As she was talking, a man entered. Joe was the mirror image of Scott—without the wheelchair. She put her hand out to shake his hand, which he did slowly. Like Scott, he examined her from head to toe.

"Joe, perfect timing. This is the lawyer for Cheri Kline's kid. The lady wants to know where you work. Where do you work, Joe?" Scott laughed. Joe didn't.

She briefly introduced herself. Joe took two mints from the table and sat down on an adjacent chair, folding his arms.

"I work for change. Our sovereignty needs to be secured.

Many support our cause. Are you here about the lawsuit against Buyland?"

"The employment lawsuit? No."

"Buyland hurt its employees and didn't want to listen to us. We've our own courts, our own police force, our own judges, and government. Anyone who does business here needs to understand that. So, why are you here?"

"I represent Naomi, who was being removed from her mother's care. Her mother passed away unexpectedly here at the reservation." She sighed, folded her hands, and looked them in the eye. "I'm going to be straight with you. I've been threatened, and my car vandalized. I've also been told to drop the case and stay away from here. And frankly, I should. But I want to understand what happened here before I do anything. It's the only way I know to help Naomi and myself."

Scott and Joe looked at each other. "Tough lady," Joe said.

"Yeah, real tough," Scott agreed.

"You're not a Buyland lawyer?" Joe said.

"Something doesn't add up with Cheri's death. I'd like to ask something a bit indelicate. Did Cheri deliver envelopes to you or anyone else you know on the reservation?"

"Envelopes? Who said that?" Scott asked.

"Her daughter."

Joe switched the cross of his legs and then cleared his throat. "Our group accepts donations from those willing to give. I have nothing. If a person wants to donate to our cause, I won't say no."

He had all but admitted he received envelopes. He could have been mixed up with Cheri's death.

"Cheri contributed to your cause and delivered the donation in an envelope to you?" Bridget asked.

"Cheri is Osage, and she handed over her headright money. That is what she told me. Nothing wrong with that. Cheri also knew the monkeys. Maybe she got too close to them." Joe stood still, his arms still crossed.

"Monkeys?"

"White people. Monkeys because you are hairy and you talk too much," Scott said with a mischievous grin on his face. Bridget smoothed her frizzy hair.

"Any other monkeys, other than myself? A person that Cheri knew?"

Joe paused.

"That night, she got a call that made her upset." Joe sighed as fatigue seemed to overcome him. "On the phone, she said her donation was bad and made the fighting worse. She was real angry and left the house. I never saw her again. I felt bad because it was a lot of money."

"How much?"

"You need to understand that I lead a legitimate organization. That money helped pay the lawyers and other costs because that family lost a good job at Buyland. It also helped to organize—"

"—against the tribal leadership. How much?" she asked again. Joe folded his arms. "Was it more than three thousand?"

"That night was about five thousand. But in total, it was over thirty thousand."

"That's a lot more than headright payments," she said.

"Yes, it is," said Scott. "Where did that extra money come from? That would be interesting to find out because that cash helped to stir the pot here, right, Joe?"

After a few minutes of awkward silence, Bridget took that as her cue to leave.

"Did you tell Officer Bennett this?"

"Some of it. I didn't mention the donation. But I told Bennett she left on foot to meet someone after receiving the call," Joe said.

"Thank you for speaking with me. I'll go," Bridget handed Scott her card. "And by the way. I'm not hairy, just curly. If you've more information, please call. I cook and do dishes, too."

"My type of lawyer."

\*\*\*

As she left the reservation, she turned on the radio and found only static-laden radio stations with elevator music, disgruntled talk show hosts, or the current agricultural report. Her thoughts darted from Barshefsky to Scott and Joe Monroe. Joe Monroe had been straight about receiving money from Cheri and wasn't apologetic. She wondered if Elaine Kline got wind of Cheri's financial support of the tribe and interfered. That might be something for a family to argue over. As a legal guardian of a person with mental illness, Elaine probably had a different idea of how Cheri should spend the money.

Bridget phoned Walter.

"How was your interview?" he asked.

Bridget said she was going to the law firm to meet the backers of Sun Foundation, and Walter naturally concluded it was an interview. She never corrected him.

"I, uh, just got done. Could you do me a favor and check on Aunt Irene? She's not answering her phone."

"Irene's probably outside, tackling weeds again."

Only one more stop before heading back to Broken River. She tucked the phone into her tote bag and pulled the car into a rest stop.

"Not bad," she said to herself, splashing water on her face.

She slipped on heels and buttoned her suit jacket, once again dressed like a professional. She needed to because she had an interview, except she would be asking the questions.

# Chapter 29

Buyland's corporate office was in a large industrial park outside of Cedar Town. The offices were unremarkable, sandwiched between other mid-sized retail offices.

"I'm here to see Cal Roberts," she told the receptionist.

"And you are?"

She introduced herself and handed her a business card. The receptionist examined it and looked her up and down.

"You're a lawyer."

"I am. I'm conducting a little research, some background information, and would be grateful for five minutes of Mr. Robert's time."

The woman raised an eyebrow and then retreated to a back office. Pictures of Buyland stores across the state lined the pale blue and yellow walls that matched Buyland's logo.

"Ms. McGarrity?" A man dressed in khakis and a short-sleeved polo with the company logo came to the front with her card in hand.

"That's me." They shook hands.

"I'd like to thank you for your interest in our company. Right now, we're not looking for corporate counsel," he said.

"Sorry, there's a misunderstanding. I'm not looking for a job." Not yet, she thought. "I represent a child. Her mother died on the Wisaka Reservation. If you wouldn't mind answering a few questions."

He looked her up and down. "The reservation? A death? Hmm. I've had my fill of lawyers. Did she, the deceased, work at the store?"

"No. And I'm trying to understand the dynamics on the reservation. I was in the area, so I thought we might talk. Sorry for the inconvenience. I can assure you that there's no pending litigation against Buyland from my client."

"You represent kids?"

"And families."

"Guess so. Since you're here, we can talk."

She followed him to his office.

Bridget had researched every company and group associated with the reservation. A logical place to start was the Buyland's headquarters. The company was a family-owned and comparatively small regional retailer that serviced rural communities. Buyland's most remarkable feature was its exclusive contracts with two reservations, contracts threatened by protracted litigation with the Wisaka Nation.

Cal sat down and picked up a pen from a white Formica desk. He clicked the pen in an irregular rhythm. His gray hair curled in loose strands over the collar. Behind him were a couple of photos, a black and white one of a stern man standing next to an older Buyland store and one with a younger looking Cal cutting a ribbon amongst them.

Bridget continued. "I read about your case in the paper and wanted to ask whether you knew about my client's mother."

He slumped at his desk. "I thought we had the entire case

settled and then things exploded. It costs a fortune and is bad for business. I mean, the U.S. Marshals—incredible. Why did this get so out of hand? You're a lawyer. How would you handle it?"

Cal didn't want to talk about her case. He wanted to talk about the store's lawsuit. She hesitated to give legal advice in any area outside her expertise, but she didn't want to irritate him.

"Again, not my area. But negotiating and settling are always good ideas. The Wisaka Nation wants Buyland to acknowledge tribal jurisdiction and handle the matter in its courts. That issue is important to them and makes sense that they do. The federal government isn't paying attention much. Not that I've seen. Heck, their courthouse is in better shape than many counties here."

Bridget found herself waving her finger and retracted it.

Cal sighed, "Ms. McGarrity, Bridget? I agree. That's what we tried. We welcomed the protesters, gave 'em free drinks and ordered pizza."

"Seriously?"

"OK, only water."

She was surprised. She had expected his corporate evil self to unfold, belittle the Wisaka Nation, and reveal a link to Cheri.

He continued. "Working with the Wisaka Nation is a fantastic opportunity. We won the contract over our bigger competitors and were revising our contract to agree to their court, including a big chunk of change to the employee who brought the suit. Then everything fell apart. Before we knew it, a line in the sand was drawn. Now we're barely keeping the doors open."

Cal's strategy was sensible, not sinister. Difficult public litigation was a situation to avoid and not good business. Buyland had hoped to settle, pay for its misdeeds and be a good friend to the reservation. She had assumed that Buyland would be patronizing and defensive. It wasn't, and neither was Cal.

"Would the name Cheri Kline mean anything to you? Did she work for you?"

"No, but I'll double-check," Cal booted up his computer. "Sorry, no."

"Did you hear anything about her death?"

"I read about it. Bridget, I'm not sure what you're getting at here, and frankly, I don't think I like it."

Bridget nodded. She didn't want to anger him or make false accusations. But she couldn't shake the feeling that the store was somehow involved.

"Cal, my client is only fourteen. Her mother has died, and she needs to understand what happened to her. And it has, well, affected my law practice as well." Cal raised his eyebrows in interest. "Her mother, Cheri Kline, may have funded the protests against the store and the tribal government—"

"No surprise there. The former Buyland employee who filed suit against us wanted to settle early on because she wanted the money. That changed. Now she is apparently flush with cash from somewhere, I don't know where. She's decided not to settle for the bundle of cash we offered and now has new lawyers. The protesters also got a second wind, and the tribal government will not budge. And get this, the last lawyers that visited my offices were a bunch of lobbyists."

"Lobbyists? Like politicians?"

"Yeah, lobbyists representing the Wisaka Nation. Last I heard, even the grocers' association has its own. And everyone has lawyered up. I can barely keep up. Frankly, I think that's why this thing hasn't settled."

"Litigation and conflict can cost."

"And we're paying. To be honest, it's damaging our bottom line. You wouldn't believe the checks we're sending to big law firms, and it's detracting me from what I love to do: running grocery stores. Right now, we're damaged goods. My grandfather would be rolling in his grave. And the competition is hovering in the wings."

"Competition. Such as—?"

"Penny General. They're big players," he answered.

"Penny General might love to have its stores on the reservation."

"And how d'you come to that?" He folded his arms and squinted his eyes. "Did Penny General send you?"

"Of course not, no. I don't deal with messed-up companies, just messed-up families.

Cal chuckled. "I'm a bit paranoid these days. It's hard for the smaller companies to fight off the big guys. You're a small fry, too."

Bridget's cell phone vibrated in her tote bag. It was Aunt Irene.

"Sorry, family beckons."

Cal stood and put out his hand. "I guess we're done here. You'll find your way out?"

"Thank you so much for your time, and please call if you think of anything."

"Will do. Let me know if you find anything out."

\*\*\*

Outside their offices, Bridget walked briskly towards her car.

"Good news, Aunt Irene! I'm alive and not in jail. And I've acted out my fantasy life as a detective." The line was silent. "Hello? Aunt Irene?"

After a long pause, a deep voice spoke. "Interesting." A male voice. The blood drained from Bridget's head, pooling to her feet.

"Who is this? Where's Aunt Irene?" she said, her voice a

mere whisper.

"Your aunt and I have become acquainted. We're discussing the proper use of using borax weed killer. Charming woman," he said slowly, deliberately.

"Chet Russell?"

"You recognize me! We're becoming friends, and I needed to see your family. I thought I'd visit Walter and your son next."

"Hand the phone to Irene," Bridget said.

"Was I too bold coming here? I truly thought you would be here. You see, I'm on a mission to make sure your family understands how truly talented you are. You need their support. I understand that."

"Hand Irene's phone over."

"Now, don't you forget you're a leader waiting to be born. I get to know your family and make sure you'll receive the support you deserve while you're on your field trip to Cedar Town."

Every cell in her body screamed that Chet Russell was dangerous. Had he just threatened Aiden while complimenting her at the same time? He knew she was in Cedar Town and had spoken with Barshefsky.

"I noticed you hesitate. You did ruffle some feathers with Mr. Barshefsky, but what's done is done. They're only a small part."

"What's the name of the other investors?"

"The donors? Clients require discretion. That information will become available once you sign the papers and start enjoying success."

"And I drop all my cases."

"Exactly."

"That can't happen."

"Tsk, tsk. That is fear speaking again. Time to think out of the box, imagine your new world with you in control. Admit it, Bridget, you barely make ends meet, a son to support, and a husband, as well. You deserve—"

Rustling and static pierced her ears, and the phone went silent.

"Oh, god." Bridget redialed, getting nothing. She redialed, and finally, her phone rang.

"Got cut off." It was Aunt Irene's voice. Bridget sighed. "Mr. Chet was pruning the apple tree. He's got more muscles than Prince Edward Island. Think he'd go for an older woman?"

She leaned on the side of the car, not caring what sort of dirt stained her pantsuit. It was at least an hour-and-a-half away from Broken River, and that's if she sped.

"Chet is not a friend. Tell him to leave. I'm serious," said Bridget.

"I can tell that you're serious. And anyone can tell that he's a pompous jerk. The way he showed up, with no introduction, and that sales talk. It's maddening, but I played along. I'm not as naïve as you think, dear."

"As long as you are OK."

"At least I got him to prune the hedges. Who's fooling who? I thought about antifreeze in his pop, but I decided against it. He's already left, and no, you're not coming here because I'm taking Aiden to his soccer game."

Bridget fished keys out of her tote bag, got in the car, and drove off with a screech. She weaved through the congested lanes of traffic which meant about ten cars in Lincoln County.

\*\*\*

Aunt Irene sounded like herself, but she had had enough of Chet Russell and called the Broken River police and requested a wellness check at Aunt Irene's house to ease her mind and ensure

Aunt Irene's safety. She then asked to be connected to Chief French.

"I was wondering whether you could check a name for me."

"A name check? What about our agreement that you're not to investigate? You leave these matters to me."

"That's why I'm calling. His name is Chet Russell."

"I'll take a look," said French, exhaling with a slight whistle. "Are you driving and talking on the phone?"

"I'm out of town at the moment, near Cedar Town."

"Don't tell me you're investigating that case."

"It's not your jurisdiction. That's what you said. And the punk who smashed my car is too petty for your staff to give any serious attention."

"I've known you a long time. You act impulsively when things don't go your way. You're a lawyer now, so act like one. Lawyers have other resources so use them."

She snorted. Yes, she was a lawyer—a lawyer whose car got smashed and was being sued for malpractice by a client who couldn't even remember her attorney's name.

"I don't see why I have to apologize for my former teenage self. But I have no lawyer fairy dust. Should I sue? For what? Attempted fraud? How about you file charges against Chet Russell for impersonating a nice guy?"

"There's no such thing."

"Exactly. See my problem?"

"You ask your clients to trust the system and to trust you. Now it's time to trust me. If it's true what you're saying that someone's after you. We're here. Don't do it alone."

Her throat clenched. "Just check on my aunt."

She tossed the cell phone on the passenger seat in disgust. Chief French didn't want her to investigate the punk, yet Chet Russell didn't want her to practice law. She was sick of other people's advice. She was on her own, and she knew it.

Bridget called Diane at the office.

"You know the withdrawals from all my cases Chet Russell dropped off? Prepare them all for my signature. I want to see where a check for two hundred thousand dollars will take us."

# Chapter 30

With nothing but blue sky for the rest of the drive, Bridget hatched a plan to collect solid evidence to connect Chet Russell with the Klines to hand over to Chief French. Years ago, Bridget managed a settlement for a client who had burned down a warehouse, supposedly by accident. Settlement papers were signed, her client wrote a big check to the guy who owned the warehouse, and another check went to Bridget for legal services. Once the checks cleared, she never saw her client again.

The bank was frantic. Not enough money was in his account to cover the check, but the bank had mistakenly honored it. Her client had written other high-sum checks, but those had cleared. Midwest Bank & Trust assumed the other check would clear as he made a deposit from another bank to his account, a nasty little trick called check kiting.

The bank had a difficult conversation with its insurance company about why it honored the check and was defrauded to the tune of two hundred and fifty thousand dollars. Bridget cooperated with the bank. She knew them. Midwest Bank also held all her law practice and personal accounts, a mortgage, and a credit card.

The bank compared signature cards with the second account, which showed it had acted correctly and saved its insurance claim. During the entire ordeal, the bank shared many details about the account. The transferring bank did the same, and her client was eventually caught. Bridget learned that checks and bank accounts could reveal a lot about a person.

She pulled over to the side of the road, fished through her tote bag for Chet Russell's card, and dialed.

"My friend, excited about your future?" Chet said.

"You're right. I have been letting fear of change control me, afraid of moving ahead. No reason to wait. I accept! When can I expect the check? Sooner would be better. I've had car trouble."

"As soon as I see immediate compliance. First, you need to stop working on your cases."

She hesitated, but she needed to know.

"Any particular case you're worried about?" she asked.

"Cases that consume too much of your time. Like the one you are working on now."

"You mean the Sullivan dissolution?"

"No, Bridget, let's not be coy. You don't need to be traveling around the state to Cedar Town and the Wisaka Reservation."

"I've been warned off that case, and my car was vandalized. You wouldn't know anything about that?"

"Terrible, how awful. Did anyone get hurt?" Chet's voice dropped, sounding so sincere. "You're worried about leaving your clients behind and working for a foundation—I get that. The question is, how can you not? The public will have the best access to a person of your skill. You're a leader which this community needs. For the moment, this may be overwhelming, and a lot is going on in your life right now. And that is exactly the reason you need to act now. See you soon, at your office."

Bridget squeezed the phone and got back in the car, slamming the door. The Kline case, and Chet had confirmed that was the case that most concerned him. *I'm over my head.* That's what Barshefsky told her. Maybe he was right. Yet Chet was so friendly and showed genuine concern. The way he talked set her head spinning. The fact was, she wanted him to be legit.

As the sun dipped into the western sky behind a curtain of corn, she finally reached home. She lingered a moment in the driveway. Aiden was at soccer, and Walter had started his painting job at the Victorian home, so the house was hers. At least it should have been.

Why was the front door wide open?

# Chapter 31

Bridget pushed the door open slowly and tiptoed inside. The front hall and living rooms were their usual mess; she walked to the kitchen and gulped. The kitchen looked like rats had ravaged her cupboard. A cereal box lay sideways, its contents scattered on the counter and on the floor. A dirty glass of juice sat next to it. She stepped on a cheese stick wrapper that stuck to her foot. This had not been Walter. He had his faults, but a slob he was not.

A breeze of hot air brushed her face, colliding with the cool air-conditioned house. The sliding French glass door to the backyard was wide open and a swarm of gnats hovered. She took in slow, calming breaths while reassuring herself that the fluttering in her chest was an overreaction caused by the attack on her car. Yet her internal conversation did nothing to calm her. She fished for the pepper spray in her tote bag and tiptoed outside.

Someone laid on the lawn chair sound asleep, her face covered with a disheveled sheath of black hair, the chatter of katydids indifferent to the sleeping child. It was Naomi.

"Wake up, sweetie."

She gently laid a hand on her foot. Naomi jerked upward in panic; her reddened, tired eyes darted side to side.

"Where am I?"

Bridget moved a tangled lock of hair from her face.

"You're at my place. You must have fallen asleep."

Naomi's eyes scanned the backyard wildly. She was ready to sprint, not talk. Bridget placed a hand lightly on her back, directing her inside the house. This was unfamiliar territory. She had never had a child just show up at her home.

"First things first. Everything's fine. You're safe. Let's get a meal down you."

"I ate," Naomi said.

"A bowl of cereal is what mothers call a snack. You need a meal."

Naomi frowned, and Bridget immediately regretted the comment. Mentioning a mother was a mistake, now that Naomi was facing life without one.

She gently led her inside and sat her on the couch, ignoring her dirt-caked shoes. In the kitchen, she plopped a frozen patty in a pan, found two slices of white bread, cut off the crusts, and put them in the toaster. She opened the fridge, dug out pickles, lettuce, and ketchup.

"Mustard? No? You look like a ketchup-only kid to me. Would you like to watch TV?"

"I can't go back there."

Bridget stepped closer to Naomi and gave her a gentle hug. "I'm glad you came. Stay here for now and eat something. I don't think anyone would force you to go back there now. We'll figure this out."

Naomi's shoulders dropped as she said no to the TV and then drank a large glass of water. She lived on the other side of town. Given the state of her hair and smudged face, she had been through an ordeal.

Aunt Irene and Aiden came home like thunder and lightning in a cornfield—big, loud and dangerous to ignore.

"Hamburgers! With potato chips?" Aiden stopped in his tracks. "Who are you?"

Bridget made introductions and asked Naomi to help Aiden with emptying his backpack. She squinted but then took his hand, and they looked for his homework. Aiden gazed up at her adoringly.

"Are you my babysitter?"

"No, sorry."

"Do you play video games?"

"Depends on the game."

Aiden's eyes softened. It was love at first sight. Naomi laughed at his silly questions. The two retreated to the couch and sat quietly, mesmerized by the video graphics and eerie gaming melodies.

Bridget called Nick Harmon's phone but didn't reach him. She left a message on his voicemail that Naomi was with her and then called Elaine Kline and left a similar message.

Aunt Irene drew a big question mark in the air.

"I'll make the burgers and vegetables," she said to herself. After the food was ready, she shooed the kids to the kitchen table.

Aunt Irene pinched Bridget's elbow and pointed to the French doors, and they walked outside.

"Don't like hamburgers?" she asked.

"What's going on?" Aunt Irene said.

"Not sure and don't care. Right now, all is peaceful, and I'm having a great evening. So is Naomi."

"She's your client, right?"

"Yes, she is. Importantly, I look great. Don't you like the apron? It's checkered. If you want to help me, buy me an apron with skull and crossbones on it to shake things up."

"Please be serious. The girl could stay with me."

"Not a good idea. I just got that creep, Chet Russell, away from you."

"The child's in trouble, and troubled kids get hurt."

"Harboring a runaway child is a felony."

"Better me than you. I'm sure you've already called your people. And you're a lawyer. You can do something about that."

Yes, her lawyer fairy dust. Sprinkle litigious flakes of golden magic, and all will be well. Aunt Irene walked back into the house and faced Naomi with her arms crossed and brows furrowed.

"Where you headed to, sweetie? To the reservation?" Aunt Irene asked.

Naomi found a loose thread on her shirt and unraveled the seam. Aiden interrupted.

"Reservation? Like an Indian reservation? Really? You're a princess. Indian princess?" Aiden said in a hushed tone, bewildered. "This is awesome! Wait till Jordan hears!"

"Enough. And you'll say nothing to Jordan. Shower, Aiden!" she said, pointing her finger towards the stairs.

Naomi gave Aiden a high five. "That's right, buddy, I'm royalty."

Aiden skipped upstairs, belting a song from a Disney musical.

"Seriously? Are you really singing 'Pocahontas'?" asked Naomi.

Bridget shook her head. "So sorry. Stay a little longer, and I'm sure you'll flee from here, too. Aiden, enough."

"What did I do? You still like me, right?"

"Chill, baby boy," Naomi laughed and then came a genuine smile. It was lovely.

"We have to talk, but I don't want you to worry. It can wait, though, if you like."

Naomi spun her back to Bridget and cast her head down, examining the kitchen tile. Bridget immediately regretted the question. Her lovely smile vanished as tears formed on her cheeks, and then she cried. But she didn't cry like a teenager or child. She wept like an old woman, silently, discreetly.

"I'm so tired. I can't go back there," said Naomi. "I kept my mom's check and here it is. I asked whether my mom was Indian, but she sent me outside while she cleaned. She says I'm dirty. She bought new furniture."

"Odd. Strange, though, about the furniture. Everything looked new."

"Elaine talked on the phone and said I would 'be handled.' She said I don't know nothing. But I do. I know about the money going to the reservation. I went, too. Elaine's taking mom's money."

Naomi curled up in a ball on the couch.

"Do you know who she was talking to?"

"Not sure, but she talks to Uncle Jay a lot."

Aunt Irene stood up like she had decided. "I would love for you to stay at my place. I have a spare bedroom. No TV, but I've got a ton of books."

"We have to coordinate with social services, and I haven't heard from Nick. I'll call him again and let him know that Aunt Irene is offering to put you up for the night."

Bridget didn't say she should probably call the cops, but they would only take her back to Elaine or the shelter. Aunt Irene was as good as anyone and had been a foster parent once.

"How about that? Aunt Irene loves kids. And tomorrow morning, we have an errand bright and early."

***

After Aunt Irene left with Naomi, Bridget stepped outside. The moon was bright, casting shadows across her front lawn. Nick, unfortunately, hadn't called back. She thought about calling Chief French, but she was exhausted trying to explain herself to him again.

"Officer Bennett, thanks for taking my call. I know it's late."

Bridget brought Officer Bennett up to speed about the case, the headright, and Elaine never having adopted Cheri but was her legal guardian instead.

Officer Bennett offered his insight. "Back in the 70s, life was tough. On many reservations, social services took native kids away from their parents. While kids were too often given up for adoption by their parents. That changed later, and that's why social services must identify if the child is Native American. Cheri's parents probably had trouble, and she was given up for adoption. A legal guardianship is different."

"Not so strange if the child is independently wealthy. They probably wanted to make sure Cheri kept her headright."

"I'll let the Attorney General know Cheri is Native American," said Bennett.

"Will you investigate the crime then and link it to a child in need? That may give you jurisdiction."

"Clever, but I can't make promises. Right now, I'm fighting with the neighboring county. They refused to process the evidence from the site, but I have it here in storage."

"Cheri received a call that night. Could you run her cell phone, see who called her?"

Officer Bennett chuckled. "Playing police officer? I already did that. Elaine called her, but the two last calls were unknown."

Bridget's heart sunk. She thanked him for the information, although things still didn't connect. It was interesting but didn't add up to who had wrecked her car.

She walked to the curb and looked at the street. An SUV turned on its headlights and drove off. With the yellow glow of the streetlight, the exact color was hard to see, but it was a light color. Was it the white SUV? She squinted at the license plate; it wasn't local.

She walked back inside and locked the door.

# Chapter 32

Naomi brushed the wall of Aunt Irene's mudroom as Bridget stood inside waiting. She resisted the urge to hurry her along. Naomi needed to linger—she was just getting a sense of the place.

If it was in her power, a happy Department of Human Services was a priority. Happy social workers might follow her lead and secure a place for Naomi away from Elaine's grasp and not in the shelter. Unfortunately, Nick hadn't called, so she decided to go to social services with Naomi herself.

"Now I won't have to worry about you two," said Aunt Irene as she opened the front door, and the morning sun blinded the trio as they stepped on the porch. Aunt Irene gasped.

A large silhouette of a man holding handcuffs blocked the doorway. Bridget raised her hand to her brow, blocking the sun.

It was Rob Small, the JCO. He swayed slightly like he was preparing for a fight, and the wooden porch creaked like an old ship every time he shifted his weight.

Rob's presence meant one thing—Naomi was about to be

arrested and charged with committing a crime. No youth shelter, no foster home, no home with her father, but the detention center—jail for kids.

"Playing ding-dong ditch, Rob?"

"Cute. This juvenile delinquent is a runaway and you're with her, which is strange. We won't dwell on that right now. I came myself instead of sending the police. I told them, no problem. I know the kid. I know the lawyer with her." He swung keys around his finger and cracked a wad of gum in his mouth. "Got yourself in trouble, didn't you, kiddo?"

Bridget folded her arms defiantly. Aunt Irene stepped outside and surveyed the street, then placed her hand on the door frame to steady herself.

"That white SUV looks familiar," Aunt Irene whispered.

In the clear daylight, it looked like the same white SUV belonging to Chet and the one at her house last night.

"The charges for auto theft were dropped at the Wisaka Reservation, remember?" said Bridget.

"New day, new charges. Something about stealing a three thousand dollar check? That's a big felony for a little girl."

"Social services know she's with me. And as far as the check goes, give me a break. What is a fourteen-year-old going to do with a check?"

"The kid comes with me."

"Where is Nick? He should take care of this, not you. How did you know we were here? Did Nick tell you?" Bridget asked.

"Haven't heard from him. A little bird found me and chirped," Rob revealed a smile that contained part of his breakfast. His bulbous face contorted into a taunting frown.

She took a small step closer, placing herself between him and Naomi.

"Seriously, something's wrong here. Juvenile services and social services need to figure that out themselves before arresting a child. I will not clean up this mess for you. Send the paperwork to my office and let me contact the county attorney. I promise the charges will disappear by the end of the day. If not, I'll bring her in myself."

"Step aside. We are on our way to juvenile detention," he said.

"I can't let you do that. The child is coming with me."

Rob stepped towards them and raised the cuffs. She put her palm up, slowing Rob's progress.

"One question: where's your warrant?" asked Bridget.

"I don't need a warrant."

"Certain about that, Rob? I know you were the top of your class and all."

She took one tiny step closer to him, smelling his stinking coffee breath. He had expected that Bridget or Aunt Irene would simply hand her over, and a warrant was a stretch given Naomi was charged with a felony, and she was a runaway. Rob would not hear from her whether he needed a warrant.

"Yes. I'm sure."

Sweat dripped off his face. She wasn't sure how much she could play with him and messing with him was a one-way street.

"Who's pressing charges?" Aunt Irene asked.

"I don't know. Not my job."

Rob was lying. Of course he knew about the charges.

Ladybugs swarmed around them, one making a suicidal dive into Bridget's curls, which she ignored. Her thoughts drifted to Aiden tucked happily at school, to Walter's painting job, to her law business chugging along, to a caramelly-blended iced espresso and abandoned teenagers in shelters and foster homes. After the two-second reverie, Bridget directed her gaze at him again, with one thought: *God, I hate juvenile court officers.*

"Do you own a house?" she asked.

"What?"

"You heard me. Do you own a house?"

"Yes, I own a house," Rob answered.

"Own a car, Rob?" She cocked her head to one side.

"Of course. What is this about?"

"Tell me, Rob, do you like your house? Do you like your car?" Rob looked blankly. "If you take one step towards Naomi, that car and that house will belong to me. I also like your savings account. And they will all be mine, and Naomi's, of course." Bridget pointed her finger towards Rob. "That's after Naomi sues you for false arrest, assault, and trauma. Oh, my god, the trauma. You'll be living out of a box after I'm done with you. Pinky promise."

She held up her bent pinky.

He snorted and placed the cuff keys in his pocket. He reached for his cell phone and plodded to the far end of the porch while he figured out whether he needed a warrant. Bridget and Naomi didn't wait. They headed to her car.

His head shook as he threw his keys and stomped on the ground.

What would she do with Naomi now? She's a fugitive, and I'm harboring a fugitive, she thought.

"Where are we going?" asked Naomi.

"I haven't figured that out yet."

She loved giving Rob a tough time. He was a distraction but knew this would only give them a little more time. After driving for fifteen minutes, she laughed out loud and gave a little cheer. Her glee was infectious. Naomi buckled her seatbelt, put her feet on the dashboard, and grinned.

"I got that smile back!"

"Yeah, it feels good."

Naomi cracked open the window and tipped her face towards the sun. She closed her eyes as the strength of the rays melted the tension on her youthful face. Bridget relished the quiet, ignoring the uncertainty of their future.

# Chapter 33

Her office wasn't exactly the sneakiest place to conceal themselves if they intended to hide, which she didn't. Bridget decided she wouldn't let a JCO bully her and would handle this in her own way. Diane greeted her with hands on hips and eyebrows raised.

"Dying to know what happened. Juvenile services called. Chief French called. Have I been fired yet? The suspense is killing me." Diane was unflappable, a quality Bridget sorely needed, especially now.

"No new job."

Naomi trailed behind Bridget into the office building and then sat down on the red chrome chair, giving it a quick spin. No one could resist the chrome chair.

Diane's face softened. "Let me guess, Naomi Kline? You are the cutest 14-year-old I've seen in ages. Let's get you a pop. Ms. McGarrity has work to do."

Bridget mouthed a thank you and retreated to her office. Diane walked in with a printed email from the juvenile county district attorney. Naomi was facing a Class D Felony for stealing a check of over three thousand dollars.

"She's fourteen. Naomi wouldn't even be able to cash it," said Diane.

Bridget peeked outside through the shades in her office and didn't see the white SUV.

"If anyone asks or calls, tell them you 'don't know' or 'no comment.' Make sure that Naomi stays in the kitchen."

"Of course. Anything else? Is there a body I should bury? Evidence to stash? Cocaine to flush down the toilet?"

The entrance door buzzer clanged.

"It's Nick Harmon," said Diane.

Bridget sighed in relief. Today Nick wore a black and orange Hawaiian shirt with splashes of bright green.

"Good news!" said Nick.

"Finally. You could have called back."

"Sorry about that. I've been ripping up the phone lines trying to find a solution, and sometimes a social worker turns off the phone at night."

"And morning. What have you got?"

"Another family member has stepped forward. Her uncle, Jay Kline, lives out of state in Washington, D.C. He's agreed to take care of Naomi and we're running checks on him now. Mr. Kline will be here tomorrow."

"The uncle who lives in D.C.? Opens arms, a family reunion? That is a stretch."

"He checks out. Successful, decent job and is critical of Elaine. They'll have time to get acquainted. Much better than the shelter."

"You mean detention center, not a youth shelter. Did you even talk to Rob Small? Or didn't you know they charged Naomi with felony theft?" Nick's bright smile descended into a frown. "So, you didn't know. Then how did he find out Naomi was at my aunt's? She should stay with her until you and the JCO have a little chat."

She summarized the confrontation with Rob.

"Where's Naomi?"

"She's here."

"She needs to come with me. You know that. But I love your passion."

"Detention center is pretty harsh."

"It is, but she will be safe. Travis swung a baseball bat at you." Nick shook his head. "Ever since he threatened to out me, this case scares me. Naomi is safest in detention or the shelter until we get her settled."

"I don't know."

"She won't be there for long. You'll sort out the charges and her uncle might help. You do your job and I do mine, Sister Justice."

Nick's eyes pierced right through her. She walked to the window, peeked behind the blinds, and spotted the white SUV again.

"As long as Naomi agrees. And you're going to pull your car around back. I don't want anyone to see you leave with her."

Naomi stepped into her office; she had probably heard everything. "I'm fine with the shelter or the detention center, whatever. I'm not going to Elaine's."

"Well, that's settled then," said Nick.

"I want to meet this uncle and check him out for myself. Can you share his number?" asked Bridget.

"Uncle Jay? He's terrible."

"Let's let you two talk first," said Nick.

"I don't think so," said Naomi.

"We should go Naomi. How about a hug, Sister Justice?"

Nick and his hugs. She relented. If anyone had told her as a teenager that she would hug a social worker, she would've punched them.

Bridget watched Naomi get into Nick's car and felt a sense of relief. She'd talk with the county attorney about dropping the criminal charges against Naomi.

After Nick had left, Bridget retreated to her office. She dialed the number for Jay Kline and it went to voice mail. She searched the internet and found nothing under his name or in Washington, D.C. Elaine said he was into politics and fundraising. But what did that mean? Maybe he worked for a politician or a party. Or lobbying.

On a whim, she ran Jay Kline's name on a government website that required lobbyists to disclose their work, yet she found nothing.

*What am I missing?*

Diane walked into the office.

"Could you do some digging on Jay Kline, Naomi's uncle? I didn't find him listed anywhere on the internet. He works in Washington, D. C."

Diane looked pale. "A man called about Nick and hung up. There's been an accident. Naomi was with him, right?"

The phone shook in Bridget's trembling hand.

"Nick? You there?"

The answer was heavy breathing. A faint ding pulsed, like from an indicator that a car door was open.

Nick gasped like he was in pain. "My car window...glass everywhere. I'm bleeding."

Bridget pressed the phone to her chest.

"Diane, call the police, tell them to find Nick Harmon. He's been in a car accident." She paused, afraid of the answer.

"Where's Naomi?"

"So sorry."

"What do you mean, Nick? My job is to protect her."

Nick coughed and gasped. "He's here, Bridget. Evil man."

"Travis? The clerk?"

Nick breathed into the phone, his voice inaudible. The dinging receded into the background, and she heard footsteps followed by the sound of a car door opening and closing.

"Bridget McGarrity, we're disappointed. You didn't file that paperwork," said a nasal voice.

The paperwork would have gotten Bridget off all of her cases. And away from Naomi. "Skinny Boy. Travis, or whatever you are," Bridget said flatly.

"How's your car windshield? Breaks easily with the right force. Anything breaks with the right force. Isn't that right, Nick? Too bad, lover."

There was another crash. Bridget sunk to her knees as fear crept up her spine like a snake coiling itself around its prey. Nick whimpered in the background.

"Where's the girl, McGarrity?"

A surge of energy flowed through her like all her neurons were firing, trying to make connections. Travis didn't have Naomi.

"I don't know," said Bridget.

"Don't be stupid, McGarrity. The police have been informed that a juvenile delinquent attacked a social worker. Find her."

A thud and crash sounded. Nick.

"What do you want? I'll do it."

The line went silent. What have I gotten myself into? Bridget ran outside and breathed, panting. The SUV was gone. She froze, not knowing what to do. If Nick was in danger, so was Naomi. Diane followed her.

"Call Chief French. Tell them Naomi will be blamed for hurting Nick, but she's being set up. Tell him to check that SUV, a white SUV."

"SUV? What are you talking about?"

"The one that was here, the one that's been following me. The one that Chet Russell had. Or like it, I don't know."

Puffy white clouds danced in the sky as a line of rolling dark clouds followed. Although it might miss them, a storm was coming. Maybe it was best to run.

Diane handed Bridget her purse and car keys. "I'll make the calls. Drive safe."

Bridget drove slowly, searching the side streets, looking for Naomi. She guessed what route Nick had taken. After ten minutes, which seemed like an hour, Bridget spotted police lights flashing and the sound of an ambulance. It was undoubtedly Nick. She wanted to see him, explain what had happened, but she hesitated. Would that help Naomi?

She had passed a gas station with ice slushies. Bridget turned the car around and drove into the station. She went inside and asked whether anyone had seen Naomi, and they hadn't. A strip mall was next to the gas station, and she looked inside the stores—also, no luck.

In the distance, police lights flashed.

Her phone rang. "Naomi's here," Aunt Irene said immediately.

"On my way," said Bridget.

***

Naomi had made it to her house across town, and Aunt Irene's house wasn't far for a track team medal winner. She drove straight to Aunt Irene's, and to her relief, Naomi was sitting on the couch with a soda. They embraced.

"You're OK."

Bridget repeatedly whispered, patting Naomi's head lightly.

"He grabbed me, but I got away."

"Are you hurt?"

Aunt Irene and Bridget examined her arm, which was red. Bruising was starting. Bridget closed the curtains to the house, sure that the skinny guy Travis would follow her.

"Call the police," said Aunt Irene.

"I did. And Diane is calling Chief French. I'm not sure it's going to help. The police will think that Naomi did something bad to Nick. And take her to the detention center. Although that's not so bad, at least she should be safe there."

"You think so? Didn't you say that guy worked in the courthouse? He knows everything about you, every case, every file."

"Oh god, I didn't think about that."

"What are you going to do?"

"The only thing I can do. Cooperate."

"You're what?" demanded Naomi.

She was in a daze, as if living another person's life, another reality.

"Nick calls me Sister Justice."

"Please don't talk crazy," said Naomi.

"A crisis? Of course! Oh, Mighty Isis!"

"Dedicated foe of evil!" said Aunt Irene.

"Defender of the weak," Bridget answered.

"Champion of the truth and justice." They said in unison. "Oh, Mighty Isis!"

Both laughed as Naomi's mouth dropped. "Interesting."

Aunt Irene nodded her head to Bridget as if giving her permission.

She held a finger over her mouth, shushing Naomi as she pressed the numbers into her cell phone. She stood rigid like she was tough, strong, and wearing battle gear. If only.

"Hi, Chet, this is Bridget McGarrity. There's a conversation we should finish."

"I'm all ears, Ms. McGarrity."

She could imagine his thick-lipped grin smiling on a mountain of cash.

"All ears? Well, that is a noble status in the corn belt." She was feigning fearlessness as much as she could muster. Hopefully, that sounded tough, she thought.

"Ah! Humor, interesting," he growled. The smooth cheeriness in his voice had disappeared.

"Is the offer still open?" asked Bridget.

"Glad to hear you ask. The offer is still open. You need to withdraw from your cases."

"Done. Diane has the paperwork."

Chet paused and said, "And one more thing. There's a certain juvenile, Naomi Kline, who needs to be delivered to the detention center. Assuming you find her."

He wanted Naomi to go to the detention center? That meant she wouldn't be safe there. Bridget clenched the phone. Who could get to her at the detention center? Lawyers, social workers, juvenile court officers, police, family. Too many.

"I can find her. Could you meet me there with my check?"

"Call me when you get there."

Bridget wiped the sweat from her neck. Had she just made a deal with the devil?

"What're you doing?" asked Naomi.

"*Necessitas non habet legem.*" Bridget shook her fist at the sky, drawing strength from the gods.

"Necessity knows no law," explained Aunt Irene.

"Someone smart said that once. I think it was me," said Bridget. "What it means is forget the rules, the law. This is an emergency." After several minutes, she broke the silence.

"I have a delicate question to ask. How sneaky can you be?"

# Chapter 34

The Grand Am was parked near the front entrance of the Lincoln County Juvenile Detention Center. Naomi slumped in the passenger seat, looking genuinely upset. However, upon closer inspection, someone might have detected a sly smile like she had a secret, a knowing Mona Lisa grin. Bridget popped open the hood of her newly repaired car.

A white SUV was parked about a mile away, clearly visible across the flat horizon. She called Chet.

"I'm here with that kid. This is so exciting. I'm ready for a change. Thank you for your assurances. I was getting nervous about a threat against me in one of my cases, but I looked up Sun Family Foundation, and it's already a registered business!"

There was silence on the other end of the line. A suburban pulled into the lot. Aunt Irene.

"One more thing, Chet. I'm making a counteroffer, and the price is now $220,000. I need a new car because I damaged the engine. I've been too scattered-brained to put oil in the damn thing."

"I can meet our price. I'll have to rewrite the check."

"Wonderful." Bridget shuddered. That was too easy.

"You've withdrawn from your cases?" asked Chet.

"Done! Check the online docket and you'll see a notification of withdrawal."

There was silence on the line while Chet checked, probably online or with Barshefsky's help. But that would show only half the picture. The online record would indicate that a motion to withdraw from the case was filed. However, it wouldn't reveal what she wrote, which was very different than the title—the motion requested a hearing date, not a withdrawal. If all goes to plan, she would spend the next week correcting the mistitled paperwork.

"Excellent. I'm on my way."

"I've had car trouble, so could you meet me?"

"I know where you are."

Bridget pocketed her phone and put on a cap. In case Chet was looking, she wanted to look nonchalant as possible. Hopefully, the hat would hide her nervousness. She wanted to get hold of that check to see whether it revealed anything about him.

Aunt Irene pulled close to the detention center entrance and stepped out, leaving her car door wide open.

"I'm ready to harbor a runaway again!" said Aunt Irene.

It wasn't the first time. While staying at a foster home separate from her brother, Bridget escaped. Aunt Irene was waiting there with a warm car and beverage.

"I haven't had this much fun in years. After all, you trained me well," said Aunt Irene.

"Except I always got caught."

"We're smarter now."

"I hope so."

She spotted the white SUV approaching. Naomi staggered

out of the Grand Am, dragging her feet as she headed towards the steel, fireproof doors of the juvenile detention center. Bridget yanked it open. With her back to the street, she continued to press the heavy door open, blocking the view of anyone entering the street side. And, more importantly, blocking Chet's view.

Anyone watching would have assumed that Naomi walked into the juvenile detention center.

But she didn't.

As the door obscured the view, Naomi had scrambled alongside the building, crouching low, until she reached the Suburban, where Aunt Irene calmly stood near the car, the door ajar, as if airing it on a muggy day. Naomi scrambled inside and hid in the rear. Bridget closed the entrance door, headed to her car, and nodded knowingly to Aunt Irene.

"You good, kiddo?" whispered Aunt Irene.

"Yeah. Is that guy there yet?" Naomi said, a little out of breath.

"He's coming. Stay down," Aunt Irene said.

Chet pulled into the parking lot in his white car with no license plate. He was being careful. She knew from a prior case that the quality of surveillance videos was terrible. A camera wouldn't record much other than an SUV. Without a license plate, identifying the car would be challenging, if not impossible. Chet sauntered toward her, geared in a baseball cap which cast his face in a dark shadow. The hat also would likely obscure any image of his face.

"You've made an excellent decision." His broad grin revealed impossibly big teeth. Gone was the chunky Rolex, another identifier. She squeezed her fists to stop them from trembling, then outstretched an empty hand as Chet handed her a stack of stapled papers with the fancy watermark from Whitfield & Barshefsky. Bridget looked them over briefly, signed, and handed them back.

With a wry smile, Chet dangled the check in front of her. She took it—$220,000. Made out to cash and signed by Chet Russell. The check was drawn on First Bank & Trust, her bank. Perfect. Like a police officer placing evidence in a crime bag, she folded it carefully and slid it into her pocketbook.

"Thank you. Now I can buy that minivan I never wanted," she said.

"You're welcome," he answered. Chet opened his jacket slightly, revealing a gun.

Bridget winced. "What's that?"

"Just exercising my second amendment rights." He stepped forward and gently squeezed her shoulder.

"Naomi is where?"

He let go as Bridget contemplated biting his hand. She stepped closer to him, close enough to kiss. She wanted him to look at her and not anywhere else. Invading a male's personal space usually confused them, at least for the moment.

"As demanded, Naomi is in the detention center."

Bridget bit the side of her cheek, concealing any emotion.

"Perfect," Chet smiled.

"I have to stop at my office, get my things. Tell my secretary."

"Diane? Why, I've already called her. You're to call next week and see your new offices." Chet said.

"Right. If you'll excuse me, my ride is here."

"Give my best to Irene. The check will take a day or two to clear."

"Chet, did I ever have a choice?"

"Whatever do you mean?" Chet's enormous grin dropped, and he looked genuinely concerned. "No worries. And Bridget, be sure to put your office building on the market. Today?"

Bridget stammered. Her office building, an old Maid Rite restaurant she and Walter had renovated together.

"Of course."

Chet walked to his car, keys jangling, placing a cell phone to his ear. Bridget walked as fast as she could to the Suburban, with a lightness to her movement. She sat in the driver's seat, closing the door firmly shut.

"Think it worked?" asked Aunt Irene.

"I hope so. Naomi, stay down. Don't move."

"No, duh," said Naomi, sighing. "As long as I'm not going to that detention center or ending up at Elaine's, I'm good."

"What now?" asked Aunt Irene.

Bridget held the check against the light and called Diane at the office.

"Close up the office and go buy a 'For Sale By Owner' sign. Seriously."

# Chapter 35

At the helm of the rusty Suburban, Aunt Irene drove the trio to her home and straight into the attached garage. She closed the garage door before letting Naomi out. Bridget headed to the basement office and called First National.

"I have a check for $220,000 that I plan to deposit. Could you make sure the check clears before I do anything?"

"Of course," said Lisa in a monotone, like handling a check for $220,000 was an everyday occurrence. Bridget provided Lisa with all the information from the check, including Sun Family Foundation and the account number.

Within minutes, Lisa relayed the bad news. The check from Sun Family Foundation would bounce. The account had a balance of one hundred dollars and was only opened two days ago.

"Bring the check to our main branch immediately. We'll perform an investigation on the check," said Lisa.

Feigning disbelief, Bridget said, "I'm completely at a loss. I think I've been duped."

In fact, she wasn't surprised. She had counted on it. Villains willing to vandalize property were unlikely to fork over that amount of money, at least not to her. Opening a checking account doesn't require much, as any money launderer or check kiter knows. Banks demand scant information, and she wagered that Chet gave only his name and an address. If he didn't have an address, a person with him did, and the bank might give her that information. A crook can create dummy corporations, but don't piss off banks.

"Are you sure? Could it take awhile to transfer?" asked Bridget.

"This account shows little activity. And it's a crime to write a check without sufficient funds. I don't see any related accounts. We'll contact the account holder."

"First Bank is the payor bank, so you have its file, including account signatures."

"We can verify the signature on your check."

"I can't get there right now. Is the name..." Bridget looked around and saw the Broken River Weekly Advertiser on the table. An advertisement for Kinderman Tree Removal took half the front page. "Is the name Kinderman on there? Uh, a 'Troy Kinderman', is he an owner on the account?"

"No, Ms. McGarrity. Sorry."

"There was another person, but he didn't give his name."

She pressed her lips, feeling a slight pang of guilt. Hopefully, the bank would never get wind of her little deception. Typically, a bank wouldn't freely share names of who could sign a check; however, this was a $220,000 fraud. If the bank improperly cashes a check that large and it bounces, the bank might run into trouble and be stuck paying the amount.

"Who has signing power on the account?" Bridget asked nonchalantly.

Lisa hesitated before she answered. "The name Chet Russell

is on there."

"Hmm, Russell."

"And another name, Sally Avery," said Lisa.

"Sally Avery doesn't ring a bell. I'll bring the check to you."

"The sooner, the better."

Bridget exhaled audibly as a pound of tension released from her shoulders. For the first time in weeks, she had the upper hand. Who are you, Sally Avery? Why are you and Chet working together?

Bridget sipped weak coffee as Aunt Irene tiptoed downstairs.

"Do you have instant coffee? This java needs to be resurrected," said Bridget.

"What is with your generation and coffee? You might as well chew mud."

Bridget shared the details about the check with Aunt Irene. Solid evidence of murder the bounced check was not. Nevertheless, it was a step. Bridget was confident if she could find Sally Avery, she could find a connection to the Klines. Searches on Chet Russell had so far produced nothing. Sally was different. She wasn't supposed to learn about her.

"He's made mistakes—giving me a contract using Whitfield & Barshefsky's distinctive paper stock with a watermark. This is his second—a check that would bounce."

"Maybe not," said Aunt Irene.

"What do you mean?"

"He never expected you to cash the check."

"Why not? It's two hundred grand?"

Aunt Irene gave a hard, long stare. "He told you to wait a couple of days. These are bad people."

"You mean Chet doesn't expect me to cash the check because I'll be dead." She held the check up to the sunlight, looking for something, anything. "But he signed his name."

"If it is his real name."

Bridget groaned as tension crept into her bones like a creeping vine on steroids. "There's one way, and that's forward. I can't stop now. Not when I have real, tangible evidence."

She checked on Naomi—who was sacked out on the recliner. The restful peace of the innocent. She went downstairs again and started on Aunt Irene's computer. A simple search on Sally Avery produced nothing.

"Your computer is painfully slow."

"Suits me fine, thanks."

Bridget battled the computer for the last time. In frustration, she opted for an alternative approach: delegation.

# Chapter 36

With a baseball cap tipped low, Bridget slunk into her own office and played secret agent. Her office would be closed, but Diane came in to back up computer files and documents into a cloud account, something she had resisted earlier because of the expense and online security. Now she needed access. Mobility was vital, even if the office was closed.

She resumed the hunt for Sally Avery, to no avail. On corporate filings, the secretary of state didn't list an 'Avery.' Only Chet's name. The name wasn't listed under any other corporation. Sally Avery didn't even have a traffic ticket or title to a house. A skip tracer might find her, but Bridget wanted results now.

"Back-up is done. Seriously, though, I don't know why I'm even here."

She cracked the tension out of her neck and asked Diane, "Ever hear of Sally Avery?"

"No. Should I?"

"She's a signatory on the account with Chet Russell for Sun

Family Foundation. What a stupid name. He might as well have called it 'The Dummy Foundation.'"

Bridget looked at her trusted employee, Diane—the person who knew way too much about her. The person who also had signatory power on an account. She dropped her pen.

"It's you."

"Me?"

"A person Chet trusts. You're Sally," said Bridget.

"I am? I've been called many things, but not Sally."

"Sally is like you, a trusted employee or maybe a legal secretary." Chet had to have his own Diane. Working a scheme couldn't be done without the diligence and grit of trusted support staff. Even if Chet was a fake name, one name on the account had to be authentic to open it.

"Thank you, Diane. Please make a discreet call to the Whitfield firm in Cedar Town, asking for Sally Avery."

"Whitfield? Them again? Why not you?"

"If I do, I'm going to swear at them. We need Midwest Nice right now."

"Sure, right after I finish writing my severance package and golden parachute."

"Severance package? That would be your coffee cup."

With a blank expression, Diane said, "I'm here for all the glory."

Within minutes, Diane found out that Sally Avery worked as a legal secretary for Whitfield & Barshefsky. She used a different name there, but the receptionist knew her maiden name.

"Yes!" Bridget pumped her fist. "You're going down!"

That was it. The connection. Whitfield & Barshefsky had set up a dummy foundation with Chet Russell at the helm. Barshefsky had also sued Bridget to make her life miserable enough to make leaving the practice of law an easy decision. More precious, Chet wrote a fraudulent check with the aid of a trusted secretary at the Whitfield & Barshefsky law firm. A crime. Bridget called Aunt Irene.

"We're one step closer." She brought Aunt Irene up to speed on the account information with the check.

"A bank account means murder?"

"Here's what we know. Cheri Kline recently passed away. Barshefsky starts a bogus malpractice suit and also represents Elaine Kline. Chet gives me an offer of a lifetime to walk away from my law practice. The day after refusing, my car was vandalized, and I'm warned to stay away from the reservation. Barshefsky tells me I'm in over my head, and the only case Chet Russell mentions is Naomi's. Now, he writes a fraudulent check with the help of a secretary at Whitfield & Barshefsky. All this while Nick Harmon suffers, attacked by a former clerk who swung a bat at me."

Bridget had taken out a paper and pen, writing as she talked and made bullet points. There was a long, uncomfortable silence on the phone as she waited for her cheering section. Aunt Irene wouldn't have it.

"I hate to say this. Naomi shared her mother's problems with me, and Cheri had been sick with mental health issues for a while. She was an ill lady who was difficult and fought her family and Naomi's father. The child barely saw her mother, who had only shown up in the last month, with talk of danger."

"Then why am I being threatened?"

"You've been dragged into something fishy. It's not clear to me that it's murder."

"Maybe, but Naomi was attacked. Me, too. It's Chief French's turn now."

# Chapter 37

At the Broken River PD, Bridget didn't have to wait to see Chief French this time. A clerk behind bulletproof glass called back to French's office as soon as she entered the lobby as if they'd been expecting her. The buzzer sounded and she walked towards the offices feeling calm, almost happy because the fraudulent check was in a white envelope—the smoking gun—and in her hand.

Bridget opened French's office door and immediately halted as if she had stepped her foot in wet concrete. In the chair opposite Chief French sat Alan Barshefsky with a sideways grin, his hands folded across his generous belly.

"Bridget, we were talking about you. Please sit down," said French.

Stunned, she looked back and forth between French and Barshefsky, her pulse quickening.

French continued. "Sit down." French made notations on a pad. "I understand you're already acquainted with Mr. Barshefsky?"

"Call me Alan."

Bridget crept her way to the chair as Chief French spoke.

"We were discussing the pro bono cases. His firm does advocacy work for the Wisaka Nation. Interesting, admirable work. We don't deal with those issues in Lincoln County." Bridget tried to force a smile; it didn't come. "You came to me. I'm so glad you did. I've been getting calls about you all morning about that CINA, *In the Interest of N.K.* What is it?"

Bridget stammered, crinkling the envelope in her hand because she was in a quandary. If she mentioned the fraudulent check, Barshefsky would know she discovered Sally Avery, and if she mentioned Naomi was with Aunt Irene, he'd know that Bridget had deceived Chet Russell. But if she lied to Chief French about either or said she knew nothing, which would be a lie, she could face charges for obstruction of justice.

She was a bug stuck under a glass jar with Chief French and Barshefsky gawking at her. She folded the white envelope and slipped it into her back pocket.

"I came here to ask about Nick. He was hurt, and my office called it in."

"Nick Harmon had a car accident. His lung was punctured." French said softly.

"Terrible, is he...."

"I'm not sure of his condition. We're hoping for the best."

Chief French detailed Nick's so-called 'accident,' but she barely heard him.

"Would you like a glass of water?" asked French.

Bridget shook her head. "I just talked to Nick," she said in a whisper. She wanted to share everything she knew with Chief French, but how could she with Barshefsky sitting next to her? She was supposed to be shutting down her office. She couldn't sit there and tell Chief French that Nick was intentionally hurt.

"His last phone call was to you? I'll have the investigator connect with you," Chief French said.

Bridget jerked her head up and made eye contact with French. He wanted to know her activities. Did he suspect her involvement? Would Chief French never give her a break?

Barshefsky inhaled deeply with a wheeze. "Were you close to the social worker? Life's so short and fleeting. Enjoy the moments that we can. That reminds me of changes in your professional life. Are you dropping out of the Kline case? Wonderful to have closure, isn't it?"

"It's the detention center for that child. There are serious allegations against her," said Chief French.

Barshefsky nodded his head in acknowledgment and smoothed his bowtie. He looked like a gigantic birthday present adorned with a red ribbon.

Barshefsky's eyes did not waver as he stared at Bridget. She turned away. French was quiet, evaluating them both as if he enjoyed the exchange.

"Barshefsky should leave now. He is suing me, and if we are going to talk about Nick, then he shouldn't be here."

French's prominent eyebrows raised in unison with his mustache. "You're suing Bridget? Why, she is one of the finest lawyers in Broken River."

She squinted at French, unsure whether the comment was serious.

Barshefsky continued. "No problem there. A misunderstanding. Ms. McGarrity, you'll be happy to know Abby Baker insists on dropping her lawsuit. You could use some good news."

He straightened his collar from his neck and the chair creaked. Bridget unclenched her hands and sat on them to prevent herself from slapping him. The events were unfolding too quickly and were out of her control.

Bridget tried to absorb the information she had just heard. Barshefsky did advocacy work for the Wisaka Nation. Initially, she had searched for connections between herself and the law firm after Abby had sued her. I could kick myself, she thought. She hadn't considered checking whether Whitfield & Barshefsky had any clients who were Native American.

"You represent the Wisaka Nation against the Buyland store?" Chief French asked the exact question Bridget wanted to. He must have done homework on the reservation.

"One of those cases, a labor of love. Quite the kerfuffle. A faction led by Joseph Monroe challenged the council of the Wisaka Nation. They blocked the Buyland store from opening. Of course, our firm had nothing to do with that." Barshefsky grinned at Bridget.

"Advocacy—so you're a lobbyist?" she asked.

"Let's just say we represent the Wisaka Nation."

"Wisaka Nation has its own courts."

"Not in the capitol, and not in Washington, D.C. Domestic terrorism is a serious thing."

"Domestic terrorism?"

"Joseph Monroe, of course. And his brother."

She thought of their home, Scott Monroe in a wheelchair, and Bridget taking out his garbage for him and eating a mint.

Chief French leaned in his chair, contemplative, like he was listening to a fascinating lecture. The two acted like best friends. Barshefsky and his wealth had charmed the police chief and probably had given him an earful about poor, unstable McGarrity. God only knows what Barshefsky said to French before she entered the room. She could imagine their conversation. A lawyer with her troubled past, acting erratically, too emotional about her cases, gets herself sued by a disabled client. She should stay at home and try not to screw up her kid.

"Chief, another time." She stood to leave.

"You're looking a little pale, McGarrity. Talking now would be better."

"Nick is a friend and a colleague."

"Glad you're dropping the Kline case. I understand the child is facing two felonies, attacked a social worker, and stole a check?" said Barshefsky.

"A check made out to her deceased mother."

"Hmm, interesting. Where is Naomi, by the way?" asked Chief French.

Cold sweat dripped down her back as she felt Barshefsky's glare. Great, they now know she didn't bring Naomi in.

"We will talk later, Chief. When you have time."

"Never knew you to back down from a case," said Chief.

Bridget pivoted toward the door and powered-walked out of the office.

Outside the Broken River PD, she breathed deeply as her eyes moistened. She didn't know whether her distress was from Nick or raw fear. She uncoiled her spine, trying to compose herself. She couldn't. No thought came to her head other than one—time to leave.

# Chapter 38

Bridget pulled the car into the garage, walked into the house, and yelled for Aunt Irene and Naomi. She dashed to the basement storage and rifled through old suitcases and found a mid-sized backpack. Aunt Irene and Naomi followed, wide-eyed and puzzled.

"Nick Harmon is in the hospital, badly injured."

Biting her lip, she struggled to sound calm. Time to focus on the task at hand—leaving Broken River as soon as possible. She detailed her encounter with Chief French and Barshefsky to Aunt Irene and Naomi. Ignoring their inquisitive faces, Bridget jogged upstairs, skipping steps.

She laid the white envelope on the counter.

"Take the check to First Bank," Bridget said.

On the couch, Naomi folded her slender legs under her and observed the commotion without comment.

"Naomi, you and I are going on a road trip." Bridget placed her hand on top of Naomi's.

"You both?" said Aunt Irene. "Hate to be a killjoy. But are

you sure? Maybe we should hand you over."

Naomi jumped off the couch. "No way. Last time they had a cop take me back to Elaine's."

"She's right. Elaine will drop the charges again, and she could end up there by suppertime. They found another family member, an uncle, and he's volunteered to help. Plus, Chet wants her at the detention center, which is not a good sign. With Nick out of the picture and unable to communicate, his replacement will not be up to speed. Nick knew about Chet, and that punk Travis, Skinny Boy. His replacement might hand Naomi over to the Klines because that was Nick's last recommendation."

"Slow down, Bridget. Give Chief French another try," said Aunt Irene.

"No. I'm sick of begging."

Aunt Irene placed her handbag on the couch. "Alright then. But you're not giving the authorities much of a chance."

Bridget took the leather handbag from Aunt Irene. "Interesting to hear you root for the cops or social services."

"True. All right, I'll go with you."

"You're staying here."

"Don't be ridiculous," said Aunt Irene, glowering.

"I embrace the ridiculous. Plus, I need you to make bail for me in case I'm arrested," she winked at Naomi. "That's supposed to be a joke."

"If feel like this is a mistake."

"Stay here. Walter needs help with Aiden, and I don't want to make him nervous. Actually, could you call him for me?"

Bridget pressed her hands together in prayer and smiled timidly.

"You embrace the ridiculous. Call him yourself," Aunt Irene said, sighing. "This social worker, you knew him?"

Bridget continued to stuff the backpack with food and water. Stopping by her house would have been preferred, but she didn't want to be spotted.

"He was the caseworker for Naomi. He listened."

She pulled aside a corner of the curtained window. The street was quiet. She walked outside the house to the Grand Am parked at the curb.

"Walter picked up the car," said Aunt Irene.

Her lips quivered as her heart ached; she missed him, missed Aiden. Focus, she said to herself. Naomi came outside and stood by the car, kicking a swath of crabgrass overtaking the pavement. Bridget directed her inside the vehicle.

"You OK with this?" Bridget asked Naomi.

"We're getting out of here?"

"For a day or so until I figure things out and decide on the next steps."

"Cool."

Naomi pulled her hoodie up over her head and tightened the strings. Bridget scrunched her curls under a black baseball cap. Aunt Irene came outside with a windbreaker for Naomi.

"In case of bad weather, even though it's eighty degrees, we should've had this weather in July," said Aunt Irene. "And I won't say Indian summer."

"You just did," said Naomi.

"Forgive her," said Bridget as she hugged Aunt Irene. "Thanks so much for your help."

"We need to talk. About things, the past." Aunt Irene shook her head. "I guess it can wait. Come back soon. Who will mow my lawn?"

*** 

With the prairie sun burning their backs and the radio playing, Bridget and Naomi headed east. Flanked by fields of corn, her breathing smoothed. Hiding felt right and was the only option she could think of. She could get on a computer, make phone calls, and talk to the police and social services without worrying about Chet and Barshefsky. She could sue someone to get attention—the thought made her smile.

But first things first. Bridget called Walter.

"Aunt Irene's coming over to help. It might be a good idea if Aiden could stay the weekend at George's place."

"Aiden loves the pool, and I wouldn't mind a dip myself."

Bridget waited for the next question, like why she wasn't coming home and why they would need to leave.

"I'll have time to work on that Victorian. The weather looks like it will cooperate. But the garage—"

"It's important that I get away for a couple of days," she whispered. "I love you."

"I love you, too."

"Thanks for picking up the car."

"Sure." After a long pause, he said, "Don't worry. I know when to call the police. Even the FBI."

\*\*\*

Bridget powered down her phone, afraid Skinny Guy or Chet could track her. The phone contained adorable pictures of Aiden and many phone numbers she no longer had the ability or desire to remember by heart. With no connection, it felt like the old days. The absence of the cellular tether was liberating. The interstate was empty and a smooth ride, having rarely seen a traffic jam in its long life. A pin-straight highway—she could almost close her eyes and still be squarely on the road. The chaos of the last days softened to white noise. Naomi was quiet in the reclined seat. There was a single, distant car in the rearview mirror and no cars ahead.

"Where are we going?"

"We'll get a hotel room. I'll make calls, talk to the police…"

The explosion was loud, followed by the sound of rubber flapping on the pavement. Locking arms, she tightened her grip on the steering wheel and held the car steady. Naomi screamed, held tight to the seatbelt, and ducked low.

In the rearview mirror, she saw trouble: a white SUV.

"Keep down!"

A man with a baseball cap hung an arm outside the window, and a shotgun reflected in the sun's glare. Despite the unstable wheel, she maintained some speed. Then came the second pop. Another tire blew and rubber slapped the pavement.

Fields of corn flanked her, reminding her of summers spent detasseling corn. Detasseling field corn was usually good money, depending on the seed company, which hired hordes of high school students. Every summer, teenagers descended on the cornfields to rip off the pollen-producing corn tassels to allow different varieties of corn to create special hybrid corn. The work was tedious. For three summers in a row, Bridget woke at the crack of dawn to catch a yellow school bus to take her to the fields, hours away. A rite of passage for corn belt youth, detasseling was not for the faint of heart.

Bridget knew the ins and outs of a cornfield.

The white car was still behind them and coming closer. Yellow hair spiked out under a cap matching her attacker with the baseball bat at Aunt Irene's. It was Skinny Boy. The driver, probably Chet, was barely visible.

"Let's see if these guys appreciate corn."

Bridget braked as Naomi clutched the dashboard. With tires screeching, she made a sharp right and drove straight into the cornfield.

She counted aloud how many rows of corn they had crossed,

making mental calculations to plot her course.

"What are you doing?" Naomi looked at her as if she was crazy. Bridget ignored her and continued counting.

Each row of corn was about two and a half feet apart. After half a mile with tire flapping, she steered the car, taking a hard left. And after another three hundred yards, she took another hard left, forming an enormous square. She drove almost another half mile, according to the odometer. The car's tires struggled through the mud and cornstalks as she tried to maintain speed. Turning left again, she turned another hundred yards and took a soft left, making a diagonal path towards the corner of her square, and finally, she encircled her creation—a makeshift corn maze.

She reversed the car through the maze until the car came to a stumbling halt. The car was stuck, unable to go forward or backward on the poor, beaten-up wheel frame. The wheels were encased in corn stalks and mud, like an adobe cocoon.

The eight-foot-tall corn stalks dwarfed the Grand Am, concealing it. The pursuing car also was nowhere, hopefully, lost in the dizzy pursuit through the corn labyrinth. She couldn't be sure. She apologized silently to the farmer for the lost bushels of corn.

"Maybe, I did enough damage for a nice insurance claim," she whispered as she nudged Naomi, still stunned by their corn odyssey.

"You're worried about corn?" said Naomi.

"You OK?"

"Just great."

Naomi clutched the seatbelt, and Bridget got out of the car, walked to the passenger door, and gently loosened Naomi's grip. She gestured for her to be quiet as they tiptoed away and abandoned the vehicle.

In the distance, a car door slammed with deep, male voices. Bridget swore to herself. She forgot the backpack in the car and her phone. It was too dangerous to go back. At least her wallet was in her pocket. A hike through cornfields was their only choice.

"Time to run. You game?" whispered Bridget.

Naomi said nothing, her face pale, as the towering corn stalks concealed them. Bridget squinted at the sun and noted her shadow.

She knew exactly which direction to go and took Naomi's hand.

# Chapter 39

On foot, the pair headed into the dense cornfield. A bright
evening sun cast long shadows, guiding their direction. They
took an irregular path, turning left and right, and Bridget
counted the rows in her head to keep track of their general
course. About two hundred feet to one side of an acre was about
eighty-five rows of corn. Corn leaves slapped their faces as they
dodged drooping stalks, heavy with ears of corn and vermin. After
twenty minutes of trudging through cornfields in an irregular
pattern, Naomi stopped and shook her hair to rid herself of
debris.

Bridget wiped the sweat from her brow. "The beetles look
worse than they are. They won't hurt you."

Corn rootworm beetles were black and yellow, nasty and
hairy looking, some with spots. They looked venomous and
dangerous but only annoyed farmers and corn.

"I'm thirsty. I'm hungry," she panted.

"I thought you were a good runner?"

"Track. I do hurdles. And I hate cross country."

She wished for a lemonade stand to sprout itself in the middle of the cornfield to rid herself of the pasty dryness in her mouth. She handed Naomi an ear of corn.

"Corn?" Naomi stomped a foot in disgust.

"Corn feeds the world; it can feed you." She ripped off another ear and shucked the corn. "Not the time to be picky. Field corn has its advantages; it's taller than sweet corn, providing better camouflage. A better hideout for both of us. Still, a field of sweet corn would've been nicer on the taste buds."

"Whatever," said Naomi, who took the corn and wiped away a tear she was trying to conceal. She was a tough kid.

"Sorry, that was the best Rachel Ray I could muster."

Together they sat pensively, eating the fibrous field corn, and listened to the whistling wind through leaves of corn and a steady stream of highway noise in the distance.

The cornfield posed its own danger, and it was almost dark. She could hold out a long time in a cornfield, but she wasn't so sure of Naomi. After resting for ten minutes, the pilgrimage continued. They walked and jogged for an hour until after sunset. She didn't need light to count cornrows.

Then they finally met pavement, exiting the shelter of the cornstalks. The teenager stretched her arms as if being freed from a coffin.

They had landed at a T intersection, the road barely visible. Pearl-white lettering on two street signs glowed in the moonlight. She was relieved to see no white SUV.

Naomi grasped something from her pocket and turned her back to Bridget.

"A cell phone? Power it down! They might track it, especially if you had it at Elaine's."

Naomi held the phone to her chest. "Elaine never knew about this phone. I bought it. It's a prepay."

The cell phone rang, its piercing tone like a siren in a

cemetery. Before Bridget could stop her, Naomi answered.

"It may be bugged or they can trace you."

She took the phone from Naomi and listened.

"Where are you?" said the male voice. Naomi grabbed it back and sprinted, and she was fast.

"Fine!"

Bridget sat down on the cool earth. Of course, the child had a cell phone because everyone has a cell phone except for her, at the moment.

"Dad, I'm in the middle of a cornfield. There are two signs."

Naomi described the street signs for him and jogged back to Bridget.

"You just gave our location away."

"It's my dad."

"How well do you know the guy?"

"He doesn't have a white car."

Naomi folded her arms and shifted her weight on one leg. A picture of teenage insolence.

Bridget rested her head on her knees. Who was she kidding? She didn't have a plan, and they needed help. They could walk until morning before finding a phone. Aunt Irene was out of the question. If they found Bridget, they'd find Aunt Irene. She couldn't even imagine what the police might say or if they would even believe her.

A half-hour later, a sound erupted like churning bowels on a megaphone, right before spewing its contents into a toilet. The sound could be heard for miles—a motorcycle, grinding and loud, approached. Bridget didn't know whether to run or hide. Naomi's youthful limbs found energy, and she jumped, skipping towards the motorcycle.

Steve Ross's helmetless head was barely visible in the night as he slowed the bike. He dismounted the monster hog like a horse and Naomi ran towards him. His massive arms circled

Naomi, who matched his embrace, lifting her off the ground. She squealed with delight.

Their affection showed no reticence or hesitation. Ross wasn't the image of a shady convict recently sprung from the prison. He was a happy, albeit not the greatest, father. Bridget mused how much a motorcycle like that would cost, a vehicle for the single, unattached male who didn't have a home.

"Thanks for calling me," he said. Naomi rested her head on her father's shoulder and started crying. Bridget gave them space and herself time to assess Ross.

"Glad you're OK."

Ross led her to the motorcycle and retrieved two water bottles.

"Thank God!" said Naomi. She emptied it within seconds.

Ross handed Bridget a water bottle. "I told Naomi, you're going to like me."

She took the bottle. Could she trust him? She didn't know what to make of Steve, but she intended to be cautious. Bridget held the bottle, feeling its weight. She didn't have much choice. She opened the bottle and drank, pouring a little into her hands, and rubbed her face.

"Let's get you out of here," said Ross to his daughter, his voice barely audible.

"Go where?"

"I've got an idea; unless there's someplace specific you would like to go?"

Cars and semis hummed from the distant highway. Bridget had no intention of following him, but they were stuck.

"A place with a roof, a telephone, and maybe a computer."

"I can do that," said Ross.

Bridget eyed the motorcycle. She felt the blood drain from her face. She'd rather stay in the cornfield. Noticing her hesitation, Ross said, "The three of us can make it."

"Ever hear of a minivan or plain old sedan? Convertibles, they're good, too. You should invest in one."

Bridget sighed as the trio squeezed onto the motorcycle.

# Chapter 40

Bridget hung on as wind tangled her hair, quarter-sized bugs beat her face, and the smell of a freshly sprayed field made her queasy. After an agonizing half hour, the trio entered a trailer park east of Broken River, and she unglued herself from the back of Ross, their sweat mixing. She ached for the comforts of home and family, a shower. Naomi had sat in front of her father and, remarkably, had fallen asleep during the ride. When he halted the vehicle, she barely budged.

Ross picked her up like a tuckered toddler as Bridget knocked at the door of the aluminum trailer. A woman with stringy brown hair and yellowed teeth clenching a cigarette answered the door. Loose skin hung over her ashen cheekbones, and a blue lace camisole t-shirt that had seen better days revealed scabbed sores most would choose to hide. Her boney collar-bones protruded from her slight frame, like nunchucks, ready to strike.

"Steve. You asshole. Get the fuck out of here," said the lady, enfolding her crossed arms like the limbs of a praying mantis. The bug arm abruptly took the cigarette from the lady's mouth and flicked it to the ground.

Ross, undeterred, grinned while holding his daughter like a pleading puppy dog—a look a grown man shouldn't be capable of.

"Oh, hell, get in," she said.

The woman walked into her trailer house, her stick-like arms moving silently, barely brushing her body.

With her back to Bridget, the woman asked, "Is this your newest ass?" Not waiting for an answer, the woman slithered into a room at the back of the house, leaving them alone in the living area. "Don't make a mess and don't bother me. I need sleep!" she yelled, her voice hissing. She slammed a bedroom door behind her.

"We can't stay here," said Bridget.

"It has a roof. That was one of your requirements. Check," said Ross, who placed Naomi on a worn wool couch, its coils providing little support as the center sagged to the floor from Naomi's weight.

"That lady is an addict," she said, looking nervously around.

"A recovering addict. She's harmless."

"I also asked for a telephone and computer."

"Working on that."

Bridget could spot a meth addict. Most lawyers in the area, or anyone in social services, knew. Meth was a cancer that corroded families, and some smaller towns were the hardest hit. The lady had all the telltale signs of meth addiction: sores, skinny, bad teeth, and aggressive. She sighed. What could she do? At least they survived unhurt. She couldn't say the same for Cheri or Nick.

"Steven Ross," she asked. "Tell me why I'm here."

"Something more than a spiritual journey?" said Ross, with a mischievous smile and stepped towards her. Bridget took a step back, not wanting another bear hug.

"What do you want to know, Lady Lawyer?"

She assessed her surroundings and decided to trust her instincts and confront Ross, although she wasn't sure what information he'd divulge, if any. His speech was clear, with no pockmarks from meth on his skin and no smell of alcohol or cigarettes. His only focus was on Naomi, which was good.

"Why did you kill Cheri?"

"Whoa, there!" he said, shaking his head. "That isn't helping, Lady Lawyer."

She didn't think Steve hurt Cheri but testing his reaction to her question might reveal whether he was an ally or not. He hung out with addicts, always a bad sign.

"I had to ask."

"If you say so," he said.

Bewildered, Naomi awoke and rubbed her eyes. "I'm hungry." Bridget's stomach growled in agreement.

Ross walked behind a wall to the kitchen, and cabinets snapped open and shut, followed by a refrigerator door squeaking like a captured pig. He came out with two clear plastic glasses filled with water.

"There's nothing to eat here," said Ross.

"There must be something."

She walked into the kitchen. The mess was pervasive, dishes piled in the sink; large swaths of mold erupted from the crevices. The fridge was empty. The poor woman ate nothing and, unfortunately, looked like it. There was a pile of stuff in the trailer's corner, mostly junk, like a palm-sized piece of twisted metal that you might find along the side of the road. A shard of glass, about the size of a thumbnail, might have come from the seashore, its edges smoothed from its many days of sand and sea. Other objects were a street sign, clothing, rocks, a green bottle, and several shiny bits of twisted metal.

A strong smell drifted from the hallway. She knew that

stench—cat litter or what smelled like cat litter. Yet no cat was to be found. That smell could mean someone had been cooking meth.

Ross said she was a recovering addict, yet the house, how she looked, told a different story. The woman was actively using drugs. Just being there, a room where meth was consumed or made, meant that the residue could unleash its poison on the unsuspecting and innocent. She shuddered at the thought of being at the house when a drug addict's drug supply ran dry.

"Let's order a pizza and eat outside," said Bridget.

Naomi's eyebrows raised. "Pizza. Oh, but why? I think I still have corn kernels in my pocket."

"I know! I thought I'd shake your diet up a bit. I'm setting an example of perfect parenting. Your cell phone, please. I'll give it back."

Stepping outside, she assessed her surroundings—tiny mobile homes with tiki lights, potted plants, and lawn chairs. Cigarette smoke wafted from the neighboring trailer. Another unit had plastic wrap for a window with glass shards scattered on the ground. How much would the residents be watching them?

"Steve, you deal with the pizza."

Back in the house, she handed the cell phone to Steve. Ordering pizza wasn't necessarily risky but being spotted was something she'd hope to avoid.

***

After the pizza delivery, Naomi and Steve sat outside, eating in silence as the katydids whistled under the black sky dotted with stars. Bridget, on the other hand, was pacing as she considered their next steps. Uncertainty crept through her as she watched Steve. How much could she trust him? A decent interrogation of Steve would be satisfying and perhaps settle her nerves, but she didn't need to interrogate him because Naomi started questioning him herself.

"Why did my mom die? Why are they after me and my lawyer?" Naomi wiped her mouth with the back of her hand and looked intently at Steve.

"I don't know." He lightly placed his hand on Naomi's back.

"When did you last talk to Cheri?" Bridget asked.

He rubbed his hands together and stood, and she held her tongue, waiting for him to answer. "Before she left for the hospital, she called me."

He opened a pop, emptying it in three gulps.

"You were at the hospital?"

"Don't look at me that way. Like I'm guilty. I may be some things, but I'm not about hurting her or anyone." He crushed the can with his hand. "We argued and I hated social services being around. I wanted to deal with the situation without all them social workers or even Elaine. Cheri wouldn't have none of it, and, man, I was too late. Her head was so messed up, and she done the only thing she could."

"Which was?"

"She called social services, and they got to watching Naomi, and people started to pay attention to what was happening there. Cheri had herself a lawyer appointed." He stared directly into her eyes, his face stone cold. "She knew she couldn't help Naomi. Those social workers told her the government would."

"Why get away from Elaine? She has raised Naomi since she was a child."

"The two fought constantly."

"It's the money, isn't it? That headright money?" said Naomi. She emptied her can of pop and crushed it, just like Steve.

"Cowboys always take the money. That's what Cheri used to say," Steve said.

Bridget scratched her head in confusion. Could he be any more cryptic? "Pretend I'm dumb. That shouldn't be hard. Could you explain exactly who the cowboys are?"

Steve paused as if in thought and headed toward his bike. He started fiddling with the gears and cleaned the chrome with a rag cloth. She followed him.

"Steve?"

He continued to work on his motorcycle, and he didn't abandon his vigil until he methodically examined every inch of his motorbike. After a long silence, he faced Bridget.

"I think it's time that Naomi and I head off. You go and do your own thing."

He spoke slowly, without emotion. She laughed until her eyes teared, unable to contain herself.

"That's funny and wrong in so many ways. How long are you going to last on the road? You don't have custody of Naomi. The Department of Human Services does. You may not like that, but that is how it is."

Steve kicked the empty pizza box but said nothing. She continued because she could do nothing else but buzz like a fly in his ear until he reacted. Hopefully, he wouldn't swat too hard.

"The frosting on the cake is Naomi's charged with a crime. And you're assisting her in fleeing. I'll make a wild guess—you're on probation, and this detour with Naomi violates the terms of your probation. That will land you straight in jail, and it's hard to parent from prison." Steve turned his back to Bridget. "I've stood by your daughter who's in danger. And by the way, now I'm in danger, my family, and hell, I sold my law practice. We're in this together. Let's share a jail cell. Dearest, future cellmate, answer my questions. Tell us a story."

Steve's shoulders sagged. "You're pretty hot when you're

angry."

She groaned. "If that's a compliment, thanks. You can answer my question."

"Can't shake the lawyer out of you." Steve rubbed his chin thoughtfully. "The money, some of it, I know about. Elaine uses Cheri's money and controls it."

"Her brother? Tell me about him."

"Jay? He's a suit. Your type and does politics or business. He's a lawyer or business guy."

"Is he Indigenous?"

"Not a drop. Jay is Elaine's blood, and Cheri is the adopted one. Elaine favored Jay," he said. "That's why Cheri left. She couldn't get along with Jay or Elaine. Lately, though, Jay had been nice to Cheri, and they were doing things together."

He brushed the seat and removed mud from the wheels as he spoke.

"I think the people who messed with Cheri also took me out of the picture. Years ago, when I stood up for Cheri against her family, I got into a fight with Jay. I thought Jay was messing with her money, too, and he warned me to stay away. I blew him off and helped Cheri anyway. A week later, a guy in a bar put drugs in my pocket and punched me. And I punched him back, and the next thing, he fingers me for drugs. Cops show seconds later, and I end up in jail. Someone set me up. My lawyer didn't believe me and said a jury wouldn't either. So, I took the deal and did my time."

"The Klines put you in jail? A week ago, I wouldn't have believed you." She shook her head. "The headright isn't enough money to commit murder or set you up for the crime."

"People have done worse for less. They got me out of the way. I was out of the picture and away from Naomi."

Exhaustion permeated every cell of her body. She'd been tired before, but not like this. She knew that families could be cruel, but this cruelty was different—it was orchestrated. Hard to believe Elaine, a medical assistant who raised an orphaned child with mental illness, could hurt Cheri. She rubbed her grubby hands on her grimy neck.

"Time to go."

Taking the hint, Naomi hopped up; she also was eager to leave.

"We're going to spend money I don't have. I'll bill the state for it. 'Expenses related to madman chase in cornfield.'"

"Really?" asked Naomi.

"Not really."

"We can stay longer here," Steve winked.

Bridget still wasn't sure about him. If he had the money to buy a motorcycle, he could chip in and find his own place to sleep.

"This is no place for a child. You should know that," said Bridget, unleashing the scolding mother in her.

"One more ride on the wild hog?" asked Steve.

Bridget grinned, trying to embrace the joy of the open road. The joy never came.

# Chapter 41

At the Captain's suite at Marquette Inn the following day, Bridget had a striking view of the Mississippi. She sat on a fluffy hotel bed in a terry cloth robe, wiggling squeaky clean toes, with glossy skin beaming a healthy pink after soaking herself in the tub for an hour. Naomi lay sacked out on the pull-out bed in the adjacent room. Steve had, thankfully, declined the hotel room and slept somewhere in town. She daydreamed of a canoe. Could they float down to New Orleans, escape the madness?

A light knock broke her reverie, and she tiptoed to the door, opening only an inch. It was a hotel attendant. "Your laundered clothes, ma'am. Sorry about your car accident. Will there be anything else?"

She felt a slight tinge of guilt for her deception with the hotel staff. She gave them a story of a hit-and-run car collision, not entirely false, to explain their rumpled appearance.

"Laundered clothes and a room with a view of the Mississippi. That'll do."

Last night, she was too dismayed to watch local news or

contact the family. Exhaustion was the only emotion left, unable to face anything other than sleep. Bridget borrowed Naomi's phone, and as the child stirred, she called Aunt Irene.

"Where are you?" Aunt Irene said breathlessly, like she had been running.

"I'm somewhere safe and doing fine. How's Aiden and Walter?"

"Great, should I get Walter?"

"Later, OK?"

At least that part of the plan, where the safety of Aunt Irene, Walter, and Aiden was ensured, was a success. She told Aunt Irene everything about her awful day—she was having a lot of them lately. The wrecked Grand Am was news to Aunt Irene, which probably meant the police had found nothing. She wasn't sure whether that was bad or good.

"There must've been tire marks or other signs of an accident. I'm surprised the highway patrol didn't notice."

"True, dear. But, honey, are you sitting down?

She cradled her head in her hand; she was tired and hungry. "Yes."

"Good, you will not like this. The police issued an AMBER Alert."

It was as if she had been slapped across the face. Of course they'd issue an AMBER Alert. She could imagine Chief French with a smug smile as Barshefsky congratulated him, both commiserating about her wretchedness.

"I'm named?"

"Yes."

"What about Steve?"

"No."

"What a disaster. I knew there was a possibility that this could happen, but I didn't believe the police would follow through."

"Honey, you should have called the police. What choice did they have?" answered Aunt Irene.

As a lawyer, her clients came to her after the harm was done, after the blood was spilled, after the infidelity or drug sale. In the peace and safety of an office, she could ponder man's depravity. Not today. Now she was the depraved, a child snatcher, a target of the police, a most wanted. And like anyone who was arrested, she overwhelmingly needed to explain herself.

"Ha! Like the system ever works how it should. You should know better than anyone else. How long did Tim and I languish in foster care?"

"About that, you, um...."

"What?"

"Probably best to blame me for that delay in getting you and your brother out of foster care, not the judge or the social workers."

She sat down on the bed and tucked herself back under the fluffy blanket. "What are we talking about?"

"I didn't think it was important."

"Please take your time. It's only been twenty years."

"I guess I deserve that. Bridget, honey, I had a tiny drug problem back then, and the courts demanded a clean drug test from me before they would put you and Tim in my care."

"Who didn't smoke marijuana in California?"

"No, it was something else. I, um—"

"Yes."

"I told the courts that I couldn't take care of you, that I wasn't ready. But I changed with Uncle Billy's help—he really was a saint. We bought the house together and changed our habits. It was a blessing in disguise. Social services also were so helpful they even—"

"Enough."

"Please, let me—"

"I said enough."

She held the phone to her chest, trying not to hang up on Aunt Irene. Did it matter? Besides her decades-long hatred of social services, she built her career choice on the premise that the government is cruel and incompetent. Should she trust social services and the police more? She was living proof that they were failures, and now Aunt Irene was telling her otherwise.

Yes, she should have looped Chief French in much earlier, despite his budding relationship with Barshefsky.

"Fine, I'll give them a chance to prove themselves. I need to get back in the courtroom. I can't remember her cell phone number, so have Diane call this number," said Bridget.

After an agonizingly long, awkward silence, Aunt Irene said, "You bet. I got your number!"

Bridget found a pillow and screamed into it with thoughts of pounding her head on the wall. Instead, she got dressed, made coffee, and fixated on her spectacular view. What Aunt Irene had told her didn't matter—she would process that another day.

Minutes later, Diane called, and her voice was untroubled, like a bright light guiding her through the dark.

"I'm not sure whether you watch the news—"

"What do you need?" Diane asked.

"A judge. And soon."

Over the phone, Bridget dictated a motion for an emergency hearing. Diane churned out the paperwork, along with four subpoenas, and emailed it to Bridget. Court administration would set a court date later when Diane submitted the paperwork.

With her hair scrunched under a baseball cap, she headed downstairs to the hotel business center to use the computer. The center was empty. She logged into her email, reviewed the paperwork from Diane, and emailed it back.

Bridget cringed with the thought that her face was

broadcast across the Midwest. Not what she had in mind for advertising. Her best hope was to arrive at the courthouse unannounced and cancel the alert before they found her. She only needed one peaceful morning and a decent meal.

She punched in the number for the police station for Broken River and asked for Chief French, who wasn't available per the drone answering the phone.

"I have a message for him. Have a sharpened pencil? Tell him Bridget McGarrity called and Naomi Kline is fine and with me. By the way, I'm fine, too."

The drone gasped. "Hold on. One moment, I'll connect you."

She smirked. For once, her name was receiving attention—if only the circumstances were better. Way to make that happen, she thought.

"Where the hell are you, McGarrity?" yelled French, not wasting time on introductions or the weather.

"Sorry to ruffle your feathers. You'll see Naomi and me in court. I'm setting up an emergency hearing, and you should receive a subpoena by lunch. And a special helper could put a word in with court administration to get me a court date, like for this afternoon?"

"Me? Yes, I will do that." Chief French cleared his throat, and after a long pause, he finally spoke. "Continue, please."

She described the attack on the highway and the description of her car and the location. She omitted information about Steve, the trailer park, and the hotel.

"Pay special attention to the car wheels. Only a gun would do that," she urged.

Chief French was quiet, and she hoped silence meant police hadn't discovered the car. French cleared his throat again.

"Just bring the child in, and we'll protect her."

"You'll investigate? Now that I've been shot at?"

"One second, McGarrity." It sounded like Chief French covered the telephone mouthpiece as he spoke to another person. After a minute, French said, "Medical records that you subpoenaed came in. The records about Cheri Kline's stay in the hospital. The hospital confirms she had no history of substance abuse, and blood, urine, and hair analysis showed no trace of fentanyl or opioids."

"My goal is keeping Naomi safe and myself as well, and you weren't helping. Chief, about that AMBER Alert—"

"The Department of Human Services requested it."

"And let me guess, urged by Elaine Kline or her lawyer, Barshefsky—your lover?"

"Skip the sarcasm."

"Barshefsky had no input on that decision?"

He didn't respond, which was confirmation enough that Barshefsky had influenced him. "If Nick Harmon were OK, the alert wouldn't have been issued," said Bridget.

"You spoke to him last, McGarrity," said French.

"And I'm still alive to talk about it. Locate my car and arrange protective custody for Naomi. See you in court."

She ended the call, shaking. How had it come this far? She wasn't sure who had the authority to cancel the AMBER Alert, the police, or DHS. By now, he knew Naomi's number unless the cops didn't have caller ID. Let him call.

She walked back to her room through the majestic hotel lobby decorated in warm reds with golden accents. Tucked in a cozy corner next to a soft rust-colored leather loveseat was a glass canister of ice water spiked with cucumber. She could spend the day on that sofa. Instead, she made a beeline to the elevator, keeping her head low. A tap on her shoulder startled her. She spun around, and the cap flew off her head.

"Your cell phone, ma'am. You left it in the business center. It was ringing; you might've missed a call."

Bridget's pulse raced through her even though it was hotel staff, not a police officer with guns drawn.

"Right, thank you." Bridget ignored the cap like it wasn't hers, and she had meant it to fly to the floor.

"Of course," he grinned.

She smiled awkwardly, feeling unsteady. She didn't recognize the number; it wasn't from Broken River. She pressed redial.

"Hello? I missed this call and pressed redial," she said.

"You didn't give your name. Cautious. That's smart."

"This is who?"

"John Wapello, the attorney general for the Wisaka Nation."

"Mr. Wapello, I—"

"Call me John."

"John. I'm..."

Her voice gave out. She sat on the leather sofa in the discreet corner of the hotel lobby. She wedged the phone between her ear and shoulder as she greedily eyed cucumber spa water.

"Officer Bennett had Naomi's number from when she was with us here on the reservation. How is Naomi?"

"She's fine."

"And you?"

"I've been better."

"The AMBER Alert was a surprise." His tone was sympathetic. "As an officer of the court, I encourage you to turn yourself in, but I'm here to help if you need it."

The thought of seeking the reservation's help hadn't occurred to her.

"A solution should come as soon as I wrangle up a judge. Could you give me insight into Buyland? Or the dispute between Monroe and your council," asked Bridget.

"I would need to write a book on that one. Buyland is privately held and not interesting for an individual investor. Its small, independent operation appealed to the Elder council. Other companies approached us."

"Like who?"

"Penny General. However, it didn't offer much on fresh produce, which we need here."

"Makes sense."

"One concern we had was another chain, that we hadn't approved of, might take over Buyland."

"You sound more like an investment banker than an attorney general."

"Jack of all trades. I'm sworn to protect this community, covering everything from child support or petty crimes to major companies lobbying their interests. I've had my suspicions in this case. Hear me out?"

His clarity was like a jolt of energy.

"Buyland is interesting. It's developing a nice niche servicing Indian reservations, surrounded by rural areas that also shop there. I'm sure the bigger guys are envious. Buyland is the only store of its kind within an hour's drive. And another thing, the reservations are big business for lawsuits and lawyers."

"And lobbyists?"

"Sure. Grocers and the reservation need lobbyists like every other industry."

She walked back to the business center, sat on the rickety office chair, and typed into the computer as she searched Barshefsky's law firm and found a list of their clients.

"About the protests at the reservation. It was about a discrimination lawsuit only?"

"A Wisaka teenager sued Buyland for retaliation, alleging it fired her for complaining about sexual harassment. Buyland alleged she was a poor employee and stole something. If appealed, that would be an important case on jurisdiction. Many people, including Native Americans, don't want this thing to settle and hope the matter makes it to the appellate court. Maybe even the U.S. Supreme Court," he said.

Bridget rubbed her eyes and then resumed searching on the internet. "I'm putting you on speaker phone while I type. The lawsuit is a big case if appealed."

"Exactly. Buyland argues the dispute should not be in our courts. The tribal council believes that Buyland's position threatens the ability of Wisaka Nation ability to protect itself. Monroe just wants the store gone and a new tribal council that agrees with him."

Bridget shook her head; it was Cheri's death all over again, flashing in her consciousness, the visions of her lifeless body.

"That's three different entities, Buyland, Monroe, and the tribal council. How does Cheri's death fit in? She subsidized Joe Monroe and the protestors."

"Monroe's supporters came into funding, which fueled the already simmering fire. Buyland, last I heard, tried to settle, but the offer was rejected. The case could eventually end up in an appeal. And I'm not sure that's a bad thing."

"Unless you lose on appeal."

"True. And another thing, there's one more factor. A lot of time and a shiny penny went to lobbyists who are supposed to help us change the laws in the state to ensure our sovereignty."

"A constant fight for jurisdiction. The tribe's hands were tied because it couldn't prosecute murder. The FBI couldn't be bothered with investigating a poor woman who died because of substance abuse. Crime and discrimination go unchecked, again and again." John said nothing, letting her draw her own conclusion. "Whoever did this knew about the lack of jurisdiction and benefited from the infighting."

"It's a theory," he said. "And you wouldn't be the first person to think of it."

Bridget put her feet on the table and examined a perforated

ceiling tile as her stomach growled.

"John, why are you being so nice?"

He laughed. "Rarely I hear that. Officer Bennett and I agree that something is wrong with the AMBER Alert. Naomi and her mother may have been involved with a larger issue. The discrimination lawsuit has become political," said John, sighing. "The victim's family was going to settle, but something changed their mind. They found new lawyers, and the fight is still on."

"That's what Cal Roberts said, too. Lawyers, politicians, and lobbyists. Whitfield & Barshefsky are lobbyists for the Wisaka Nation."

"We need people in this state and Washington representing our interests. Can I arrange a peaceful return for you and Naomi?"

"Thanks, John, but I'm working on that now."

After promising to share information, John hung up. The humming of the computer prodded her to research more. On the government website, she got a hit on the mandatory disclosure statements for lobbyists. Sure enough, the website listed Barshefsky's firm as a lobbyist for the Wisaka Nation. Then she plugged in every name she could conjure but found nothing.

She searched for Washington, DC, and her stomach flipped—Jay Kline. Mandatory disclosures for lobbyists listed him as a lobbyist for the Osage Nation in Oklahoma. He was the one family member who mysteriously appeared to take care of Naomi.

"Jay Kline. Naomi's uncle. He has to be involved. Was that why he was being nice to Cheri?" she said out loud.

He was lobbying for the Osage in Oklahoma, and Naomi and her mother were Osage. Cheri had probably opened doors for him with the Wisaka Nation and the Osage. Cheri could have been a moneymaker for Jay, a lobbyist who needed access.

Bridget wiped the sleep from her eyes, wondering how she had become entangled in this web. After sharing the links in an email with John Wapello, she stuffed the phone in her back pocket, pushed her cap brim low, and headed again to the lobby, looking down as she walked.

"Lady Lawyer, Bridget!"

It was Steve, in the open, standing proudly with Naomi, with a toothpick in her mouth. They just finished breakfast, so carefree.

"They gave me free toothpaste," Naomi smiled.

"Are you two mad? We need to be discreet. Let's go upstairs," said Bridget.

Steve's sizable arms encircled Naomi and Bridget, one under each. He held them tight.

"My ladies."

Bridget guffawed as she slipped from his grasp. She grabbed Naomi's hand, leading the way.

"Upstairs, now."

She nodded to the friendly hotel attendant and smiled, even though she wanted to cry. Once in the elevator, she spoke.

"There's an AMBER Alert. You need to stay hidden. I thought I made that clear."

"AMBER Alert? For me?" asked Steve.

"No, it's for me," answered Bridget.

"Oh, got a problem there, don't ya!"

"AMBER Alert? Who's Amber?" Naomi asked.

She looked out the hotel window and spotted nothing out of the ordinary. Steve whistled a tune and scratched his scruffy chin and stretched, probably shaking off wherever he spent the night. He sat on a chair and put his boots on the edge of the bed.

"What's the plan?" asked Steve.

"I have a couple of ideas."

***

She rubbed her face, exhaustion and hunger gnawing at her stomach. She looked Naomi in the eye.

"The plan is to tell me exactly what happened that night. You have information and knowledge that those bad guys in the car think are dangerous. We should figure out what that is."

Naomi sat down on the bed and studied the floor. Steve cleared his throat while he and Naomi looked at one another. Steve nodded, and she hugged her knees to her chest.

"Mom said she was working on the reservation. She called herself 'Errand Girl.' Like it was a superpower, and she was on a mission. She had errands—delivering papers and envelopes."

"I'm guessing the envelopes was money," said Steve.

"For the cause—that's what my mom called it." With her fingers, Naomi mimicked quotations at the word 'cause.' "One time, there was a bunch of envelopes in a bag, like a suitcase."

Steve patted Naomi's shoulder. "Rumor was that Cheri was doing something with Joe Monroe. I used to work with him at the casino doing security. He was a straight-up guy, and I thought nothing of it."

Monroe voiced strong opinions against Buyland and said he knew Cheri. He wasn't shy about her help and the money.

"Joe Monroe confirmed that Cheri gave money and if it was a suitcase...Well, a suitcase holds a lot more money than Cheri had from a headright. Where was all the money coming from? Why would Cheri have that much cash? She did have her own income, but it was not like she was rich," said Bridget.

Tears escaped from Naomi's eyes, and Steve put his arm around her as her chest rattled when she inhaled.

"My mom, 'Errand Girl,'" Naomi again showed quotation marks.

"Why did you run to my house?"

"I was afraid. Before I ran, Elaine said on the phone that I knew nothing about the money. But I do know! Elaine was upset, and she screamed that she wanted it to stop."

Steve fetched water for Naomi, and she emptied the plastic cup, crushed it in her hands, and threw it to the floor.

"I was there, too," said Steve.

"What?"

Bridget took a step back from Steve. Naomi withheld information from her, valuable information.

"Where were you?" she said firmly.

"I was at the reservation that night when Cheri and Naomi were there."

"Why am I hearing this for the first time?" Bridget shook her finger at Naomi. "We've been shot at, threatened, and I have been sued. And Steve, I don't know what to make of you."

Steve's face was expressionless. "It's OK, Naomi. My little girl was covering for me because I was at the reservation that night. Cheri and me argued when she went to Monroe's house. I didn't want Naomi mixed up in all that. Cheri had problems and I wanted Naomi away from her, and I thought she was better off with Elaine."

"I didn't say anything because I thought they'd take my dad away, and nobody wants me to live with him."

He continued, "When I got to Monroe's, Cheri had left. I searched for her on the bike but had no such luck. When I made it back to Monroe's, Naomi and the car were gone."

Bridget didn't know whether to believe them. If Steve meant to harm her, he already had plenty of opportunities.

"They had tried to silence Cheri."

"Someone was using her, whoever gave her that money, and she had figured that out. She wanted to tell everyone," said Steve.

"Whoever is behind this never anticipated Cheri would seek help from social services with Naomi. As soon as I and social services came into the picture, they had new adversaries. Whoever is behind this never anticipated dealing with Nick or me." said

Bridget.

"And me," said Naomi.

They sat in silence, taking it all in. Having this information earlier would have been better, but there had not been much time to put things together.

"It should be pretty easy to figure out who Elaine was talking to on the phone. Chief French or Officer Bennett could subpoena Elaine's phone records."

Bridget's stomach grumbled loudly; she hadn't eaten since the pizza the night before. Naomi giggled at the sound despite the tension, returning to her teenage self.

"That breakfast buffet is calling me." She shook her head, trying to contain her anger and focus. "This information should come out. We should be in front of a judge this afternoon, and we'll get Naomi into protective custody."

"I'm staying with my dad."

"Do you have an address yet?"

"Working on that," said Steve.

"Please do."

"It's a plan then," Steve said.

Bridget handed Naomi her cell phone, put her cap on, and opened the door to the hotel room. She gasped. Two grim-faced police officers stood stiffly, hands hovering over their pistols at their hips as a radio crackled.

# Chapter 42

"Bridget McGarrity?"

"Yes, I am."

"Are you aware of an AMBER Alert?"

No, she would not answer that question. Or any questions. The officer held up handcuffs, and she put her hands out.

"Oh, joy!"

Two more officers marched into the hotel room. A female officer headed to Naomi and guided her to the hallway.

"What's going on? Am I being arrested?" Naomi asked.

"No, dear, I am. I thought I'd take the hit this time. It looks like I will save money on renting a car. I found my ride back to Broken River."

"You can't take her! She's my guardian ad litem!" screamed Naomi.

"Give me a minute, please," Bridget asked.

"Sorry, no."

"Naomi, look at me. I'm fine. You're also fine. You are safe, and this woman here will take good care of you, and your dad will follow. Just cooperate with her, OK?"

"But I—"

"No buts. We're on this roller coaster, and there's no way to jump off. Take the ride until it stops."

The officer led Bridget out of the hotel room, away from Naomi.

"Bridget McGarrity, you are charged with the abduction of Naomi Kline in violation of code—" The officer cuffed her and recited her rights, which got her thinking.

"Officer, you can't arrest me."

She wiggled the cuffs around her wrists and raised her finger the best she could, like a schoolteacher trying to teach a disobedient student a lesson.

The officer continued his colloquy of reciting Miranda rights as if he was afraid that if he stopped midway, he'd have to start all over again. She waited for him to finish.

"Now that you've gotten that off your chest, let me explain. I'm an officer of the court on my way to a judicial proceeding. You can't arrest me on my way to court because that would constitute obstruction of a judicial process."

The officer laughed. "Really? You can share that one with the judge yourself."

"I would settle for no cuffs." Her stomach growled again. "Could we grab a bagel on the way?"

\*\*\*

Handcuffs and a flock of local TV station reporters foiled the plan for a quiet arrival at Lincoln County Courthouse. To the many reporters' questions, she chanted over and over, like a mantra, 'no comment, no comment.'

"Did you kidnap Naomi Kline?"

"Any comment about the death of the girl's mother? Are you involved?"

"Ms. McGarrity, have you spoken with your husband, Walter? What about your son!"

She stopped cold in her tracks. Should she keep her head down? Cover her face? After all, she was handcuffed, like a hungover bad girl movie star. Instead, she eyed the young reporter with a blunt bob haircut and dark eyeglass frames the size of truck headlights.

"There's something I'd like to say." She looked past them, pondering the proper phrasing, and said, "Promise you will air it?" The reporters nodded their wanting bobbleheads in unison. "If the public knew what cheap cologne you guys wear, they wouldn't think so highly of you."

"Cut that!"

"Did that go out?" said another.

She maneuvered her way past the flocking reporters as two police officers flanked her approach. They slipped into the courthouse, greeted by Mark Evans, the county attorney. He guided her through the judges' hallway behind the courtroom, conveniently constructed to keep judges and county attorneys from the disgruntled public.

"Mark, I didn't know county attorneys moonlighted as greeters, but thanks for not sending me straight to jail," said Bridget.

"I hope you know what you're doing," said Mark.

"So do I. You can cut me loose, please."

She raised her wrists and rattled the handcuffs. Mark scratched the short stubble on his chin and smirked.

"Handcuffs. Nice. That should be mandatory attire for all defense attorneys," he said.

"God, you are clever."

Mark chuckled, as well as a police officer following them. It was going to be a long, impossible day.

In the hour-and-a-half ride in the squad car, she'd convinced the officers to contact court administration, and somewhere, a little guardian angel organized a hearing for that afternoon. She entered the courtroom, and the police directed her to the designated table for defendants and their attorneys. Mark examined a stack of files on the opposite table. She raised her bound hands, rattling her handcuffs at the police officers.

"Officer, am I conducting this hearing shackled?" she asked.

"You'll need to wait for the judge."

"Second thought, let's keep 'em. I enjoy protecting the public, too. Silver brings out the hazel in my eyes. Stop smiling, Mark."

She tried to smooth her hair without bashing her face with the cuffs. Her outfit wasn't very professional, but she had little choice. At least she had had a bath at the hotel.

Courthouse security blocked the courtroom entrance, providing a temporary respite from the hungry press hovering outside where the usual players assembled. Rob, the juvenile court officer, leered, his gum popping with a goofy grin on his face. A court-appointed attorney stood next to Steve shaking his finger at him. So much for attorney-client bonding. And by Steve's wild expression, the attorney did not impress him. He threw his hands up in the air and marched toward Bridget.

"I don't like this squirrelly lawyer. Why do I need him when Naomi's got you?" Steve gave her a pat on the back, and she steadied herself as the handcuffs clattered against the wooden defense table.

"Annoying how the chains rattle. Expect bruises." Steve winked at her.

She gave him a low five. "Thanks for the tip. Good to have a bonding experience from one convict to cuffed arrestee."

A low hum of voices filled the courtroom. This courtroom was usually reserved for trials that attracted attention and required larger attendance, not the type of trial where only the families showed.

Steve sat in the front pew on the aisle side next to Elaine as she adjusted buttons on her sweater and avoided Steve's intense gaze. A handful of witnesses, nurse Connie from 5E and Chief French, were there, and Connie waved as if Bridget was paparazzi. Connie's bright orange lipstick and bushy pigtails were as noticeable as an orange construction sign.

Diane had spent the morning serving subpoenas for them to testify, and incredibly, they all showed. She met Chief French's critical eye, and he walked towards her; she braced herself for the usual verbal lashing.

"Good afternoon, Bridget. What does one say?" French smoothed his mustache and adjusted his holster. He scanned the room like he was king and owned the courtroom.

"I'll try not to call you to testify, but I need you here just in case. Sit there and look scary like you usually do."

"Cute bracelets, McGarrity. And your wrecked car? We never found it, if it was ever there."

Her sore arms fell to her lap like a monk in prayer. Stay on the roller coaster, she thought. You can't get off. The courtroom was her only ride, even though Chet and Skinny Boy were trying to make her look crazy and were doing an excellent job at it.

"I'm not lying."

"Didn't say that you were." French clasped his hands behind his back like he was about to give a lecture. "I received a call from an Officer Bennett of the Wisaka Nation. Most interesting."

The press filled the back pews. French didn't wait for her answer and walked past the press, glaring at them with his best spaghetti Western scowl.

Naomi entered the courtroom and heads turned; a young

woman, presumably a social worker, guided her to the seat next to Bridget. Her heart wrenched as she noted Nick's absence. He should be here. Naomi sat down, screeched the chair across the wood floor, and turned her back to Bridget.

With her back still turned, she said, "Did you kidnap me?"

"Did you feel kidnapped? We fled from the people who hurt Nick and probably your mother. You and I were next on their list."

Naomi turned; her eyes were red. "This better work. I'm living with my dad, no matter what they say. Why are you clenching your fists?"

She loosened her grip, and blood returned to her hands. Elaine tiptoed to Naomi, arms outstretched, the vision of grandmotherly concern.

"Naomi, silly girl. What have you gotten yourself into? Are you alright?" She smoothed Naomi's hair.

Naomi jerked her head from her hand. "Ew. Go away."

Elaine covered her mouth like she was about to cry. "Of course you're upset," she mumbled as she returned to the wooden pew.

Across the courtroom, Diane squeezed by the police officers. She plopped two legal pads on the defense table—one for Bridget, one for Naomi—and a thick file folder labeled *In the Interest of N.K.*, a water bottle, and a granola bar.

"I sent everyone notice of today's hearing, and I followed up with a phone call. Court admin set up the hearing once I told them the press might come," said Diane, pausing as she saw the cuffs. "And here are pens. I suppose you still can write with handcuffs." Bridget opened her mouth to explain, but Diane held up her hand. "I don't want to know. I have a couple of messages."

She held up a notepad and read, her reading glasses balancing on her nose.

"From your Aunt Irene: 'Chin up, even if your neck is dirty.'

Or when your wrists are cuffed. And she's got the bail money. Next message from Walter. He says, 'I have the car. Why'd you buy new tires?'"

Diane peered over her glasses.

"What?" Naomi grabbed the note and read it. "That's so messed up."

"I left the car in a cornfield with the tires shot out. The car wasn't drivable," she explained to Diane.

"Maybe it was an alien invasion? Too bad they didn't get you a new car."

She opened the water bottle, drained it, and ripped open the granola bar. She stole another glance at French. Did he presume she was lying when she reported her car? Did French know the car was now at her house?

Mark interrupted her musings. "McGarrity, the press is in the courtroom. What's your position on publicity?"

"The press? You hold them down while I kick."

"Seriously. The newspaper's lawyer contacted our office." Mark folded his arms.

"I hold the reporters down while you kick? I'm a little rusty on first amendment law, but Naomi is a child, and protecting her interests is a compelling interest. Her name or picture cannot appear anywhere. Let's be straight: the press doesn't care about the kid. They like pictures with attorneys in handcuffs, and I think they got plenty already. What judge do we have?"

"Strickland. He cleared his calendar for you."

Great, she thought as she devoured the granola bar. "Strickland and I are BFFs for life. He probably has already decided. What about Naomi's request to be placed with her dad?"

"Social services are against it, and so is the state."

Naomi screeched the chair across the floor again.

"Is there any information that I could provide to persuade you otherwise?" asked Bridget.

The creak of an oak door and the sucking sounds of rubber orthopedic shoes on a wooden floor interrupted their conversation.

# Chapter 43

"ALL RISE! The Honorable Judge Strickland presiding."

"Thank you. Please sit down. Bailiff, open the doors," said Strickland, his sonorous voice projecting through the courtroom.

A herd of reporters and cameramen shuffled into the courtroom. Judge Strickland sat, hands folded on the bench, quietly observing. As soon as the press assembled in the gallery rows, he began the proceedings. Anticipating an argument, Strickland addressed the press.

"There's nothing in our state or federal constitutions that bars the press at a juvenile hearing. However, statutes and regulations are replete with protections for the child, and all are constitutionally sound."

"Do you have a supporting case law for that proposition, Judge?" shouted one journalist.

"Who said that?" Strickland's glare could melt ice.

"I did," waved one reporter, a younger man, with a yellow Hawkeye cap on his head. He looked more independent blogger than a TV reporter.

"Please stand and identify yourself."

"Todd Arnold from *Cedar Town Reporter.*"

"Mr. Arnold, next time you interrupt these proceedings, you'll have a police escort out of this courtroom. Is that clear?"

The reporter nodded. "I get it."

"Good, I'm glad you 'get it.' Remove your hat, Mr. Arnold."

He slowly removed his hat as he sat down. The other reporters barely moved, like straight-A students.

"You can write that in your article as well." Strickland's full bass voice resonated through the now-crowded courtroom. "As I was saying, no law bars the press in juvenile proceedings. However, the identity of the child shall remain unknown. Therefore, I allow the press, but no cameras or any other recording devices. And I mean any. Pens only, reporters."

"Judge, we can edit out the child's face. We've done it before," said a reporter holding a camera.

"Interrupting again? Bailiff, escort this man from the courtroom."

"Oh, come on, I just—"

"Say another word, and I'll hold you in contempt. Neither you nor your colleagues will disturb this proceeding."

The room fell silent as the bailiff escorted the reporter out the door.

"Who's that?" asked Naomi. Heads turned as a large-bellied man in a gray suit with a bow tie opened the courtroom doors with a whoosh.

"Nobody good," said Bridget.

"I apologize to the court for my tardiness. I just arrived from Cedar Town and didn't receive notice of today's proceedings. I hereby enter my appearance on behalf of Elaine Kline. My name is Alan Barshefsky of Whitfield & Barshefsky." He turned his head to Bridget, looking calm as a python ready to strike. "Good to see you again, counselor."

Bridget bit the inside of her cheek. Barshefsky wasn't on the case and wouldn't get notice of the hearings. There was no reason to send him anything. Elaine knew, however. Barshefsky's comments confused the press and made her look bad. She stood to speak.

"Sit down, counselor. You'll get your turn, Ms. McGarrity," Strickland said.

She quieted, heeding the judge's advice as lights hummed and the air thickened from the packed courtroom.

After giving the "who's who" in the courtroom as the reporters diligently scribbled their notes, the judge directed Bridget to proceed.

"Ms. McGarrity, all the parties received and reviewed your request to transfer placement of the child from her grandmother, Elaine Kline, to her father. You may proceed, Ms. McGarrity."

She looked around the courtroom and contemplated everyone there—the social worker sitting in the front row; Mark Evans, the county attorney, shuffling through papers; Judge Strickland; and Chief French—her self-proclaimed adversaries. The same people and the institutions they represented that she had been fighting since she was a child. But were they the enemy? The fallacy that she languished in foster care because of a faulty system was just that—a fantasy. Aunt Irene hadn't wanted her and her brother, not at the beginning. Truth was that family could be no better than strangers.

"I call Elaine Kline to the stand."

Calling Elaine first to the stand was risky. The usual protocol dictated that she offer background testimony and recommendations from a social worker, maybe the parents, or even the child. Bridget didn't have the luxury because the emergency hearing was set only for an hour.

Alan Barshefsky stood slowly and deliberately. His awkward posture drew attention as he cleared his throat. Bridget squinted her eyes at him, wanting to pounce. He was deliberately stalling. He knew Bridget had little time.

"Your Honor, on behalf of my client, Elaine Kline, we object to these entire proceedings. The allegations made by the child and Ms. McGarrity are misdirected and false. There's no emergency."

Strickland interrupted, "Are you saying that I was incorrect in granting this hearing?"

"No, Judge, I—"

"Good. Need I remind you, Mr. Barshefsky, the child's mother has died. A review is necessary. Your objection is noted."

"Elaine Kline should not have to testify at all. And I didn't receive notice of the hearing!"

Bridget couldn't hold back. "Golly gee, Mr. Barshefsky, maybe you should fire that secretary of yours, Sally Avery? You know, the one who set up the bank account for Sun Family Foundation. I look forward to meeting her."

"You're crazy," said Barshefsky.

"You mean Sally Avery doesn't work at Whitfield & Barshefsky, Al?" She wished she had the entire day for this hearing. This was the most fun she'd had in two weeks.

"Enough, counselors," said Strickland. "Mr. Barshefsky, you were not the attorney of record and, therefore, not entitled to notice. However, your client is here, so she did receive notice, correct?"

"Yes."

"The venerable office of Whitfield & Barshefsky employs perhaps one, two, or maybe no attorneys who regularly practice juvenile law? I'll refrain from determining your requisite competency to represent Ms. Kline in this proceeding. If you are not qualified, you will self-report your ethics violation to the Office of Professional Regulation."

Barshefsky sat down and avoided Bridget, who beamed,

relishing his dismal performance.

The judge continued. "Ms. McGarrity is one of the preeminent attorney advocates for children in this county. Mr. Barshefsky, I suggest you consult her on honing your skills."

Snickers erupted in the gallery, and Bridget stood a little straighter. Positive recognition from Strickland, while shackled, was unexpected and welcomed.

"Thank you, Judge." She hoisted her sore arms. "Could someone please remove these?"

Judge Strickland's mouth slackened, which was the closest thing to shock that she had ever seen from Strickland.

"Chief French? Explanation?" asked Strickland.

French stood, hanging a thumb on his belt. "That's standard for AMBER Alert."

"An alert that has been canceled, of course?"

French coughed. "Sure, Judge."

"Bailiff, remove the cuffs."

As the officer removed Bridget's cuffs, the courtroom quieted. Bridget rubbed her sore wrists, fresh with bruises.

Elaine Kline walked to the witness stand, rubbing her hands on synthetic slacks. She frowned at her lawyer, who had failed to keep her off the stand. Bridget turned briefly to the gallery, ensuring all backup witnesses were in place. They were. She gathered her thoughts. A lawyer could spend up to an hour soliciting background information from the witness asking questions like name, age, occupation, residence, family, and the like. However, being direct and fast was essential as she had limited time. She figured she had about five minutes before chaos erupted.

"You are the legal guardian of Cheri Kline, correct?"

"Yes, I'm Elaine Kline. My daughter is, I mean, was Cheri Kline. When we lived in Oklah—"

"'Yes' will suffice," she interrupted. "But you're not Cheri's birth mother or adoptive mother? You're the legal guardian, correct?"

"Those things are not important."

"Please answer what I ask. You set up a guardianship for Cheri, correct?" asked Bridget.

"Why, yes, she was two years old. An orphan. And she needed—"

"As a legal guardian, you managed any money she would receive or inherit. Correct?" Elaine clasped her hands together to her chest and looked down. "Mrs. Kline, please answer."

"Yes." Elaine's gaze shifted from the judge to Naomi to her attorney.

"If you had adopted her, she wouldn't have received any inheritance. Correct?"

Elaine cast her eyes downward as she buttoned and re-buttoned the top of her jacket. "I guess."

"Because she had a lot of money, correct?"

"No. Not a lot," said Elaine.

"When Cheri turned eighteen, you established a conservatorship?"

"She couldn't care for the baby because she was gone all the time. In the end, she agreed to it, to the conservatorship."

"Ms. Kline, Cheri is an enrolled member of the Osage Nation, correct?"

Elaine whispered, "I don't—"

"You're under oath."

"Yes."

"Cheri, like other tribal members, is entitled to headright payments, correct?"

"I'm not sure how it works."

"But you know how to cash a check, don't you? Last year's payment to Cheri was approximately eighteen thousand?"

"About," whispered Elaine.

"And eighteen thousand is not much money?"

"Why are you asking these things?"

Elaine pulled tissues from her purse, and Barshefsky cleared his throat. "I object, Your Honor. The line of questioning is irrelevant and harassing."

The judge removed his reading glasses, balancing them on his hand, and yawned.

Bridget quickly responded before Judge Strickland could rule. "Financial resources have everything to do with raising children. Also, this is a CINA case, not a criminal proceeding. The evidence standard differs."

"Overruled. Sit down, Mr. Barshefsky."

Bridget continued her questioning. "Now that Cheri is deceased, you want her daughter to let you manage her money, correct?"

"I guess so."

Elaine smoothed her skirt and removed a piece of lint from the armchair. Naomi tugged Bridget's shirt, and after the third tug, Bridget excused herself.

"Can it wait?" Bridget asked Naomi.

"I don't want to live with him. Why is he here?"

"Who?"

"My uncle. He's in the back," Naomi whispered.

Bridget glanced back over her shoulder and spotted the back of a man leaving the courtroom--tall with broad shoulders, wearing unassuming corduroy pants, leather dress boots. And a watch big as a dumbbell reflected in the light.

*Damn.*

Bridget swung around and looked at Elaine, stiff as a board. Her fidgeting had paused. Barshefsky chuckled.

"That can't be your uncle, Jay Kline. Because that—"

"Ms. McGarrity? Do try to focus," said Strickland.

Bridget reached for a water bottle, but it was empty. She

clenched her shaking hand and looked at the back of the courtroom again to Naomi's uncle, who had turned his head. His eyes met Bridget's and a cruel grin stretched across his face. Realization surged through her like an electromagnetic pulse. She had been played from the beginning. How could she be so stupid?

She knew the man, but not as Jay Kline. She knew him by another name—Chet Russell.

\*\*\*

"Ms. McGarrity? Please proceed. You did state that was an emergency hearing."

"Yes," Bridget said, her voice barely audible.

Her eyes closed for a moment as realization set in. She had been played from the beginning. Chet had done everything to distract her—from dangling promising new opportunities, a malpractice suit, Nick, to running them off the road, all of it. And his dear mother, Elaine, had helped him. Chet/Jay had done everything to divert her from the one thing she was supposed to do—protect Naomi.

How could she continue? Jay/Chet had to be stopped, arrested, or at least detained. She looked to the judge, to Naomi, and Chief French. She would have to stop the proceeding to have him detained, but she wasn't sure it would even work. Who would believe her?

The most urgent matter was Naomi, who had to have her day in court, and her first step was to get her away from the grips of Elaine Kline.

*Let's get to it.*

"Isn't it true that a medical assistant has access to fentanyl?"

asked Bridget.

Elaine's face turned pale with a faint yellow hue.

"I'm only a medical assistant."

"You're in daily contact with medication like fentanyl and oxycodone, isn't that correct?" Bridget gestured toward Connie in the gallery. "Your colleagues at the hospital would confirm that, wouldn't they?"

Her eyes dashed from her attorney to the beaming face of Connie. Elaine's shoulders sagged as if something had been taken from her, and she then looked longingly at the man who had just entered the door, her son, Jay Kline.

She shook her head. "I didn't do this."

"And Cheri wasn't a drinker, was she?"

"No. She never drank booze because it messed with the psych meds."

"Isn't it true that fentanyl can be lethal? Especially if mixed with other prescriptions?"

Elaine wiped her hands on her slacks and cast a pleading glance at Barshefsky, as did the judge, waiting for him to make an objection. None came.

Bridget continued. "Fentanyl combined with her psychiatric medications could be lethal."

"I didn't mean it! I mean, I don't know."

Animated conversation erupted in the gallery. Bridget waited, allowing everyone in the room to digest what they had heard.

"Mean what, Elaine? What did you do?" she asked softly.

Barshefsky's corporal self stood abruptly, almost tipping the table in front of him. The action may have surprised others, but she had expected him to object much sooner, and she could tell the judge did, too. He should have never let Bridget ask those questions unless, of course, he wanted Elaine to admit her role.

"I must object. This hearing is about transferring custody of the child away from Ms. Kline, not crazy accusations of foul play."

"What role Elaine Kline had in Cheri's life is relevant as to whether Naomi should live with her or any of the Klines," said Bridget.

Strickland's face smoothed. She knew what Barshefsky did not know, that Strickland enjoyed the exchange between attorneys and the palpable energy of the courtroom. Many judges would halt the banter between attorneys, but Strickland embraced it.

Bridget continued. "And relevant are criminal charges against Naomi originating from Elaine Kline. Accusations range from theft of a headright check to a stolen car. I'll take a wild guess that you requested the AMBER Alert, Mrs. Kline?"

"I object and demand a five-minute break to consult with my client," said Barshefsky.

He was stalling again. The hair raised on her neck as she briefly glanced back to the rear of the courtroom. Chet's eyes shifted from Bridget to Elaine, like a cat spotting a bird.

"Ms. McGarrity, are you with us?" asked Judge Strickland.

"The only reason Barshefsky needs a break is to provide his client with answers to my questions, which is improper."

"The inquiry seeks solely to incriminate. She's entitled to the protection of the fifth amendment," he said.

"The questions benefit the child. It's her interests that we're concerned with in this proceeding, not Elaine Kline's," she retorted.

"I agree. Ms. McGarrity, you may continue."

So far, Bridget did what she had intended—expose Elaine's financial interest. Implicating her in Cheri's death was not planned, but the words had been uttered, although not quite a confession. There finally would be an investigation into Cheri's death, and that revelation should keep Naomi from Elaine's reach. She could stop now. But why? She had been given the green light. The roller coaster ride was not over.

"You talked Cheri into leaving the hospital, didn't you? Convinced the staff you were by her side, so they would be comfortable with her leaving. Isn't that correct?"

"Leading, Your Honor," objected Barshefsky.

"She's a hostile witness. It's allowed," defended Bridget.

"I take the fifth. Is that right? The fifth?" said Elaine, who had paid attention to her lawyer's objection about incrimination and now figured out what to say.

"At the hospital, you gave Cheri your car keys, didn't you? And then you called the police and told them Naomi stole your car."

Elaine was speechless and wiped a tear. The courtroom was silent as she covered her face with her hands, wilting in the chair. She seemed to age before them.

"Or was someone else giving you instructions, like your son?" asked Bridget.

"No, it's me. It's all true," said Elaine, burying her face in her hands.

"You killed Cheri Kline, didn't you?" said Bridget, gripping the table.

"No. I didn't mean it, and it shouldn't have hurt Cheri. I had to do something. Naomi stays with me and not in a shelter...a little less pain, oxycodone. She was so troubled and should have stayed away. That's all it was. Something to relax her."

# Chapter 44

"No!" Naomi screamed, slapping her hand on the defense table, ready for a reckoning with Elaine. "I hate you!"

Naomi moved toward Elaine, but her dad was not a millisecond behind her. Steve jumped over the front guard pew, landing next to Naomi. His protective arms encircled her, consoling her and giving her privacy from inquisitive reporters. He guided her to the chair.

Gasps and hushed comments pounded through the gallery, and a few reporters slid from their seats, alerting editors. Bridget sat down, her body folding in fatigue but trying to maintain her composure. Elaine's admission didn't escape the child, and she understood it all.

Not skipping a heartbeat, Chief French walked towards Elaine with a solemnness that would make the dead cry. A reverent silence fell over the courtroom as Chief French requested Elaine to come with him. Barshefsky, frowning, rose to speak, awaiting silence in the courtroom so all could admire his posturing. It didn't come. Instead, Barshefsky slammed his folder on the table and walked to Bridget.

"You are in way over your head. This isn't over," he hissed.

She recoiled as she felt the heat of his stale breath. Judge Strickland pounded the wooden gavel until silence enveloped them.

"Mr. Barshefsky, you'd better accompany your client. Ms. McGarrity, I grant your application. I will transfer placement of Naomi Kline to be with her father, Stephen Ross, with custody to remain with the Department of Human Services. The Department may continue to offer services to the family."

Daughter and father embraced, and Bridget sighed in relief. Naomi could be with her dad, no longer the orphan.

Strickland continued. "Any other objections from the Department of Human Services or the State?"

Mark Evans and the DHS quickly consented, which wasn't surprising. Bridget had saved them from returning Naomi to a dangerous home.

Bridget hugged Naomi, feeling strength return, and then hugged her a little tighter as if she were her own daughter. She turned towards the gallery. Connie, cracking gum, gave her the thumbs up, and she mouthed a thank you in return. Connie's presence in the courtroom worked. Just her being present had rattled Elaine.

Naomi sobbed into Bridget's shoulder, and she wiped tears from her own eyes. Tissues appeared out of nowhere for both of them.

A knot in her stomach loosened slightly. She recalled Aunt Irene's advice—keep your chin up, even if your neck is dirty. She rose to speak, straightening her spine, despite tousled hair and wrinkled clothes. She continued to hold Naomi's hand.

"Ms. McGarrity?" Judge Strickland asked.

"Given the circumstances and my... 'trip' with Naomi, I agree to withdraw as Naomi's attorney and guardian ad litem."

Judge Strickland placed his reading glasses on the bench as the gallery quieted.

"Your actions protected this child when this court and every other professional in this room could not. I deny your request. These proceedings are ended."

The judge exited and a rush of reporters stood in the courtroom, some approaching the defense table, but the bailiff shooed them outside.

"You're still my lawyer?" asked Naomi.

"Yes, but there won't be too much to do now. Good news, right?"

"Are they going to put Elaine in jail? I hope they do, forever."

A caseworker walked over to them. "I'm Rachel from the Department of Human Services. We can have you meet a coworker today about housing, Mr. Ross, and talk about job placement. The Department will make sure Mr. Ross knows of the many resources out there."

"Wow. OK, then. Can you fix my bike as well?" said Steve.

Bridget continued, "Speaking of which, buy a helmet for Naomi if you're going to be riding around on that thing." Bridget gently nudged Naomi. "I'm only trying to save you from endless bad hair days."

Naomi didn't seem to hear them as she watched the flow of people moving in and out of the courtroom. Bridget looked as well. Chet/Jay was not among them, but she expected she would not see him again. She would have to have a long talk with Naomi and Steve about him, but she didn't think Naomi could have the conversation now.

How did she not know that Chet Russell was Jay Kline? The file, of course, never had a picture of him. When she met Chet at the detention center, Naomi didn't see him since she hid in the Suburban. Elaine had also taken down all of her pictures in her house before Bridget visited. She searched for Chief French, but he had already left.

Jay had to be detained, and Bridget needed to tell someone about him, but an intense need to see her own family grew. She'd been gone only two days, but it felt like years.

The assistant county attorney, Mark Evans, walked over to Bridget.

"You can leave through the back if you need to. Take your time. The bailiff will show the way out."

"You need to find Naomi's uncle and arrest him. His name is Jay Kline. He tried to detract me from this case."

"Distracting an attorney from the case. Sounds like a felony."

"Funny, but he's involved in this. I think he was behind all this, and he was directing his mother. Please talk to Chief French or any police officer. They'll listen to you quicker than me."

"Sure, McGarrity. Anybody else you want to be arrested or confess to murder?" asked Mark.

She buried her hands in her jacket pocket and found a fistful of compressed cornhusk and dirt. She let the soil run through her fingers and shook the debris off her hands. Had she really been shot at and forced to trash her car in a cornfield? It felt unreal, yet her jacket pocket was full of dirt. Would she be able to explain everything that happened?

"I'm not even going to ask why you have that much dirt in your pocket."

She took his hand and placed the mass into his palm. "It's cornhusk and pure Midwest topsoil. Do me a favor, Mark, give it to Chief French. Tell him it's from me."

"Do what?"

"You owe me." Bridget batted her eyelashes.

"For what?"

"You almost placed this child with a killer."

"Fine. I'll deliver dirt and corn. This day couldn't get any stranger. Stay safe, McGarrity."

Mark poured the crushed cornhusk and dirt into an envelope and left through the back of the courtroom.

The new social worker, Rachel, continued to counsel Steve and Naomi, informing them of what to expect. Naomi would be in a new school district and would have temporary housing that would remain confidential and unlisted. Neither the media nor Elaine would know their location.

Bridget and Naomi hugged.

"This is a terrible shock. I'm so sorry about your mother. At least you're safe now. No one will know where you and Dad are staying. Not even me."

"What about that social worker, Nick?" asked Naomi. Her voice was flat, and her face pale.

"He's still sedated," answered Rachel.

Naomi stared past them, her thoughts elsewhere, and they couldn't shake the child from her solemn contemplation. Bridget considered telling Naomi about her uncle, but she didn't see how it could help her at this moment. She was dealing with enough.

"Come on, you two, lighten up. You best be on your way. I got this," said Steve.

"Right, you go ahead, Bridget," said Rachel, probably relieved not to be dealing with a lawyer.

"Glad this is over," Bridget said.

A man behind her cleared his voice.

"Excuse me, Ms. McGarrity?"

Bridget placed her hand on her stomach; the knot still hadn't loosened. What now?

\*\*\*

"Perhaps you'd like to dabble more in corporate law?" said a voice behind her.

"Mr..... I'm sorry, I can't remember your name." I need food, Bridget thought.

"Cal Roberts, from Buyland." He stood ten feet from her, his hands buried in khaki pant pockets. "I saw you on the news. Somewhat curious, you being at our office, and Buyland's lawsuit with the reservation. Did that kid's grandma admit to murder?"

"Looks that way, yes."

He buried his hands deeper into his pockets. "Why were you really at my office?"

Bridget rubbed her sore wrists as she pondered what to say. "I was looking for a connection with Buyland's lawsuit and her death. I didn't find one. I thought maybe Buyland was responsible. Sorry, I was wrong."

He scratched the stubble on his chin. He looked like he hadn't shaved since the last time she saw him.

"Maybe you're not wrong," he said. "Buyland is being bought out. Penny General, our competitor, made an offer we couldn't refuse. Penny will handle the lawsuit with the reservation, so no more lawyer fees for us."

Bridget steadied herself on the bench while longing for water, a decent meal, a shower, and maybe a bath, too. Naomi left the courtroom with her father and social worker. She felt guilty for trying to drag Cal Roberts into her investigation. He still had questions like she did. Finding Elaine had been involved was surprising but unsatisfying.

Penny General was the same company John Wapello mentioned because they'd worried that Buyland would sell or was a target for a takeover.

He focused on the ceiling like he was somewhere else, searching, and he said, "I told the lawyers about you when I pressed for settlement. I said another attorney thought agreeing to the tribal court's jurisdiction was an excellent strategy."

"The attorneys, let me guess, Whitfield & Barshefsky?"

He resumed scratching his beard and directed his gaze from the ceiling to the window. "Huh. Whitfield & Barshefsky lobbies for the Wisaka Nation. How d'you know?"

"Elaine Kline's lawyer is Alan Barshefsky. He sued me for malpractice in a different case, and that was him up there today. I can't say that I'm feeling any professional admiration."

Cal shook his head. "Whitfield & Barshefsky's name showed up during the negotiations with Penny General—both lawyer and lobbyists. That's double-dipping. Stinks, doesn't it? The Wisaka Nation must also be paying a fortune. There's something fishy going on here, and I can't figure out how I lost my family's company. As soon as we got this contract with the reservation, we were done for."

Bridget thought about the envelopes of money, which stank of corruption, but nailing Barshefsky hadn't happened. At least Naomi and her own family were safe, even if the victory felt hollow.

"My client is safe, and my family is safe," she said.

"They ran right over us, like a freight train. You don't look so hot."

Diane saved the day. "I'm kicking you out. Bridget, you look like hell, and you can't afford to pay me overtime. I'll bring everything back to the office, and your ride is outside. Sir, here's her card. Call her. Like next month, unless you're a paying client."

Diane handed Roberts a business card. She then felt Diane's hand on her back as she guided her toward the door.

"I wish you the best," Bridget said, but he had already turned to leave.

It was all over. But why didn't she feel better?

# Chapter 45

She exited the building through the back and directly into the parking lot. Despite her years of practice, she had never left the Lincoln County Courthouse other than through the main entrance. Rarely were her cases in the spotlight.

The parking lot was quiet, and except for the cars, there was nothing. She stopped cold in her tracks. How did that get there? Over the cracked blacktop parking lot was her Pontiac Grand Am, fixed and new and without a scratch.

Then a man stepped out from behind the car. Hands in jeans and a brushed ponytail at his neck, he winked at her.

"Walter! Thank God it's you. Everything OK?" Bridget and Walter embraced, long but casually, as only life partners could. "You weren't in the courtroom, were you?"

He shook his head. "Not my scene."

"Good. And I'm sorry for all this, for being gone," she said.

"You missed a ton. Aiden did a front flip off the diving board. They finally chose an accent color for the Victorian—"

Bridget embraced him again.

"Aiden is with Aunt Irene, and he's sure eager to see you. Could we sneak a little 'us time' first?"

"That would be amazing."

"You let me in on the details. I don't think Diane will ever speak to me again. I called her, um, more than once. You weren't answering. She covers for you well."

Walter's pale eyes reflected the clear blue sky, and his arm encircled her waist.

"I didn't tell Diane much."

"The grandma did it?"

"Yes, the grandma did it." A random reporter snapped a photo. Hand in hand, they walked faster towards the car.

\*\*\*

At home, Bridget relished the chance to be the queen of her house once more. She took a roast from the freezer, fantasizing about a feast for her family. Grilled vegetables, potatoes with fresh rosemary sprigs that were big enough for Aiden to pick off, and a sliced medium-rare roast. She'd skip corn this time. A bottle of sparkling apple juice cooled in the fridge, and a glass of red wine rested in her scratched hands.

Aiden ran inside, his backpack bouncing on his back. "Mommeeee! You were gone! You came back." He paused and frowned. "Colby says you're in trouble."

Aiden's questions and comments fired one after another, and she nodded without answering a single one.

"Did you want hors d'oeuvres before your dinner?"

"'Hor' what? What's that?"

"Let's start with another hug."

Aiden squealed in delight, running from the house into the

backyard. All was quiet, and everything was where it should be. Determined not to be disturbed, she ignored every phone call, although they all twitched every time the house phone rang. A lost cell phone was the least of her worries.

After their perfect meal, Walter could ignore the phone no longer. "So much for the unlisted phone number. Let me take care of this."

Walter hadn't retreated to the garage once. It was so lovely, she thought. He answered the phone and then hung up in frustration.

"Another hang-up."

He took two steps, and it rang again. He answered it.

"Another hang-up! That's what happened last week, before your, um, 'vacation.'"

She barely heard him. Her thoughts ricocheted from images of Naomi's uncle in the courtroom to Cal Robert's conversation at the courthouse. Elaine admitted to harming, maybe even murdering, Cheri. Yet Naomi's uncle was free as a bird, and Cal Robert had lost his family business. Although 'lost' was likely a stretch because Cal probably made a lot of money on the deal, even if selling his family business wasn't something he wanted. Who was winning here? And why did Bridget feel like she lost? At least she was home, safe with her family. Naomi was also safe.

The phone rang again, and Walter walked toward the phone.

"Leave it," she said.

"The caller ID says the Department of Human Services."

"I'll get it." Bridget skipped to the phone. "Since when do you guys hound attorneys at home? Can we talk about boundaries?"

"Bridget McGarrity? This is Rachel, from social services, Naomi's new caseworker. Sorry to bother you at home. We tried your mobile."

"My phone went missing, and I was enjoying that." Bridget pictured her abandoned phone in her car and sighed.

"Is Naomi Kline with you?"

"What? Naomi Kline? She's not with me. She's with her father, of course, while social services hovers over her like a hungry guard dog."

Walter shooed Aiden out of the room. Rachel cleared her throat.

"Um, well... no one's seen her since the courthouse. Naomi apparently ran away again."

"Apparently? And again? She didn't run away; she fled. Have you considered she was taken?"

Rachel launched into a sing-song voice like she was reading a prepared statement. "Teenagers in her situation may run, as you know. Naomi chose to argue with me at the courthouse, distressed about delays in finding housing."

"You need to consider that you're wrong. Dead wrong. Naomi's been taken."

"The police were notified." Rachel cleared her throat again. "We thought, perhaps, you two took off again, but now we know that's not the case. You deny she's with you?"

Bridget's eyes narrowed. "Yes, I deny. Are you accusing me, Rachel?"

"Do call us if she shows."

"I will." Bridget slammed the phone.

Bridget didn't know whether to cry or punch a wall. Social services wasn't taking Naomi's absence seriously. This ordeal was supposed to be over because Elaine had confessed, yet many questions remained unanswered. She buried her hands in her hair, thinking where Naomi could be.

Unfortunately, the conversation about Naomi's uncle would have to wait because Elaine was in custody and confronting her wasn't an option. Because of her imminent criminal charges,

Barshefsky would never allow Bridget near her.

Walter placed a cell phone on the table. "Here's your phone. It was in the car, and I forgot to tell you about it. It's charged." He rubbed her shoulders and kissed her neck. "I missed you."

"You kept Aiden safe during my, what did you call it, 'vacation'? Thank you."

She thumbed through the missed calls. A number she didn't recognize called twice. As she placed the phone back on the table, the phone vibrated—the same unknown number again. Her happy, sated stomach soured.

"It's me."

"Naomi? You have everyone worried. Where are you?"

A rustling was in the background and cicadas were chirping. Naomi was outside.

"I don't want to... I sort of ran away again. Can you come get me? But you can't call the police. It's so dark," she said through faint sobs.

Bridget should wait for social services and the police to respond. She knew it wasn't her job to get Naomi. What was her job?

"I understand, Naomi, more than you realize. Where are you?"

"On the reservation. Near where my mom—"

The line went dead. The reservation, where else? It was the perfect place.

She scurried to the kitchen, drank a generous glass of water, and looked outside, seeing only her pale reflection in the windowpane. Night had descended—the long days of late summer were never long enough. She opened the front closet, laced her gym shoes, and skipped down to the basement as Walter followed.

"Everything OK?" asked Walter.

"Naomi. I'm going to pick her up."

She dusted off a metal stool and dragged it to the storage cabinets, which contained years of accumulated mess: a baby crib and bath, old clothing, toys—a shotgun.

She stretched her torso and stretched her arm over the top shelf. Walter paced behind her. After finding the shotgun, she pulled it out from the shelf along with a bucketful of plastic dinosaurs tumbling to the floor.

"Is that Uncle Billy's shotgun? I thought you threw that thing away," stammered Walter.

"I couldn't bring myself to throw it out."

"You hated pheasant hunting. You never hunted with Billy again."

"I know. I hated it, so I said."

She gathered several items that hadn't been touched for years, including a heavy metal flashlight and a hunting knife.

"Let somebody else take care of this. You can't handle a gun," he said.

"I don't intend to use it. I'll call 911 and social services."

She dialed 911 and gave them Naomi's cell phone number and Bridget's best guess as to the location where she identified Cheri. The dispatcher promised to connect the reservation for a response. She dialed Rachel but reached voicemail. She left a detailed message with the same information.

"You've called, and that's enough."

"The police will be there before me. I want to see that she is safe and make sure this is over. As far as the gun goes, consider it my alternative lifestyle—an accessory to my drab wardrobe. I prefer a shotgun in my car after the last couple of days." She balanced on her toes and kissed Walter. "Everything will be fine."

"Call that police chief or the kid's dad."

"Great idea, but I don't have Chief French's home number on speed dial. I'm not even sure Steve has a phone," she said.

She found fresh batteries for the flashlight in the kitchen

drawer and stuffed the items into the duffel bag.

Walter put a trembling hand on her shoulder. "I can't stand this. Why go? Please stay."

"When Aunt Irene took us in, Uncle Billy didn't have to do a thing for me like taking me pheasant hunting, helping with college, fixing up the house, any of it. What was I to him—his lover's niece? But he did. He took care of us. He did everything for us. And I recently learned he cleaned up Aunt Irene, too." She found a rag and wiped years of dust from the barrel. "I couldn't bring myself to give the gun away. Uncle Billy was a good guy. And I miss him."

"You don't need to do this," Walter said.

"No, I don't. Neither did Billy." She gently pulled him toward her, giving him a long deep kiss, burying a hand in his thick hair.

"We haven't talked about the car and the chase through a cornfield and blown tires? The car looks better than ever. The police chief thought I was crazy," he said.

"I was set up, and it worked. I looked like a crazy kid-snatching lawyer and was put in handcuffs! Do me a favor, if Chief French calls, ask him whether he got my present from the county attorney, Mark Evans."

Walter's eyebrows drew together. "Your present? I don't understand."

"It'll be fine. I'm sorry, but I have to go."

Walter's head was downcast, studying the floor. He raised his hand as in mid-thought and followed her up the staircase and headed to the garage.

# Chapter 46

The Indian reservation had attracted all sorts: philanthropists, hippies, opportunists, priests promising salvation, and, too often, the greedy. Bridget didn't fit into any category. The reservation was the last place she wanted to be, and she knew Naomi would not go there, not willingly.

On the state highway, a straight stretch of a hundred miles, Bridget sped along the road towards the reservation. If the police pulled her over, that would be fine. At least she would have company. She detangled her matted curls as she ran through all the events and people she'd dealt with: Barshefsky, Chet, the family that sued Buyland, Scott, and Joe Monroe, who supported them. She couldn't shake Cal Robert's words—they ran right over her, like a freight train.

She called the number Naomi used several times, but no response. She then called a number for the reservation but reached only a recorded message with the community center's hours. She was confident 911 reached whom they needed to and was already there. Calling Walter also crossed her mind, but she decided against it. He might talk her into turning around.

After an hour, Bridget reached the reservation and drove past the casino and the Buyland store. She followed the single-lane road deep into the reservation as the full moon emerged from under a cloud, illuminating the tangled brush. A faint glow emanated from the closest town of 10,000 people fifteen miles away. Any action for the next fifty square miles would be at the casino—a windowless fortress encasing a cacophony of slot machines, piped music, and nervous gamblers.

The reservation was quiet, dead quiet. She expected sirens or flashing lights, but there was nothing. Why weren't the police there? That was well over an hour ago. Something should've happened by now. Then again, possibly they had already secured Naomi and left.

Bridget parked the car because navigating in the dark and while on a cell phone wasn't safe. The last time she was here, a tribal police officer flanked her. Now she was alone, which was not the plan. She swallowed to rid herself of the foul taste forming in her mouth. She put the hunting knife in her back pocket and pulled her shirt over the blade as her mobile rang.

"Bridget McGarrity?"

"Who is this?" Bridget stepped out of the car.

"This is Officer Blake with Lincoln County. We understand that Naomi Kline is with you, and we're asking that you cooperate."

"Are you serious? Officer, I'm sorry, Blake? You've been misled—"

"Two witnesses identified you leaving Lincoln County with Naomi Kline."

"I left, yes, but alone. The report is a lie." She nervously searched around her; all was black. "Did you attend the hearing today?"

"No. My officers informed me how they brought you in—

handcuffed."

"Please call Chief French."

"Mrs. McGarrity, bring in the child. We can handle this."

"Listen to my words." She talked slowly as if she were addressing a toddler. "I do not have her. She is in danger, and you have been misled. I'm at the Wisaka Reservation."

"Turn yourself in, Bridget—"

She heard a twig crack, and she tucked the phone into her front pocket. She was right near where they found Cheri. A cloud covered the moon as the hair on her neck rose. Behind her, a man coughed. She froze.

"Naomi?"

Her voice bounced off the brush and traveled nowhere. The night was still, and the brushwood crunched under her feet. She called Naomi's name again. Her voice fell flat. Everything was quiet, like she was under an airless dome.

She slowly searched around her as she retreated toward her car, spotted her gun through the window, and opened the driver's door. Bridget didn't get far. The car door slammed on her legs behind her, and a hand grabbed her hair. The attacker shoved her away from him. As she struggled for balance, she spotted Naomi.

# Chapter 47

Naomi lay on the ground, her hair disheveled with duct tape binding her mouth, ankles, and wrists. She gazed up, her eyes wide and fearful. Bridget was too shocked to move, and her heart raced, but fear was morphing into anger. How can anyone do this to a child? She spun around as her aggressor had scurried away like a shifty squirrel. She stepped carefully towards Naomi.

The brush rustled behind her, and with a swoosh of air, a sharp pain seared in her calves. Her feet soared toward the sky, and she landed flat on her back, gasping for air. The fall had knocked the wind out of her. A piercing white moon momentarily distracted her as she struggled to move. She cursed her carelessness as a face materialized above her, blocking the glow of the moon.

"Kill two birds with one stone. This is too easy."

She squinted, trying to focus on the dark silhouette, and raised her hand to block the moonlight.

"What I'm not sure is whether the kid is going to kill you or you're going to kill the kid. Perhaps a double suicide. How about a note? Did you bring your pen, Bridget?"

She edged closer to Naomi, placing herself between him and the child. The fight should be two against one, but Naomi lay silent, her slender shape, a dark crescent figure entangled in the brush, only yards away from where her mother's body was found. The child couldn't move much, but her eyes reflected the intensity of the moon.

Like she was confronting a rabid dog, she looked up at him. She had met his type before, and there wasn't much negotiation that could happen. A deep feeling stirred, a wave of violent anger that she had long buried. Whatever she intended to do, it had to be quick and unexpected. She stood slowly like a cat arching its back.

"Yes, I have a pen. Even paper. I also have a foot."

She aimed as high as she could, and her foot met his gut. He winced in pain as his mouth hung agape. She surprised herself, elated her kick connected.

That kick was an old friend, a skill cultivated decades ago, essential as water in the foster home. She silently thanked the perverted foster home thug that made kicking a necessary skill in her early life. But that was then, and this was now. And she wasn't supposed to have to kick her way out of trouble. She had become a professional, a pencil pusher where the only kick she looked for was in a spicy bowl of chili. Yet years later, she was still facing villains.

She took a slight step forward and kicked again, angling her foot a little higher. Her unpracticed hip missed his chin but hit his chest. Fear and adrenaline pumping in her chest gave her strength.

The kick wasn't enough. The impact only delayed him while he overcame the shock of being hit. His raised arm swung towards her head.

Bridget ducked.

Ducking punches was a skill she learned before kicking. Ducking and running protected her and her little brother in the foster home until the other kids got bored and used new tactics. Running wasn't an option, not with Naomi here. Now if she could just crack a rib.

No such luck. He stumbled back and grabbed a gun, aiming at her face.

Bridget sighed long and low. "Really, Chet? Or may I call you by your real name? Jay Kline."

"You're slow, aren't you?"

"Jay Kline, Cheri's big brother, and Naomi's uncle. You're a busy man—killing mothers, assaulting children, filing frivolous lawsuits. How do you do it all? Working women would like to know how you find the time—"

Jay pointed a gun at her head and shoved her toward the ground. Bridget lowered herself slowly, meeting Jay's cold stare, and scooted back towards Naomi. Ignoring him, she ripped the tape off Naomi's mouth and loosened the tape around Naomi's wrists. If she could delay his actions, maybe the police might come.

"Scream. No one will hear you."

Naomi scrunched her face. "I hate you. You'll never get away with this!"

Jay shoved Naomi with his heavy leather boot and then kicked Bridget. He tossed her a roll of duct tape. "Start with your feet."

"You expect me to tie myself up? You can't be—"

She didn't see his foot coming. Before she knew it, she was on the ground, tasting blood. After cradling her jaw, she spat blood into the earth. She sat up, took the tape, and fumbled with the roll. Anger pulsed through her body.

"You must have been a real joy to grow up with. No wonder Cheri had mental health problems. She threatened to rat you out, didn't she, and expose your scheme to the tribal council?"

"Crazy Cheri was meant to deliver cash to Monroe. That was her only job. A little fentanyl from Elaine took care of that problem."

Naomi kicked the earth, trying to cover him with dirt. "I hate you. So did Mom."

"You're a misfit like your mom who had to bring her brat kid along, making her an eyewitness. Too bad you got a lawyer. It was only a matter of time until the money would be connected to me." Spit streamed from his mouth as he barked at them. "Crazy Cheri. I'll save the world from your kind—crazy and pregnant at eighteen. You'll be no different."

Jay fidgeted with his gold watch as Bridget ripped off a large strip of tape, but it stuck together, and she ripped off another shorter piece. She wrapped the tape around her leg, trying to look as if she were complying. She needed to stall.

"I don't think I understand," Bridget said. "Cheri gave your money to Joe Monroe, so the protest had a fresh flow of cash, and the employee refused to settle with plenty of money and new lawyers. A fight that you financed. And in comes Penny General with a hero offer and takes over Buyland. Who's paying you? Penny General? Or is it Barshefsky, the lobbyist for the Wisaka Nation?"

Jay laughed loudly and stretched. "Who isn't paying me? The tribe pays Barshefsky. Barshefsky pays me. Cheri pays Monroe for me. Of course, Penny General pays me and Barshefsky's firm. Cheri thought we were getting along again. How naïve."

"Well, aren't you proud." Bridget frowned.

"And Monroe did it for us. He kept the lawsuit from settling. Buyland was easy picking after that suit. And the protests! The sweetest thing was when the US Marshals kept the store open. The publicity! Everyone was throwing money everywhere to dig themselves out of the mess."

Moving at a turtle's pace, Bridget fumbled with the tape. "You played both sides. You're listed as a lobbyist for the retail industry. Barshefsky represents the tribe. You lobbied the government, hoping to undermine the tribal court. Did Joe Monroe know he was being played?"

"He knew what I wanted him to know. Hey brat, aren't you happy your mom wasn't totally useless?" Jay sneered at Naomi while checking his watch.

"But Buyland could lose the lawsuit, and Penny General could end up in tribal courts."

"Who cares? Chaos is where lobbyists and lawyers bloom. That's quicker cash than defending juvenile delinquents."

Bridget clenched her teeth. No, this was not for the money. She wanted to empower the powerless against the system. It turned out family was worse than corporate corruption.

"All this for a corporate takeover. To take over Buyland's contract with the reservation. You killed your sister for this."

"Foster child, not sister. Growing up with her was miserable, with all the attention and energy on her."

A pickup truck drove down the gravel road, and Bridget's hopes for help quickly crumbled when the driver emerged from the truck. A black cap, tattooed neck, and baggy jeans hanging down halfway. Skinny Boy, also known as Travis.

"Girls, our ride is here. Get up, McGarrity. I know you're stalling. We need to catch a train."

Bridget tossed the tape into the brush. "Have your dog fetch it."

"That's your escape attempt?"

Skinny Boy found the roll of tape in the brush. Jay came behind and held her while Skinny Boy taped her hands and wrists and then around her torso and arms.

"My next gig is Oklahoma. Companies are interested in me.

You know, my poor deceased, so-called foster sister is Osage. I care deeply."

"And Nick, he—"

Jay kneeled on one knee, looking at Bridget at eye level.

"Nick, the faggot social worker? Yes, he believed you and interfered with my ability to control the brat. Nick was putting Naomi into protective custody, where even my mother couldn't reach her."

Naomi jackknifed her legs and kicked, hitting Jay in the knee. He winced and shoved her.

"Spoiled brat!"

"And your buddy Barshefsky? Doesn't he like to get his suspenders tangled in this mess?"

Jay spun around, hissing at Bridget. "Keep up the struggle, ladies, because those are your last words. I have the gun and I have the time. When the deal closes on the Buyland's sale, I'll cash in nicely. They've already paid a hefty retainer."

She felt the knife in her back pocket, and the cell phone was in the front. Jay opened a backpack that contained a plastic bottle of Black Velvet whiskey. He snapped surgical gloves on his hands.

Bridget laughed. "What's that? It's not Whiskey Wednesday. You've brought the wrong bottle. Let's go on an alcohol run and we'll have a proper drink. How about it?"

He opened the bottle and poured whiskey over her. He then meticulously wiped the bottle clean of his fingerprints. He grabbed Bridget's hand and pressed her fingers on it. If tested, only her prints would show.

"Bridget McGarrity, a nice Irish name but a sad drunk."

"It will not work, Jay. Everyone knows I'm a single malt girl. And Black Velvet? Please, it's Canadian, not Irish. I understand your confusion."

Jay shoved Bridget, her body toppling. She lay motionless, oddly relishing the warmth of the earth. Whiskey didn't seem so bad.

"Do you ever shut up? Get in the truck. We have a train to catch."

"Both of us being bound don't quite make sense."

Jay winked at Bridget and Naomi. "Haven't you learned your lesson about jurisdiction? There's not going to be an investigation. The feds will not bother, and you've developed quite a reputation. And the tape can be removed once you're dead."

"Help is headed here now!"

Jay sneered. "Dear, stupid Bridget. Two concerned citizens called 911 when they spotted you speeding in your car with a distressed child and reported you traveling east. The same direction you fled last time, which is the opposite direction from here. Tell me about your last phone call? What was the officer's name?"

Naomi screamed as they both realized his ruse could work.

Jay dragged her by her feet toward the pickup, and Skinny Boy grabbed her torso. Bridget squirmed and twisted as Skinny Boy's wiry arms touched her.

Skinny Boy whispered in her ear. "I think I'll steal your car. I towed it, and now I own it."

"Thanks for the new tires."

Bridget jerked her body forcefully as if electrocuted and slipped from their hands, landing hard on the truck bed. The knife from her back pocket tumbled out, and she scrambled to roll on top of it. Jay grabbed it and waved it in her face, his cruel face smiling.

"Oh, my, what's this? A hunting knife? Didn't know you were a boy scout."

"No. A juvenile delinquent," she groaned, the side of her body throbbing from being dropped.

Jay tossed the knife into his black bag, and Skinny Boy

rubbed his hands together as they headed back for Naomi. Bridget struggled to loosen the tape around her wrists. The truck bed was empty—no tools or weapons. If she jumped out, she wouldn't get far with taped legs. Naomi squirmed and writhed from their grasp. They could barely hold her down as she tried to bite them.

"Little Naomi. You know how to run, but you can't do that now, can you?" growled Jay, and he took a fistful of hair and dragged her toward the truck. She screamed. Skinny Boy sat in the cab front after putting them in the truck bed. Jay hopped on the edge of the truck bed with them and pulled brass knuckles from a backpack.

"Do you like trains? I love trains. Did you know it chugs through the reservation daily but never stops? The train splits the reservation into two sections, just like the train will slice you in two."

Naomi dove to the side of the pickup truck, trying to slip over the side, but Jay and his brass knuckles were too fast. Naomi gasped as a punch landed on her back.

"I don't want to die."

"Neither do I."

Bridget's head smacked on the metal as the truck accelerated over the bumpy road. They both tried to brace themselves as they bounced about like balls for the ten-minute trip toward the railroad tracks. The brakes screeched as they halted, spewing a plume of dirt over them. Jay popped open the tailgate, and Skinny Boy hit the gas again. They tumbled out, and Bridget curled herself in a ball, bracing for the impact. She opened her eyes and saw train tracks. A couple of feet away was Jay's backpack with her knife in it.

"You won't get away with this," said Naomi.

"People know too much," said Bridget. "I've already talked to Chief French."

"You should have cashed the check. Dropped the case and stayed out of my way," said Jay.

"The check would have bounced. You never meant for me to cash it."

"Huh, that's true. I had a plan for that, too. Terrible to resort to this, not usually my style. I prefer bribery."

In the distance, the ominous horn of the train heralded a tragedy to come. Jay kneeled on one knee, dark shadows cast across his face.

"The feds will not pay attention to a dead kid on a reservation with her dead drunk lawyer. You've already shown the world you're a wild one, haven't you, McGarrity? Concocting stories about a wrecked car in a cornfield and even an AMBER Alert. That was a gift, and I didn't even plan that one."

Bridget wished she could cover her ears. She turned her head away towards Naomi. As their eyes met, Naomi stopped panting. Bridget eyed the backpack that had tumbled out of the truck, as did Naomi.

"Time to accept your fate."

As Jay turned around, Naomi jackknifed her feet forward, slamming Jay in the back of the knees. They buckled, and he stumbled. Bridget sprang to her feet and heaved her body toward him, bringing him to the earth before he could regain his balance.

With the precision of an Olympic hurdler, Naomi leaped high and long. She dropped her entire body flat on top of him—a body slam a professional wrestler would envy. Jay groaned as bone cracked against a railroad tie. Bridget rolled towards his backpack and loosened the zipper with her teeth. She found what she needed—her hunting knife. Bridget wedged the knife under the duct tape and freed her legs.

"What the—get over here now!"

Skinny Boy opened the cab door and ran toward them. Jay shifted his weight as he moaned in pain. With a bloody hand to his head, Jay staggered over the tracks towards them. She clenched her fists, and like a bull who had been taunted, teased, and wounded, she charged at Jay, and they both tumbled to the ground.

"The knife!" She pointed with her chin toward the knife.

Bridget faced Skinny Boy, who held a hammer in his scrawny hands, and he contorted his face into a wicked smile. Naomi was cutting her legs free.

*Come toward me, Skinny Boy, not Naomi.*

He waved the hammer at Naomi. "I'm gonna pound you into a pulp."

"You'll miss your train," yelled Bridget as she sprinted over the tracks, and Skinny Boy followed. He was fast and ran past her, twirling the hammer in his hand.

"Now, we're going to have fun—"

He was a bit shorter than Jay. She took a slight step back and kicked high—hitting him straight in the face. He stumbled backward towards the railroad tracks but regained his footing and swung the hammer at her. She ducked down, which he anticipated, and it hit her on the back. The train whistled, and the earth throbbed with vibrations from the locomotive.

Bridget ran, stealing a glance at Naomi, to lead Skinny Boy away. Naomi removed the tape and glowered over Jay, who was face down, spitting dirt from his mouth. His head oozed blood from hitting the railroad tie.

Naomi's hands clasped the knife and held it high in the air. She plunged the blade deep into his calf. Jay yelled, and his shrill voice matched the screech of the train whistle. She clapped her hands like she had just been handed a present.

Bridget ran towards her as Jay prepared to stand, but she stepped on the knife, sinking it deeper into the flesh of his leg. They stepped away from him, keeping clear. Jay rolled off the tracks, away from the approaching train. He stood, pulled the knife from his leg, hobbled toward them, and hollered for Skinny Boy, who sprinted back to the truck. He revved the engine and turned the vehicle around. White headlights blinded them, and the pickup charged toward them.

Bridget and Naomi sprinted into the brush, and the truck swerved towards them. Jay pointed frantically toward their direction, signaling to Skinny Boy.

The pickup truck stopped, and Jay limped towards it.

Bridget spotted something—a single light emerged behind them from a distance, followed by an ear pounding, a low rumble throbbing in the distance. She turned a complete 360, unsure whether it was a train or something else.

"I know that sound!" Naomi jumped up and down. It wasn't a train but a motorcycle. Like an animal trapped in the middle of the road, Jay looked wildly about; the motorcycle headlight covered him in light.

She led Naomi away from the train, and they concealed themselves in the darkness behind a tree. They both breathed hard.

"Are you OK?"

"They're getting away." Naomi's fists clenched.

"Let them. I'm glad we're breathing."

"This will never end, and they got to answer for it."

"They will answer. Let's go!"

"You said it yourself. No one can help...jurisdiction. Uncle Jay said it, too."

With spine straight and chin up, Naomi walked out from behind the tree and straight toward the pickup truck, her figure blurred by its headlights.

Jay turned and scowled, stepped in the pickup truck, nodded to Skinny Boy. The truck wheels spun in the dirt, spewing gravel behind it, and it crossed the tracks heading toward Naomi. The front of the train was visible and whistling.

Jay held on to the side of the open pickup door, leaning out, ready to grab Naomi.

"Help is on the way! Don't, Naomi!" The sound of the train drowned Bridget's voice.

Jay stepped out from the pickup to confront her. Naomi did not slow or change her course. She headed toward Jay and barreled into him, pushing him. He tumbled, and both lay in a heap on the railroad ties between the steel rails. The train seconds away. Bridget screamed.

Naomi rolled off the rail and stood. Jay scrambled to stand, but as he stood, Naomi kicked him, and then she sprinted away as Jay stumbled and fell backward on the rails. The freight train drove right over Jay.

He was gone.

Bridget finally reached Naomi and embraced her, not allowing her to look at his mangled body.

Skinny Boy, who had stepped out of the pickup truck, spun around, and fled back. A motorcycle skidded to a stop next to him, cornering him before he reached it. The man snapped off his helmet—it was Steve. He stepped off his motorbike, caught him by the collar, and threw him down with a thud. Skinny Boy groaned.

"Stay down!" Steve yelled as he stepped his leather boot on his chest.

Behind the single light of the motorcycle emerged a row of headlights with a cloud of dust pluming behind. Five SUVs, some with the emblazoned words *Tribal Police* surrounded them, bejeweled by a crown of headlights, and Bridget and Naomi were royalty. Tears pooled in Bridget's eyes as several officers hurried from their cars with guns raised. Officer Bennett was with them.

Skinny Boy waved his hands towards the police.

"Thank goodness you're here! That crazy woman attacked me! She's drunk and killed a man! The child's uncle tried to save his niece!"

Steve lifted Skinny Boy by the collar and punched him again in the face with his motorcycle helmet. Officer Bennett held Steve back.

"My turn."

Bennett handcuffed Skinny Boy. Another officer came to assist. Steve returned to Naomi while keeping watch on him.

She barely felt her arms still embracing Naomi. Skinny Boy, what he said, could they believe him? She doubted it, but the lie could deflect fault away from him and toward Bridget. She loosened her grip.

"Is he? Jay, he's—" Naomi stammered.

She gently cradled the child's face in her hands as they looked eye to eye.

"What you did was save the day. You saved me, and you. You've been beaten, shot at, mentally tortured. He took your mother. You, Naomi Kline, are perfect. And this time, I think it really is over."

She nodded her head as tears streamed. Steve put a hand on her back, and Naomi buried her face in her father's arms.

"Though, let me answer any questions. You don't need to tell anyone about that last bit—"

Bridget wanted to cry, laugh, scream but couldn't do anything other than relish the pulse of her heartbeat, ecstatic to be alive. Officer Bennett approached. It was less than two weeks ago since she first met him, almost like a memory from another life.

"Bridget McGarrity?" Officer Bennett asked.

"Yes."

"You OK?"

"Splendid." She gave a thumbs-up.

"I have a phone call for you."

# Chapter 48

Officer Bennett handed her the phone, and she flinched as she placed it on her ear, which was tender from smacking it on the pickup truck.

"Glad you're alive, McGarrity."

"Chief French?"

"Got the corn stalk from Evans. It'll make for one of the more unusual items in the evidence box," French said.

"I wasn't sure whether you'd believe me."

"We found the cornfield where your car must have been and traced down the tow company that pulled it out. And your aunt wouldn't leave me alone. I was afraid she's going to pitch a tent outside my house."

"Aunt Irene has her ways."

"And McGarrity, you can turn off your cell phone now."

"My what...?"

Bridget found her phone wedged in her front pocket. Her mouth dropped as she examined it—she was still on the line with 911.

"Good move, McGarrity. The dispatch heard enough. Barshefsky will never practice law again, other than as a jailhouse lawyer. Now stop playing cop and go back to practicing law."

Bridget handed the phone back to the tribal officer, who helped her stand. He took an evidence bag and put out his hand.

"Your cell phone, please."

"Really? I can't keep hold of that thing."

Steve stood beside Naomi, who had a blanket over her shoulders. He handed her a blanket and water bottle, which she happily accepted. He threw his arms around her, giving her a bear hug and lifting her slightly off the earth.

"Next time I'm arrested, I'm calling my favorite lawyer," Steve said to Bridget.

Despite her whole body aching, Bridget laughed. "Can't say I look forward to it. We should figure out another way to connect. Your daughter is pretty tough."

"It's my fault. I lost her at the courthouse." He wiped the dirt off Naomi's smudged face.

"Jay told me I had to go with him, or he would hurt my dad. So I did." Her voice shook. "It's not over."

"No, it's over. No more court, no juvenile officers, and no juvie homes. I promise. Even if that means you live with Aunt Irene or me."

Steve shook his head. "You two! I kept calling that social worker. She told me you'd been spotted with Naomi, heading east, but it made no sense. I drove to your house, and your husband said you headed to the reservation. I made good time on the bike." Steve winked at her.

"And the tribal police?" asked Bridget.

"They'd figured something already. When the train whistle blew, I had a funny feeling. Bennett told me where Cheri died, and I figured that sick jerk would head back there."

"I may still need a lawyer," said Naomi.

"What? No, I—"

Naomi threw off the blanket, marched up to Officer Bennett, and held her arms out, waiting to be handcuffed. Officer Bennett didn't move.

"Put me in jail. I killed Jay Kline and I'm happy I did."

Officer Bennett gently laid his hands on her arms and lowered them.

"I know what happened. Your mother was murdered, and you saved your own life and Ms. McGarrity's. There's only one place you are going and that is someplace warm. The casino heard what happened and will put you and your dad up for the night."

"Can he say that? I thought you're not the boss here but the FBI?" she asked.

"The feds don't pay attention much. I don't think they will this time either," said Officer Bennett.

The ambulance and squad cars bathed the scene in flashing red and blue lights. More squad cars and a fire truck arrived from the neighboring county, which had agreed to help this time. The police were taking pictures of Jay's body, and it would be only a matter of time before they wanted a statement from her. It was the crime scene, the CSI stuff Bridget had missed when she identified Cheri's body less than two weeks ago. She looked away from the train tracks, thanking her good fortune.

"Bridget?"

She turned. "Walter!"

"You're here. How?"

"Aiden is with Aunt Irene, who came once I told her what happened. The people here, they believed me, and they believed you. And Nick, I guess he's doing better and talked sense into the social worker."

"I didn't think you would—"

Walter encircled her with his warm arms, and she melted. She breathed deeply as if she hadn't taken a breath for weeks.

"I'm always there for you."

Bridget peeked at her reflection in the window of the SUV and frowned at her beat-up face.

"I'll be all the talk at the courthouse."

# Chapter 49

Walter hovered over three bicycles that lay across the front driveway. "Tires are pumped, wheels are oiled. We're good to go," he said.

Bridget walked out of the garage, balancing three bike helmets in her arms. "Aiden! Your helmet."

Aiden swatted at a maple tree with a large stick and a swell of gold-tinted leaves scattered. "I don't wanna wear it."

"Neither do I, but I do it. Pat yourself on the back for being such a wonderful person."

Aiden took the helmet, chucked it onto the matted grass, and swung at it like it was a golf ball.

"Come on, Aiden. Today's the last day of decent weather. Snow's coming next week."

"I love snow."

"I should buy snow tires for the bikes. Walter, is this one yours—"

Walter folded his arms across his chest, ignoring her outstretched arm holding the helmet. He looked behind her as his eyes focused on the street. Bridget turned as the sheriff's white SUV slowly pulled into the driveway.

"Not this again," Walter's voice shook.

Chief French stepped out of the car with papers in his hand and walked towards Bridget.

Aiden bounced lightly on his feet. "They gonna handcuff you again? Dad, can I have your phone?"

"No selfies with the sheriff." With a spring in her step, Bridget walked towards the sheriff as leaves crunched under her feet. "Got something for me, Chief?"

"Thought I'd personally serve these on my way to lunch at Irene's." He smoothed his handlebar mustache as he handed her a large manila envelope. "She's serving tempeh. I think that's what you call it."

"Aunt Irene's fried tempeh sandwiches. Brace yourself."

"Put your helmet on, young man. You have interesting women in your family, Walter." French nicked his head toward Walter.

"That's one way of putting it. Thanks for stopping by. I think."

"All is well, Walter." French returned to his car and drove off.

Walter hovered over the envelope. "And what is it this time?"

"Chief French is hanging with Aunt Irene. I'm trying to figure that out." Bridget said.

"That's not what I mean. The envelope!"

"Oh, this?" Bridget tore open the envelope, glanced at the contents, and waved the papers high, proud as Lady Liberty. "Yours truly has been subpoenaed for testimony in the matter of 'United States of America vs. Alan Barshefsky, Defendant,' and here's another subpoena for Skinny Boy.'"

Bridget pecked him on the cheek and showed him the paperwork.

"And this is a good thing?"

"Very."

"If you say so. Aiden! Let's go!"

Aiden ran through the pile of leaves as he swung in the air with his stick. Bridget rubbed her wrist even though the bruises and cuts had faded. Skinny Boy faced charges for murder, kidnapping, and assault. Alan Barshefsky faced additional charges, including fraud, tax evasion, racketeering, and conspiracy to bribe public officials. Elaine also wasn't faring much better, and last Bridget heard, she was negotiating a plea for attempted murder, conspiracy, theft, obstruction of justice, and false reports.

Her stomach fluttered in expectation when she thought about testifying. Barshefsky and his entire law firm were hurting. He was ousted as a partner, and witnesses had lined up, from her to Abby Baker, Cal Roberts with Buyland, and even Chief French.

Penny General's takeover was on hold indefinitely, and it was rumored that Buyland was negotiating a new contract with the reservation. It'll be a switch, though, testifying, she thought. Instead of the defense table, she'd be on the witness stand, a new adventure.

"Are we going?" Walter and Aiden hopped on the bicycles.

"We need to be back at five. There's someone I'd like to visit tonight."

\*\*\*

The house was humble, near the subsidized housing subdivision on the west side. A rosy-cheeked woman opened the door, and a bashful toddler sat on her hip, his tiny hand clasping her shirt. The scent of baked apples greeted them as they entered. Bridget carried a gift box wrapped in light blue paper with a white satin bow. In a neck brace, Nick held a notepad and a manila folder.

"Thanks for letting me see him. Nothing official," she said.

Bridget's visit was social, not professional. She wanted and needed to visit the foster home of a young, energetic couple intending to adopt the boy she had rescued from Abby's home.

"Ya betchya. Great to meet you, a real pleasure. You were on the news." She took a step closer to her and whispered. "You look better in person."

The woman stuffed a binkie into the boy's mouth and put him on the floor. "We're working on losing the binkie."

Bridget placed the present next to him. The toddler's cheeks were chubby, and his brown eyes were bright and blinking. A far cry from when she had last seen him, half-starved and crying—when she took him from Abby Baker's apartment and drove off with him to the hospital.

The boy braced himself against the box and pulled himself to standing. Bridget couldn't keep her eyes off him. He looked so much better, as if untouched by his rough start in life.

"He's thriving so well under your care. He's gained weight."

The boy tumbled and howled, and the foster mom swooped him up within seconds. "Oh, my, and a stinky too. I'll be right back." She trotted off to another room with the confidence of an experienced loving parent.

"I haven't heard from Naomi lately. How is she?" asked Nick.

"No news is good news. Steve found a job and an apartment, and Naomi is babysitting Aiden on Saturday. I'm not sure it's a good idea. I think Aiden is in love."

"People never want to talk to social workers after their case is dismissed."

"No, I guess not, and usually, they tire of lawyers as well. This case is an exception."

"You are the exception, Sister Justice."

The foster mother returned with the boy and showed Bridget into the living room. The boy crawled towards the present on the floor, and he got a hold of the ribbon.

Bridget's phone buzzed at her side, breaking her from her reverie. "Hi, Bridget, it's court admin. Glad I caught you. Would you be available for a temporary removal hearing tomorrow morning?"

"Tell me more." She stepped into the entrance hallway, out of earshot.

"A mother was found asleep at the bus station with a portable meth lab in her backpack. Her two children were with her boyfriend, a registered sex offender. The children's hair tested positive for methamphetamine."

"I'd be representing who?"

"The mother. She's at the county jail, and the temporary removal hearing is tomorrow at 8:00 A.M." The clerk from court administration delivered the information in a monotone voice like it was as routine as ordering a pizza.

The little boy spat out his binkie and replaced it with the ribbon. The foster mom helped him open the box, and he tore into the tissue paper. He was in a much better place.

"Thanks. I'll be there."

# Acknowledgments

If you have made it to this page, I would like to thank you for reading my book. It is truly a compliment. If you just skipped to the back, asking yourself, what was she thinking, and is this accurate? I also thank you. But before answering that, I want to emphasize, this book is a work of fiction. All the characters, names, places are invented, that includes names, and places. The "Wisaka Nation" is a fictional place. The name "Wisaka" comes from the mythical cultural hero of the western Northeast Woodlands region, Potawatomi, Sac and Fox, and Kickapoo nations.

So back to the question, is the book's portrayal of American Indian law correct? The answer is maybe, it depends, and well, sometimes no. And if that answer is giving you flashbacks of an unsatisfactory exchange with a lawyer, my apologies. When I initially wrote this book ten years ago, I thought I had a fair understanding of the jurisdictional briar patch of Indian, state and federal law. But over the years, I have watched the courts play legal legerdemain with Indigenous sovereignty—a trend that seems to have no end in sight. As of this writing, the Supreme Court is considering gutting the Indian Child Welfare Act, which requires that Indian tribes be notified, and is mentioned in the book. That law was enacted in response to the atrocity of Indigenous children being taken from the parents without notifying their parents, relatives or tribe. And then there's the Supreme Court's 2021 finding that a large portion of Oklahoma is still an Indian reservation, and, therefore, the state had no jurisdiction over certain crimes—a win for treaty rights, Indigenous sovereignty and self-governance. Yet a year later the court somewhat reversed itself, with a *just kidding*, we meant something different. And all that does not even begin to touch Native communities' relationship on the state level.

What all that legalese may mean is that this book could be a historical piece in a matter of months. So, in a Jesus-take-the-wheel moment, I gave up rewriting. I hope that the endeavor of bringing awareness to the needlessly complex issue of jurisdiction, and the lack of respect for those it affects the most, Native communities, is worthwhile.

Many thanks to all who supported me—you are too many to mention, but here are a few. First, to my mother, Geraldine, approaching her 103rd year, who taught me more about Native American history than I ever learned in school. She drove me across this great nation, stopping at Indian reservations, and skipping Las Vegas for a grand Indian pow-wow in the Southwest. She related the stories from her mother, who told her the Osage were the richest people in the country. That gave me pause.

To my kind critics, supporters, and early readers, Geraldine, Kathleen, Johannes, Anna May, Frances, Mina, Angela Rydell, Shoshauna Shy, Mary-Louise Bajolle, and to my many writing buddies over the years, my heartfelt thanks.

## About the Author

S.A. O'Laughlin was born in Chicago and holds a Bachelor's degree from Washington University in St. Louis and a Juris Doctor from University of Arkansas School of Law. She practiced in Iowa as a general practice lawyer and in Illinois in civil litigation and class actions. Since 2018, she lives in Germany with her family. When she's not writing, O'Laughlin teaches law as an adjunct professor. *In the Interest of N. K.* is her first book.

Made in the USA
Las Vegas, NV
26 June 2023

73931975R00184